WITH ALL DUE RESPECT

WITH ALL DUE
RESPECT

Lewis Segal

Leapfolio

An imprint of Tupelo Press
North Adams, Massachusetts

Library of Congress Cataloging-in-Publication Data

Names: Segal, Lewis, 1935- author.
Title: With all due respect / Lewis Segal.
Description: North Adams, Massachusetts : Tupelo Press, [2016] |
Birth Date:
     April 26, 1935
Identifiers: LCCN 2016023822 | ISBN 9781936797868 (alk. paper)
Subjects: LCSH: Law firms--Fiction. | Neo-Nazis--Fiction. | LCGFT:
Legal
     fiction (Literature)
Classification: LCC PS3619.E375 W58 2016 | DDC 813/.6--dc23
LC record available at https://lccn.loc.gov/2016023822

ISBN: 978-1-936797-86-8

Cover designed by Josef Beery
Text designed by Hadley Kincade

First paperback edition: July 2016.

Leapfolio, an imprint of Tupelo Press
Post Office Box 1767
North Adams, Massachusetts 01247
Telephone: (413) 664–9611
editor@tupelopress.org

www.tupelopress.org

www.leapfolio.net

For Shirley
For everything

PROLOGUE

2014

*There are fathers who do not love their children; there
is no grandfather who does not adore his grandson.*

—Victor Hugo

It is a winter day. I am in the winter of my life. I am sitting near the wood stove in the home of my daughter and son-in-law, gazing out at the snow-covered trees that surround the house. The warmth from the stove gives me comfort and the presence of my eighteen-year-old grandson gives me joy. His name is Will, named after my wife's father, William O'Dwyer, a beloved primary care physician who made house calls.

I think it is the right time to tell him the story that he has asked me, over and over again, to tell him—the story of the most remarkable experience I had in more than fifty years as a lawyer in New York City. It is a story that has taken on an almost legendary quality in my family. It is a story in which I made mistakes, acted selfishly, tried to do the right thing, and—ultimately—gained an understanding of what was really important to me and, also, what mattered very little. I hope my grandson will suspend judgment of me until the end of the story, at which time I hope he will think kindly of me.

Will is a thoughtful and lively listener to the stories I tell him and he likes to jump in from time to time to ask a question or make a comment. I will certainly make room for him to do so in this story.

PART ONE

JUNE–AUGUST 1974

Rieber: Lowenthal, you know it is a historical fact
that the Jews are the basis of our misfortunes.
Lowenthal: Of course.
Rieber: You agree?
Lowenthal: Of course. The Jews and the bicycle riders.
Rieber: The bicycle riders? Why the bicycle riders?
Lowenthal: Why the Jews?

— Katherine Anne Porter
from *Ship of Fools*

ONE

The Wall Street law firm of Coburn & Perkins occupied the six uppermost stories of a fifty-story building near the New York Stock Exchange. Looking down at the bustling financial district far below its offices, the lawyers of the firm could sense that they were major actors in the great financial drama playing out around them. The cases they handled, the transactions they orchestrated, the clients they represented—these things combined with the physical elegance of the firm's offices caused many of those lawyers, including me, to think they were playing an important role in the American economy and system of justice.

A few months after I joined Coburn & Perkins as a partner in its litigation department, something happened that caused me to think that one of my partners might be a Nazi sympathizer. That was many years ago but the incident and its aftermath are still vivid memories. I'd like to tell you about it.

The luncheon room at the Graduates Club was an ideal spot for the partners in my new firm to have a casual lunch break. It was a short walk from our offices on Wall Street. Six of us were seated at a round table in the club's luncheon room, a comfortable table in a comfortable room. I had never been in the Graduates Club until I joined Coburn & Perkins and was given a Club membership as a perquisite of my new partnership. There was a relaxed atmosphere in the luncheon room. The transaction of business in that room was frowned upon and members were prohibited from bringing documents to the tables. It was a place in which lawyers, stock traders, bankers, and senior business executives could take a break from the serious and stressful work they did every day. Being a member of the Club and having lunch there at least once a week gave me a feeling of importance that, looking back on it, was a foolish and egotistical thing. But that was how I felt on the day I will tell you about.

Lunch was served by black waiters in linen serving jackets. The luncheon conversation at our table had been casual, desultory, with subjects ranging from the New York Yankees to gossip about partners who were not at the table.

The date was June 6, 1974, the thirtieth anniversary of the D-Day invasion. We were relaxing in the mahogany and leather opulence of a site designed to make successful people feel even better about themselves. In the course of the conversation, a young partner by the name of Barry Weinberg casually mentioned the D-Day anniversary. Tom Spellman, our top litigator, immediately straightened in his chair, placed both of his hands on the table, cleared his voice, and began this pronouncement: "The invasion was a catastrophic mistake. What our country and its allies should have done was align ourselves with Germany. If we had done that, we could have defeated the Soviet Union and avoided the Cold War. We would have brought an early end to the Communist threat that still hangs over Western civilization. We would have spared the captive nations of Eastern Europe the misery of Russian occupation. We made a grave mistake when we chose the wrong side in that war and we're still paying the price for it."

—

Will, I want you to understand that much of this story consists of conversations that I had with various people. Obviously, after so many years, my memory of those conversations is, to say the least, inexact. In telling this story, I have reconstructed the dialogue to the best of my ability. I assure you that—although the words may not be perfect reproductions of the actual conversations—the content is a close approximation of what the conversations were about. • *Of course I understand that, Grandpa.*

—

Spellman never simply expressed opinions. All of his opinions were expressed as indisputable facts. This statement was delivered fluently, forcefully. It was like an argument in court, like a carefully prepared speech. It wasn't just an offhand remark. This sounded like a subject that Spellman had thought about seriously and these were his conclusions.

As I usually did in those early months of my time with the firm, when Spellman took to his pulpit, I retreated into silence. Intimidated.

—

Why were you intimidated? Didn't they come after you and pressure you to join the firm? I'm sure you've told me about that. • Will, I think you'll understand, as the story unfolds, how I felt in those early months at Coburn & Perkins.

—

While Spellman was making his statement, Fred Perkins—the oldest partner in the firm, who I always thought was somewhat feeble-minded—continued to nibble at the remains of his salad. With a furrowed brow on his otherwise blank face, he appeared to be digesting Spellman's remarks.

Harry Madison and Paul Swanson continued their discussion about the Yankees, apparently oblivious to Spellman's words.

After a few moments in which the silence became unbearable to me, I said, "Surely, Tom, you must think the defeat of Nazi Germany was an essential military objective, don't you?"

Spellman responded, "Not as urgent, not as essential as the defeat of the Soviet Union. Look, Michael, I believe you're a thoughtful guy. Think about this. The Soviet Union has always had, still has, as its principal objective, the spread of its Communist ideology throughout the entire world including, without doubt, the United States. You might not want to invite Hitler to your house for dinner, but he posed no threat to our country. We simply picked the wrong enemy."

Weinberg looked stunned. After a pause of at least half a minute, he asked, "What about the Jews of Europe?"

"I knew someone would ask that question, Barry, and, frankly, I knew it would be you. I'm certain that the Allies could have made some sort of a deal with the Germans that would have provided a solution to that question," Spellman pointed out, sighing, as if this issue was barely relevant to the strategic vision that he had shared with us.

"A final solution?" Weinberg muttered.

"Correct," said Spellman, wiping his mouth with a linen napkin and rising from the table.

"I have to be in court at two o'clock."

———

Isn't that how Hitler and the German Nazis referred to the Holocaust? • Exactly.

———

So, did I have a Nazi sympathizer as a partner? This was not a question I expected to ask myself when I joined the firm in a lateral move from a smaller firm five months earlier.

———

I'll bet that was a question you didn't expect to have to deal with. How troubled were you by that question? • I wish I had been more troubled than I actually was. This is what I recall thinking at the time: I wondered what it might mean to me personally if it turned out that Spellman really was a Nazi sympathizer. Would it mean anything it all? I knew almost nothing—no, I knew absolutely nothing—about Nazi sympathizers in America in 1974. It was twenty-nine years since the end of the war against Nazi Germany. The truth is that my greatest concern was that Spellman's views might be harmful to the firm. • *Frankly, Grandpa, I think you missed the point about how weird it was to have a Nazi partner. That had nothing to do with the effect on your law firm. Didn't you care about the kind of people you had around you—the kind of people you had lunch with?*

—

In any event, I still had a lot to learn about my new partners. Now, forty years later, I am comfortably retired. I might say I'm a survivor of the practice of law. My experience in the firm was very different from what I expected and most of that difference revolved around Spellman's lecture at that luncheon table.

TWO

Tom Spellman became a central figure in my life. I made an effort to get to know him but he always kept his distance from me when it came to his private life. I have two theories to explain his reticence. It's possible that Tom's refusal to describe his background, his family, his feelings, or anything else that might help me get closer to him may have been an indication of the low regard he had for me; I simply may not have been deemed worthy of sharing the painful truths about his family that I later learned from others. But I think it is more likely that Tom was concealing things from himself because they were inconsistent with the image he had of himself and that he projected publicly.

I would have to describe his public demeanor as aristocratic. Tom looked like a successful lawyer. He was large—tall and well-built—with a shock of well-groomed light brown hair, a handsome face, a graceful, ambling manner of moving around. He was never natural or informal; he seemed always to be posing, projecting an image of importance, stature, breeding, confidence. These, by the way, were all qualities that no one would ascribe to me. Tom dressed in conservative, well-tailored suits that looked—and probably were—expensive. His posture was perfect. His wing-tip shoes were always polished. He displayed—in his every word and every movement—supreme self-confidence bordering on a swagger. His speaking voice was deep and resonant. If I compared myself to Tom—which I couldn't help myself from doing—I came out second best.

—

I don't agree with that. You're being too modest, Grandpa.
- Flattery will get you no place.

—

Lest I sound unduly modest, I want you to know that I was a highly regarded trial lawyer with a record of success in handling complex corporate litigation over a period of sixteen years. You correctly remember that I told you that I agreed to join the firm only after it had made repeated efforts to recruit me away from my previous firm. The firm offered me an immediate partnership and a guaranteed minimum income that was higher than the most money I had ever earned in the old firm. Although I was happy in the old firm, I was now at an age when playing in the major leagues of corporate law seemed like the career I was destined to have. The fact that Tom Spellman was a powerful person and a highly influential partner in my new firm was part of the professional environment I had moved into when I agreed to join the firm. He was intimidating, not only to me but to virtually everyone else in the firm. But you shouldn't understand that to mean that I was an insignificant speck in the firm. I knew my new partners needed and wanted me for my legal skills and because they needed someone who was strong enough to work with Spellman and to counterbalance his flair and bravado with good solid lawyering.

I learned from Tom that the Spellman family home on Long Island was known as Two Oaks. Both trees were destroyed in a hurricane when Tom was a young boy. But the name remained—I suppose in memory of the trees. I was impressed that his house had a name; my childhood apartment in the Bronx had a number.

Tom told me that he spent a happy boyhood at Two Oaks. As Tom described it, Two Oaks stood alone in a park-like setting that was once a farm and there were no close neighbors. Nevertheless, Tom was able to assemble a group of friends from the area—schoolmates generally—and he enjoyed an unofficial leadership status in his circle of friends. He was rarely alone and seldom idle. He attended an excellent, and expensive, private day school from kindergarten through grade 12, graduating near the top of his class. He played for the school football team but admitted that he was not a "natural athlete."

According to Tom, the Spellman family lived a good life. His father, John Spellman, commuted into the city where he worked as an investment banker. He commuted by train and often returned to Two Oaks late at night. John Spellman earned a great deal of money. He had lost a fortune in the

1929 crash but gradually rebuilt his wealth, struggling to hold things together in the years immediately following Tom's birth in 1928. Politically, Tom's father was a notable figure in the Republican Party on both a national and state level. A generous contributor to the party, he was considered an insider although he never ran for or held public office. He was a vehement opponent of Franklin Roosevelt's New Deal. No one doubted that he hated Roosevelt with a passion. He was an adherent of the isolationist wing of the party and was vocal in his advocacy of America's neutrality as the specter of another war in Europe appeared. Tom's description of his father and his politics was presented to me in a manner that I can only describe as boastful. I couldn't tell whether it was his father's business acumen or his politics, or both, but it was clear that Tom Spellman was proud to be the son of John Spellman.

Tom described his mother as an attractive and interesting woman. An independent thinker with a perky demeanor, Liz Spellman was active in—of all things—Long Island Democratic politics. Despite their deep differences in political outlook, Liz and John were, according to Tom, a happy and compatible couple.

I thought the picture of his family life as Tom described it to me was a bit too ideal to be entirely accurate. Ozzie and Harriet were a popular radio couple during Tom's boyhood but they certainly didn't live at Two Oaks.

It turns out, as I later learned from several of the other partners, that Tom grew up in a toxic household environment. I was told that John Spellman traveled extensively, purportedly on business, and was absent from the home for weeks at a time and that Liz Spellman took advantage of these long absences to develop close—and eventually intimate—relationships with at least three of the men whom she met at Democratic headquarters. One was a state senator, the other two were a vice chairman of the local party and the candidate in the then current congressional election. The Long Island newspapers I had occasion to read years later reported that she was the spirited plaything of the Long Island Democratic Party. It was reported that Tom was sixteen years old when the news of his mother's relationship with the candidate leaked out during the election campaign and that he sent the newspaper clipping to his father's office.

The story in the press was that when John returned to his office and found the newspaper clipping his son had sent him, he became enraged. He went immediately to Two Oaks and tore the house apart, smashing lamps, ripping the upholstered furniture, tearing down drapes, breaking windows. Tom walked into the house and saw his father at the point in this rampage when John was trying to set fire to the drapes. This horrific scene was described to me by the reporter for the *Long Island Press*, one of a swarm of news people who had covered the story of the trashing of the iconic Two Oaks and the ensuing protracted divorce proceedings of its wealthy and high-profile occupants. Tom was portrayed in this story as the victim, the bright and beautiful son of selfish, immoral parents. There's no doubt that Tom was the victim. But what were his injuries and where are his scars? And why on earth did he think that this story, this fateful chapter in his life, could be concealed from me and others who thought they knew him well? Those were the questions that buzzed around my head when I first learned about those events and those are the questions that have intrigued me—and troubled me—in the decades since then.

John Spellman was no ideal husband. I heard reports from people who knew the Spellmans that John was physically and emotionally abusive to Liz and to Tom. A lawyer I knew told me that Tom had told him that he loved his birthday as a boy because it was the only day of the year that he felt completely safe from physical abuse from his father.

Tom as a lawyer, a litigator, the chairman of our firm's formidable litigation department—I grew to know that Tom Spellman in great detail and with real insights. It's possible that eventually I knew him better than anyone else did, including his wife. Starting with the day I arrived in the firm, I worked with him every day. I wrote every brief he submitted, always over his own signature, by the way. I mapped out the strategy for every case he appeared in. I constructed every argument he delivered. I prepared every case he tried. I was Tom's brain.

Now, don't get me wrong. Tom was a very smart guy and an extraordinarily effective trial lawyer. And he was the most prodigious rainmaker in the firm, attracting important clients as if he were a magnet and they were iron filings. His clients loved him. They had supreme confidence in him. I actually saw one of our clients consoling Tom when he was sitting in the empty courtroom, stunned, after a jury ruled against his client. Tom was distraught while the client, facing financial ruin, was comforting him. That doesn't usually happen in our business when you lose a case.

But Tom was intellectually lazy. He never kept up on developments in the law. In fact, the law didn't really interest him. But people did. He was a genius at identifying a person's hot button. He could look at a witness and intuitively know exactly how to maneuver him into replying with precisely the answer that would win the case for our side.

For two men with vastly different personal backgrounds who didn't particularly like each other, we were an effective team. We were respected and valued within the law firm because we produced notably good results and because Tom generated so much revenue. When it came to sharing that revenue, I got the scraps that Tom left on the table. I must note, in candor and honesty, that I resented the fact that Tom's income was appreciably higher than mine and my perspectives about Tom may well have been colored by that resentment.

I had met Tom's wife, Anne, on a number of occasions. I liked her a whole lot more than I did Tom. She had an engaging warmth and sense of humor, qualities that were totally absent from Tom's personality. She talked proudly about her Irish heritage, which, I must say, was evident on her face. That may be one of the reasons I felt a real affinity for her. The Spellmans were nominal Episcopalians, but other than elaborately decorating Two Oaks during the Christmas season, they had no meaningful religious observances. Tom converted to Roman Catholicism when he married Anne White while in law school. He took his new religion serious- ly, more seriously, in fact, than Anne did. Their children all attended Catholic schools.

There was an occasion shortly after I joined the firm when a number of partners and their spouses rented a ski lodge for a long weekend. The Spellmans were there as were my wife and I. Everyone was expected to bring wine to accompany a catered dinner on Saturday night. Tom brought several bottles but made a point of identifying one of them as special and re- served for him and Anne. This violated an unspoken rule of the weekend and was resented by most of the people in the group.

Around the dinner table were eight partners and eight spouses and on the table were four or five bottles of wine. The "special" Spellman bottle was placed—by Tom—directly in front of his place setting. Tom went into the kitchen to give some instructions to the caterer. While he was out of the dining room, my wife picked up the "special" bottle and, cheered on by everyone at the table, she filled the glasses in front of five people—including hers and mine—at the other end of the table.

—

Grandma did that? • She certainly did. I wish you could have seen her in action that evening. • *She's quite a woman, isn't she, Grandpa?* • You can bet on that.

—

We all sipped the wine, unanimously pronouncing it to be superb. The bottle, with barely a few remaining drops of wine in it, was passed along back to Tom's area. Tom returned to his seat and picked up the bottle. At first he looked confused, then stunned, then enraged. "Who the fuck drank my wine?" he bellowed. A bottle of cheap Chianti, wrapped in straw, was passed down to Tom by Eric Williams who suggested that Tom might like to try it. Tom, his face blazing red, charged at Eric. He was intercepted by Anne, who was laughing up-roariously. She put her arms around Tom and with her head against his chest—in the manner of a middle linebacker—she pushed him back to his seat. He sulked for the remainder of the weekend. I wondered what repercussions there might be from this incident beyond having to spend the remainder of the weekend in the company of a sulking Spellman.

That was one of the rare occasions when partners shared a social experience. More typically, we led our own lives outside of the firm. I had some good friends among the lawyers, but not many. Barry Weinberg, the spark of the D-Day luncheon, and his wife, Jessica, were among them. They lived in Brooklyn, not far from my home in Brooklyn Heights, and my wife and I saw them frequently and liked them a lot.

THREE

When I was in law school and thought about what life must be like in a quality law firm, the image I had in my mind was of a group of intelligent and capable people working collaboratively to solve the legal problems presented to them by clients. I thought that those lawyers—by the very nature of their cooperative efforts, performed every day they went to work—must create bonds of friendship and reciprocal care and concern.

That image might have been accurate in some firms, but it didn't come close to describing any law firm with which I had ever been affiliated. In my naiveté I gave no thought to such things as how a firm actually managed to get to represent its clients, how much the clients paid for the work done by their lawyers, how the income of a law firm was distributed among its lawyers, how the firm was managed, and all the other things that combined to make a law firm an economic engine. I had an innocence that I think must have been commonplace among lawyers from working class backgrounds who had spent their lives from kindergarten through law school with no experience with or exposure to the world of commerce and industry.

The point that I missed in my innocence was that law firms—at least the larger firms that represented corporations and banks and executives and investors—were created to make money, as much money as possible. The firms I knew about went about making money in more or less the same way. The first thing they needed to do, the *sine qua non* of success, was to be very good at what they did. Economically successful law firms did a good job for their clients. They delivered results that clients needed and expected. In order to perform at the necessary level they hired good lawyers, primarily from the so-called leading law schools. Most of the successful firms began—in the 1960s and 1970s, if not earlier—to encourage the development of specialties, areas of expertise designed to provide sophisticated professional services in areas of importance to their business clients. They organized themselves into departments or practice groups to promote efficiency in the delivery of services.

It became the standard practice of the major law firms to bill clients by the hour. This system carried with it a number of side effects that were widely recognized as undesirable but unavoidable. The longer it took to complete a task, the more expensive it was for the client. The hourly billing system relied upon the integrity of the lawyer to record his billable time accurately and honestly. Despite what many people might think, I never became aware of serious abuses of the time-keeping systems. Easily the most deleterious of the side effects of the hourly billing system was the inevitable drive to increase billable hours by working harder and longer. The heroes of the law firm were frequently those lawyers who amassed the highest number of billable hours each month and each year, often at the expense of the health, family, and quality of life of those heroes.

FOUR

The day after the D-Day lunch, Barry Weinberg walked into my office, closed the door and sat down. I was busy writing a brief for Spellman and didn't appreciate being interrupted. Barry started talking as soon as he sat down, not bothering to ask if I had time to chat with him.

"Well, what did you think of Spellman's performance at lunch yesterday?"

"He certainly can be an asshole at times."

"He was serious. He wasn't just being an asshole. He was making a point, a pro-Nazi point!" Barry raised his voice as he said this.

I have to tell you about Barry. He was the first Jew to be hired by the firm. That was in the mid-sixties and the firm was anything but a pioneer among the white-shoe law firms in that regard. In fact, Coburn & Perkins was among the last of the major New York City law firms to hire a Jew. I wasn't with the firm at the time Barry was hired but rumor had it that Spellman adamantly opposed hiring a Jew, making arguments in support of his position to the effect that collegiality, compatibility, and mutual confidence were important firm values that would be undermined if a Jew was in the firm—arguments that would be an embarrassment if they were circulated thirty years later.

Barry was the first Jew to be made a partner. He was absolutely brilliant. He was a star. A scholarship student at New York University and NYU Law School. He was first in his class at the law school and editor-in-chief of the *Law Review*. He clerked for a judge of the Second Circuit Court of Appeals. Perfect credentials. Tall, thin, graceful, curly dark hair, good looking in a typically Jewish way, an engaging manner, fluent in conversation, incisive in his legal analyses, and he had a wry sense of humor, and—I'm not sure how to say this without offending anyone—he didn't make a big deal out of his Jewishness. Jessica, his lovely wife and our good friend, was not an observant Jew and neither was Barry. Barry worked on Jewish holidays. His two wonderful children were being raised with no religion. In fact, Barry and Jessica made a point of emphasizing the fact that theirs was an "atheist" household.

Spellman didn't seem to know how to deal with Barry's ethnicity. He was aware, of course, that Barry was born Jewish. He even knew that Barry's late father was a kosher butcher. I learned that factoid from Tom, not Barry. Tom seemed to go overboard at times to display what seemed to me a pseudo-philo-Semitism. The double hyphens signified to me Tom's unresolved ambivalence in dealing with Barry—a strange specimen from an alien culture. On many more than one occasion, I heard Tom telling Barry about his experience as a convert to Roman Catholicism and asking Barry if he had ever considered becoming what Tom liked to call an "apostate Jew." Barry never quite knew how to deal with Tom's seemingly inordinate interest in a subject that had little intrinsic meaning to Barry.

For my own amusement, I once asked Tom if he ever considered himself to be an "apostate Episcopalian." That inquiry was met by bemused silence from Tom.

I should note that I was a complete non-belligerent in these occasional outbreaks of religious tension. Long before I came to the firm, I had become a "lapsed" Catholic, abandoning the faith of my Irish forefathers. My parochial school education at the hands of the nuns at St. Margaret's elementary school, my years as an altar boy, my inspiring encounter with the Jesuits at Georgetown, all fell victim to the church's insistence that my wife and I refrain from the use of contraceptives. It didn't happen instantly; rather there was a gradual erosion of my faith and my interest in the church. By the time I joined the firm, I was comfortably situated in the zone of indifference to religion that has kept me serene and untroubled all these years.

Let me now return to the conversation I had with Barry Weinberg the day following the D-Day lunch.

I urged Barry to cool off and not make an unnecessarily big deal out of Spellman's asinine remarks.

"But it is a big deal. He would have traded away the lives of every Jew in Europe in order to mount a battle against Soviet Communism."

"Barry, dear Barry, thirty years after the end of Hitler it doesn't matter what sort of war strategy one would have preferred while the real battles were raging. Spellman was speaking in a hypothetical environment. His comments were carried away in the wind. You must have noticed how little impact they had on Swanson and Madison; they barely heard a word that he said."

"Nazism was the greatest evil the world has ever experienced and Spellman is perfectly at home with it. Don't tell me it is over and done with."

"But it is."

"Bullshit! The Jews who were murdered—they're still dead. Their families still mourn them. And that poison is still in the air."

Frankly, I was surprised by the vehemence of Barry's reaction to Spellman's remarks. I felt I couldn't just dismiss the episode as a mere trifle but I knew that there was nothing that could be done about it. "Barry, tell me. What would you have us do?" I asked.

"At the very least, this should be reported to the Executive Committee and he should be expelled from the firm," he responded.

"Oh, c'mon. You know as well as I do that Spellman is a powerful person in this firm and that a few ill-considered comments at a casual lunch, overheard by no one outside of the firm, are not going to have consequences inside the firm, much less be grounds for kicking him out. Be realistic."

"So, you're strongly in favor of doing absolutely nothing, is that it? Whatever happened to the highly principled Michael Cullen, the guy to whom it was more important to do good than to do well?"

"Barry, you're being childish. There is nothing principled about chasing after unattainable objectives. I agree that Spellman can be obnoxious, perhaps even potentially dangerous. He bears watching. I think the worst thing we can do is launch a premature and undoubtedly futile attack on him. That will only make him more dangerous. When I say 'dangerous' I mean dangerous to you, more than to anyone else."

Weinberg stood up, stared at me for a moment, turned and walked to the door. As he left the room, he said, "I'm very disappointed in you, Michael."

Barry's remarks, his behavior, his "disappointment" in me were disquieting to me. I knew that every word he spoke was true. I also knew that my dismissal of his call for me to join him in seeking some sort of repudiation of Spellman's views by the firm was motivated by my anxiety about my position in the firm and not by any genuine conviction that the issue would be ignored by my partners. The more I thought about my motives the more troubled I became by my recognition of what they were. My statement to Barry that attacking Spellman would be dangerous to him might have been true but, in the deepest chambers of my conscience, it was a statement about my own fear that a debate in the firm about Spellman, about anti-Semitism, about bigotry, would turn into a storm that would damage me personally. I was not proud of that because Barry was right that we were facing a matter of principle.

I had trouble getting back into the brief I was writing and eventually gave it up and went home.

———

I don't think Mr. Weinberg was being fair to you. What you were saying to him seemed to me to be very sensible.

- Will, I'm not sure of that. You have to know how deep

his feelings were on this subject. • *I'm pretty sure I understand how Mr. Weinberg felt about Mr. Spellman. But he seemed to think you had a responsibility to attack Mr. Spellman and I don't see why that responsibility should have fallen on you.*

FIVE

Coburn & Perkins had more than a hundred lawyers when I came to the firm in 1974. Thirty-five of the lawyers were partners. I was the most recently admitted partner but because I was admitted laterally I was not the most junior partner. A meeting of the partners was held on the last Wednesday of every month in our main conference room. That room was the largest and most elegant room in our suite of offices and conference rooms. A beautiful crystal chandelier hung over the center of a large, highly polished mahogany table around which were twenty-eight comfortable chairs. Seating was arranged in accordance with a strict rule of seniority. The Presiding Partner—the title given to the firm's managing partner— sat in the center seat of the long side of the table facing the door of the conference room. The Presiding Partner was flanked on his left and right by the other two members of the firm's Executive Committee. Seated directly opposite the Presiding Partner was the most senior partner in years as a partner and fanning out on each side of him, and of the right and left side of the two Executive Committee members, were the other partners in descending order of their seniority in an elaborate array prescribed by custom and years of practice. Those partners for whom no seat at the table was available sat against the walls of the room on wheeled desk chairs brought in for that purpose. Barry Weinberg and I, among others, were relegated to the wall seats, known informally as the "bleachers." Although I had been a partner for only six months, I had been a practicing lawyer for sixteen years. I resented having been assigned a seat in the bleachers when I was many years senior to several of the partners sitting in the reserved seats. I had raised that point with the Presiding Partner who told me that the firm had no history of admitting senior level lateral partners and that, consequently, there was no tradition for "bumping" a partner from the table to the bleachers. I would have to wait until someone retired or died at which time I would be given "priority access" to the table. This may seem like a small and petty point but if there is one thing about lawyers, it is the fragility of their egos. My ego may well have been more fragile than most, a condition I ascribed to the humbleness of my origins.

Fred Perkins had the honor of the seat allocated to the most senior partner. Perkins was the grandson of one of the founders of the firm and the son of a recently deceased partner. I am absolutely certain that it was that heritage that accounted for Perkins's presence in the firm. He had neither the legal ability nor the client connections that would otherwise have justified his being a partner.

He was in his late sixties when I arrived at the firm. I noticed immediately that he was always meticulously well groomed—neatly pressed dark suits, starched white shirts, perfectly knotted striped ties, highly polished shoes. I never saw him when he wasn't wearing his suit jacket. All of us worked in our shirtsleeves except when we were seeing clients or meeting with lawyers from other firms. Not good old Fred, however, his jacket stayed on him all day long although he rarely saw a client or met with an outside lawyer. It would not have surprised me to learn that he wore his suit jacket at home. He was unfailingly courteous—not only to his partners but to the firm's associates, messengers, clerks, and, most of all, to the "girls" which is what we called the secretaries in those days. I never called him "Fred." Somehow that would have seemed impolite. Since he'll never read this—he passed away about ten years ago—I'll now refer to him as Fred.

Fred was nominally a member of the firm's litigation department because what little work he did was the settlement of estates in the Surrogate's Court. That branch of the law seemed to fit him perfectly. It was quiet and he was quiet. He rarely spoke except to exchange pleasantries with anyone he might encounter in the course of a day. I must have had lunch with him dozens of times but I don't recall a single substantive conversation. And in the three years from the date I joined the firm until Fred's retirement, he faithfully attended every monthly partners' meeting at which I was present and, I have no doubt, all of those that I managed to miss. At all of those meetings, Fred remained silent.

All, that is, except the meeting in June 1974. As that meeting was drawing to a close, Fred raised his hand and addressed the Presiding Partner. "I wonder if it would be in order if I brought to the attention of the partners remarks by one of our partners that I personally found deeply troubling." Jaws dropped around the room.

Immediately, I thought, "Oh, no. Here it comes. This isn't good."

I glanced at Barry Weinberg. He looked as shocked as everyone else. Staring straight at me, he silently mouthed the words, "Not me."

Paul Conway, our Presiding Partner, looking slightly bemused, said to Perkins, "If you think this is important enough to keep us all from returning to work, please go ahead." And then, with a wry smile, "It's not as if you've wasted much of our time at these meetings over the years, so please Fred, tell us what you have in mind."

(By the way, it was the custom of the firm that partners always referred to other partners by their first names. This was supposed to promote collegiality among the partners. I didn't think it had that effect. Lawyers who were not partners and all other employees of the firm were expected to refer to partners as "Mr. Whatever" and, in turn, were called by their first names. There was no pretense that the law firm was a classless society. Quite the contrary.)

Perkins, looking more resolute and focused than I ever remember seeing him, began: "As some of you may know, I served as an officer in the United States Navy in the Second World War. I was a relatively young man then but that experience was the most vivid event of my life."

Conway interrupted, "Fred, do we really need to hear your autobiography?"

Perkins snapped back, "Yes, you do need to hear about my service in World War Two, and I would be grateful for the opportunity to deliver my report in the manner of my choosing." That snappy remark got everyone's attention. He took a deep breath and continued, "I served as an officer in command of a landing craft at Omaha Beach on D-Day, June 6, 1944. It was my responsibility to see to the delivery to the beach of thirty-six brave young men for an amphibious landing. I must say it was a frightening responsibility, frightening because of the mortal danger awaiting my troops and frightening, I am not ashamed to say, because of the terrible danger that I was facing personally. It became impossible, because of wind and strong currents, to maneuver my craft all the way to the shore. I had to order the men—they were really just boys—to wade through turbulent water almost fifty yards to the beach. Most of them never made it. Machine gun fire cut them down as they waded defenselessly through the waves. Do you have any idea what it is like to look at the bodies of young men floating around in bloody water on all sides of the boat? Do you have any idea what that's like?"

He paused for a sip of water. "Those men—those who lived and those who died—won the war for us and preserved our liberty. They deserve to be honored. Dammit, I deserve to be honored!" Another long pause. "The remarks that I wished to bring to the attention of the partnership are remarks that dishonored me and my men. Thomas Spellman, at lunch a few days ago at the Graduates Club, characterized the D-Day invasion as a, quote, catastrophic mistake, a grave mistake. I demand an apology." Perkins leaned back in his chair, obviously spent, enervated by the effort expended in delivering these remarks.

Spellman sat stone-faced throughout Perkins's speech, not even reacting when Perkins mentioned his name. It was as if Perkins was talking about someone else.

Running true to form, Perkins used his debut presentation to the partnership to totally miss the point. Spellman's D-Day comments had nothing to do with Perkins or his men. I heard those comments and they were about policy, not people. The startling fact was that Spellman bemoaned the missed opportunity to align this country with Nazi Germany. That was clear to Barry Weinberg and it was clear to me. The fact that it wasn't clear to Perkins is unremarkable, the perennial fog around his brain was rarely penetrated by a ray of clarity. The problem now was that the partnership had the wrong issue placed before it. Instead of inquiring into the implications of having a fan of Adolf Hitler as a partner, the firm was now going to consider how to deal with the delicate feelings of Fred Perkins, war hero.

After a few moments of noise at the partnership table, Conway suggested that the issue raised by Fred Perkins should be referred to the Executive Committee "for careful examination and proper deliberation." Several partners wanted the matter to be discussed then and there, involving as it did, according to our senior corporate lawyer, Warren Worthington, "the issue of free speech when it comes to the expression of opinions about our government." Another partner countered, "Fred Perkins is a gentleman and he has a right, as a partner in this firm, to be treated as a true gentleman." The response to that was, "I hope I don't have to watch what I say at lunch so that I don't inadvertently offend the sensibilities of one of my partners." Someone made a motion to adjourn, which was greeted indignantly by a partner who remarked that "the rights of the partners to engage in vigorous debate is being eroded before my very eyes." Sam Waters observed that "at least this isn't about money." This drew a vehement response: "Who says it isn't about money? Everyone in this room knows that Perkins resents the fact that Spellman has the same income percentage that he has." I listened to this debate with a mixture of amusement and disgust. How could these graduates of some of the finest law schools, these preeminent lawyers, how could they so utterly miss the point? We had a partner sitting in that meeting room with us who seemed to be soft on Hitler and no one seemed to think that that was a subject that ought to command the attention of the partnership.

I didn't hang around for the post-meeting conversations. I returned to my office, closed the door that I usually left open, closed my eyes, and tried to wipe my mind clean of the silliness I had just witnessed.

—

Did you think about quitting the firm after that ridiculous meeting? • You have to understand, Will, that I had a family to support and a career to pursue. I couldn't just pick up and leave.

SIX

The partners' meeting was on a Wednesday. On Friday, Paul Conway, the Presiding Partner, phoned me and asked if it would be possible for me to come to his office where an "informal" meeting of the Executive Committee was taking place. I fully understood that this was not a request but, rather, a summons and that "not possible" was not an optional response. Because I was actually in the middle of some important and difficult work, I told Conway that I needed about thirty minutes to complete some urgent work before I could come to his office. I could tell he was annoyed when he said, "Well, do your best. We'll be waiting for you."

Paul Conway was an impressive person. It was not for nothing that the partners had elected him to a fourth two-year term as Presiding Partner. He was a renowned lawyer who represented our most valuable clients in their most important and complex financial transactions. He had a commanding appearance and an imposing presence.

I avoided him as much as I could without making it obvious. Quite frankly, I was afraid of him. He was one of those
people who made you wonder what you needed to apologize
for whenever you met him. Nevertheless, I was glad that he
was the leader of the firm. I had confidence in his judgment
and integrity. The firm—and my livelihood—were in good
hands with him at the helm. I truly believed that—at least
until the time I left his office after meeting with him about
the "Perkins matter."

That's what he called it when I arrived in his office in
response to his summons. This was the first time I had been
in his office and I almost gasped at its size and its elegance. I
don't know anything about furniture but Conway's desk was
a thing of beauty. The sofas and upholstered chairs arranged
tastefully around the room could have accommodated more
than twenty people. There were expensive-looking paintings
on the walls, interspersed with photographs of Conway with
important people including Presidents Eisenhower and Nixon.
The view of New York Harbor from his corner windows was
breathtaking.

"Thank you for stopping by, Michael. We've been talking
about the Perkins matter and we thought you might be in
a position to clarify what gave rise to Fred's remarkable
comments at the partners' meeting. Sit down, please.
Make yourself comfortable and tell us what you know
about this thing."

I took a seat facing the two other members of the Executive
Committee—Barnett and Schultz. I barely knew either of them
and wasn't entirely sure which one was which. They were
sitting together on a sofa across the room from the armchair
next to Conway's desk that was obviously my designated

seat. In any event, they were irrelevant and neither said a word during my time in the office. Conway remained seated at his desk. He was in charge of this interrogation.

"Tell us, Michael, using your own words, what took place at that lunch table in the Graduates Club."

"Paul, why did you have to ask me to tell you what happened, quote, using my own words? You make it sound like you think someone briefed me on what to say. I assure you that didn't happen."

"Don't be snippy. I just want to get this over with as soon as possible."

"Okay. The whole thing at the Graduates Club didn't take more than a couple of minutes. Perkins, Spellman, Barry Weinberg, Harry Madison, Paul Swanson, and I were finishing our lunch. I had a hamburger. The conversations over the lunch table were mostly about sports and a little bit about a case that Tom and I are working on. At one point Barry mentioned that the date—June 6, 1974—was the 30th anniversary of the D-Day invasion. Tom immediately responded, in what I would call his courtroom voice—articulate, fluent and forceful—that the D-Day invasion was—and I quote—a catastrophic mistake and that the U.S. and Britain should have made a deal with Germany to fight alongside each other against the Soviet Union. He said a few other things but that was the gist of his remarks. I questioned whether he thought it was important to defeat Nazi Germany and he surprised me by saying, in essence, that that was not as important as defeating the Soviet Union. A moment later, Barry said something about the Jews of Europe and Tom said that there could have been some sort of deal that would have solved the Jewish question. Yes, he called it 'the Jewish question.'

Barry looked upset. When Tom mentioned a solution to the 'Jewish question,' Barry asked—again I quote—'a final solution?' and Tom said 'that's right.' Tom totally missed the sarcasm in Barry's question and got up and left for court. That's it."

Conway, looking a bit perplexed, asked, "Well, what did Perkins say?"

"He didn't say a word about that and, as usual, he hardly spoke about anything during the lunch."

"You heard him at the partners' meeting. He was enraged."

"As I said, he didn't say a word about that subject. And, I would add, he gave no appearance of being enraged or even particularly interested."

"I find that very confusing. Do you think Weinberg might have gotten Fred all worked up?"

"I strongly doubt that. Why would I think that?"

"Weinberg is a Jew, isn't he?"

"Yes he is. So what?"

"So what? He has a biased point of view about the subject, that's what! I'm wondering whether he might have used Perkins to stir the pot. I can tell you that Tom Spellman shares that concern."

At this point, with my heart pounding and my blood pressure rising, my dismay over the way I dismissed Barry's plea for a strong response by the firm to Spellman's bigotry rose up in me. I said, hardly believing that I had the audacity to say what I was saying, "I want you to understand that I have the same 'biased' point of view that Barry has. That point of view is that Nazi Germany was evil. With all due respect, Paul, I would have thought that you and everyone in this firm would have shared that bias."

Conway, his tone sharpening, said, "Perhaps we should end this conversation so that you can think about where you stand in this law firm."

I rose from my seat, tried to calm myself, and said, "I always think about my position in this firm. Paul, I have the greatest respect for you—as a lawyer, as a leader, as a military veteran of World War Two and—most important—as a human being. I find it hard to believe that you find the notion of an alliance between our country and Nazi Germany to be anything but an obscenity."

He paused for a moment and turned to his corner window looking out onto New York Harbor. I remained standing, halfway between my chair and the door. Completely disregarding Tweedledum and Tweedledee on the sofa, he turned to me and said, "Michael, please sit down. We may both have said things that we probably regret."

I sat, and he continued, using his elder statesman voice, "One of the things that I have always prized in this law firm is the spirit of collegiality that prevails here. The mutual respect in which we hold all of our partners. That is a precious thing and we should all do everything in our power to preserve that spirit. That doesn't mean we can't have disagreements about particular issues. That's normal, especially among lawyers." He smiled as he spoke those last few words.

Paul continued these remarks, which seemed to me to be taking the form of a lecture.

"Michael, I find this Perkins thing extremely distasteful because it runs counter to the fundamental rules that govern the relationships among our partners."

"The prime directive," I interjected.

—

That was a smart-ass remark, Grandpa. Not everyone was as addicted to Star Trek as you told me you were. • You're probably right. But I was so frustrated by Conway's remarks that I just lashed out with the first thing that came to mind. Conway's speech was not only pompous; it was transparently inaccurate. The notion that the partners in Coburn & Perkins enjoyed a "spirit of collegiality" was so far from the truth that any partner would have found it to be laughable. My "smart-ass remark" was the only response I could think of that didn't involve calling Conway a jerk. Wait until you hear what he thought of my "prime directive" remark.

—

"Well put, Michael, very well put. 'Prime directive.' I like that. We need to work together to put this matter behind us. I love the image of six of my partners taking a break from their labors and having a collegial lunch together, having friendly conversations, and even having an occasional difference of opinion. That's the way a partnership should work. Let's do what we can to preserve that spirit."

"I assure you that I'll do that."

"I know you will, Michael. Even though you haven't spent the whole of your career in this firm, I believe you have embraced our values."

That was the end of the conversation. I took my leave and returned to my office where I didn't do any work for the rest of the day. The "Perkins matter" was eating into my billable hours.

SEVEN

My wife's name is Norah.

—

Do you think I don't know Grandma's name. • Oh, be quiet.

—

At the time of the "Perkins matter," we had been married for eighteen years. Our children were teenagers, a boy and a girl, and a late arrival, an utterly adorable five-year-old girl.

—

My mother. Was she your favorite? • All three were my favorites. • *Spoken like a lawyer, Grandpa.*

I loved my wife and children. We lived in a brownstone home in Brooklyn Heights on a street that has trees and good neighbors. We bought the house when I made my lateral move from my old law firm to Coburn & Perkins in January 1974. The house was expensive and we took out a large mortgage loan, all on the assumption that my income from the new firm would grow to a level that would enable us to carry that amount of debt and send the children to private schools. That had worked out, perhaps not as well as I expected, but well enough for us to enjoy an excellent quality of life. As a constant reminder of where the money came from to provide that quality of life, the view of New York's financial district across the river—especially at night when the office towers blazed brightly—was stunning.

Norah, whom I met when we were both law students at Georgetown Law, had recently gone back to work as a part-time lawyer in a small firm in Manhattan that did real estate law. She was one of the three women in our law school class. Although she was—by far—a better law student than I was, we agreed that I would be the breadwinner of the family for the simple reason that men were far more likely to succeed economically in the legal profession. That was an absolutely correct assumption at the time we married and passed the New York bar exam. And, to the disgrace of the profession, it continued to be an accurate assumption even seventeen years later at the time of the "Perkins matter."

—

Was Grandma really a better law student than you were? •
There's no question about that. I want to tell you that law

school was a seminal experience in my life. Do you know what that means? • *Grandpa, give me a break and have a little respect for my literacy.* • Okay Will, sorry. Not only did it enable me to meet and woo your grandmother, it gave me a new and exciting way to use my brain. The first-year class at Georgetown Law was divided into sections so that some of the courses were taught in seminars to small groups of about fifteen students. Your grandmother and I serendipitously wound up in the same section. I won't ask you if you know what that means. • *Thanks.* • I recall vividly the seminar in Contracts 101—one of the most important subjects in the curriculum. The teacher was a master of the Socratic method. • *Grandpa, I really don't know what that means. Stop laughing.* • I can't help it. The Socratic method is a style of teaching in which the teacher rarely, if ever, provides the answer to a problem. It's all questions designed to make the students think to develop and defend their own answers. I was not comfortable in that seminar, never sure enough to volunteer an answer or a comment and afraid to embarrass myself. I was not particularly expressive or articulate in those days. • *Well, that hasn't changed.* • Do I detect a note of sarcasm? But your grandmother was the star of the seminar. She was always ready with a sharp and incisive analysis of a problem. Everyone in the group was in awe of her. She was the only woman in the seminar and, as you know, she is beautiful to look at. You have only known your grandmother as a middle-aged woman. As a woman in her twenties, her beauty was extraordinary. Her ivory-complexioned face, sprinkled with a few freckles, was framed by long raven-black hair, no doubt evidence in her ancestry of a survivor of the defeated

Spanish Armada washed up on the shores of Ireland. I cannot account for the reason she was attracted to me, but my attraction to her occurred at the instant I first saw her face.

Although I was a bit terrified by her brilliance, I came up with a brilliant idea of my own. I asked her to give me some help on a paper I had to write for the seminar. She agreed and suggested we have dinner together to talk about my paper. Visions of a romantic evening flashed through my brain. It turned out that your grandmother's expectations were different. Our first, quote, date, was spent exploring whether a requirements contract had sufficient mutuality to be enforceable. A less romantic subject cannot be imagined. But it was a beginning. • *I'm happy that it was a beginning and not an ending.* • Me too.

———

I earned a good income as a partner in Coburn & Perkins but I certainly wasn't getting obscenely rich. I was one of the firm's "grinders," the lowest tier in the "finder," "minder," and "grinder" hierarchy. The "finders" brought in the business and were highly valued. The "minders" were responsible for maintaining client relationships—holding hands and keeping clients happy—and the "grinders" like me ground out the work by the hour. Because I was at the bottom of the value hierarchy, my income didn't rise as fast as our hourly rates did. Although I was well compensated by any normal person's standard, there were moments when I felt exploited and ill used. Norah knew that and she tried to comfort me by frequently pointing out what a good life we were enjoying, largely because of the fruits of my labor in the firm.

I mention all of this because, when I came home on the evening following my interrogation by Paul Conway, I told Norah that there was trouble in the firm and that my job might be in jeopardy. She said, "I thought partners couldn't be fired."

I gave her a warm and loving hug and told her, "A firm like Coburn & Perkins can find ways to do seemingly impossible things." I then told her about Spellman and Weinberg and Perkins and Conway.

When I finished the D-Day story, Norah said, "Unless Tom Spellman simply tossed off some ill-considered thoughts, his comments about holding hands with Hitler were absolutely horrifying."

"He never said we should 'hold hands with Hitler.'"

"That's precisely the meaning of his remarks."

"Norah, that's just one possible meaning. He may have meant something entirely different."

She looked annoyed with me. "Mike, you're deluding yourself. Don't forget, I know the guy. It never occurred to me that he might be an actual Nazi but, I must say, I'm not entirely surprised to learn that he is. The way he assumes he is in charge of everything and everyone. An authoritative personality and, don't forget, an extreme right-winger politically."

"Now really, an authoritative personality and right-wing politics don't add up to being a Nazi. If they did, half the people I deal with every day would be members of the American Nazi Party. Damn it, this thing is making everyone crazy."

Norah seemed to cool off a bit at this point. "I guess you're right. But I don't want to have anything further to do with him. I don't know how Anne can live with him. She's so nice and warm and friendly and he's such a dour person with a lot of anger lurking just beneath the surface. Remember the wine eruption."

I responded, "I'll add a fight over a wine bottle to the list of things that don't add up to being a Nazi."

"Please don't distort what I'm saying. He may or may not be a card-carrying Nazi but he certainly is a total shit as a person."

This made me laugh. I don't know how many times I thought the same thing about Tom Spellman. But I reminded myself that I work closely with the guy, that my professional life—and the income I derive from it—were absolutely linked to Tom Spellman. And that thought brought me back to where I intended my conversation with Norah to go.

"Sweetheart," I said, "we need to talk about how I handle this subject inside the firm. I need your advice; in fact, I need your wisdom."

"What do you think is going to happen?"

"I think the partners are going to squabble with each other. The majority will be the pro-Spellman faction following Conway's lead. Most of these guys are not in love with Spellman but they're loyal to Conway and concerned about avoiding discord in the firm. There will be a small Perkins faction, guys who understand that that pathetic old man feels hurt and needs to be comforted. And then there will be a few of us—right now, as far as I know, this faction consists of Weinberg and me—who perceive the issue very differently. I don't know how many partners will eventually come to the realization that Spellman's extreme views are a potential danger to the firm and are morally insupportable. That's the big question in my mind right now."

"What do you plan to do?"

"Nothing, at least until I see where this is heading inside the firm. Then, I don't have the slightest idea what to do."

"You're worried about your job, aren't you?"

"Of course I'm worried about my job. If it ever comes down to who has to go—Spellman or me—I'm out on my ass before I know what hit me."

Norah hugged me. With a big smile on her face, she said, "I have a great idea." She removed her blouse, then her bra, took my hand and led me into out bedroom. "Let's go to bed and have wild sex. They can't fire you for that."

"That's an offer I can't refuse." As we lawyers say, the details of what happened next are irrelevant. Suffice it to say, Norah knew how to comfort me whenever I was troubled or anxious.

—

Grandpa, that's substantially more information than I need.
- Well, Will, it's part of the story.

—

I went back to work the next day and the atmosphere in our offices felt normal and undisturbed. I gave no thought at all to Conway's subtle threat that I'd better fit in to the firm's culture or I might find myself outside looking in.

EIGHT

At the same time that the Perkins–Spellman matter was simmering among the partners of Coburn & Perkins, another issue was beginning to reach its boiling point. I believe I described to you one of the ways in which partner compensation was determined at our law firm—the finder, minder, grinder paradigm. But I omitted the factor that carried more weight than any other—seniority.

There was something lovely about the use of seniority as a basis for determining a partner's share of the net profits of a law firm. It removed all subjectivity from the process. It made it unnecessary and irrelevant for the partners to make invidious distinctions among one another as to the worth of a partner's contribution to the firm. It eliminated competition among the partners and the demeaning annual spectacle of the partners campaigning for a higher share of the profits by touting their value and belittling the value of the contributions of their colleagues. But seniority had as its underlying assumption that all partners were equally diligent, equally capable, equally committed to the success of the firm and of their partners, and equally respectful of the efforts and skills of their colleagues.

This assumption was always demonstrably untrue and everyone knew it. It was an assumption that might have worked when law firms were smaller, when the amount of money at stake was smaller, when the partners knew each other socially, when a law firm was an intimate group of culturally, ethnically, and equally privileged members of the same social class. Seniority no longer worked in the 1970s. It gave rise to glaring inequities in the distribution of the firm's profits and it became a source of irritation and unrest. Eventually, it was an issue that threatened to tear the law firm apart.

From the day of its founding in the nineteenth century until 1969, the share of every partner in Coburn & Perkins's profits was determined entirely on the basis of his position on the seniority ladder. There was a complex twelve-step process by which a partner's share was increased annually until his twelfth year as a partner, at which time he became entitled to what was called a "full" share. Thus all partners with twelve or more years of tenure with the firm shared equally in the profits and those partners junior to them had smaller shares correlated with their respective tenures in the firm. Thus, for example, Fred Perkins—who contributed virtually nothing to the firm's profitability—enjoyed the same full share as Tom Spellman whose contribution was prodigious. It's hardly surprising that this situation became unsustainable or that Tom Spellman became a leader in the movement for change.

In 1970—before I came to the firm—after what was described to me as a "contentious and sometimes ugly" debate, the partners voted to reserve 10 percent of the firm's annual profits to be distributed as a "merit pool" according to a determination by a Compensation Committee as to each partner's relative "productivity." The Compensation Committee was comprised of five very senior partners appointed by the Presiding Partner who, incidentally, chose not to be a member of the committee.

The elements of a partner's performance that were supposed to be considered in evaluating a partner's productivity were his annual billable hours (a "grinder" factor), the revenue associated with the partner's personal work ("grinder"), the revenue contributed by the clients that he brought into the firm ("finder"), the revenues contributed by the clients for whom he had management responsibility ("minder"), and, finally, a subjective assessment of how a partner enhanced the "collegiality, reputation and success" of the law firm.

There were numerous problems with this system as it played out in practice. Despite the system's appearance of objectivity, the Compensation Committee just did as it pleased, awarding the merit pool to cronies, departmental colleagues, and—worst of all—to themselves. Moreover, a significant number of partners regarded the 10 percent merit pool as mere tokenism that did little to correct the growing inequities of the seniority system. Tom Spellman, for example, was exasperated by the fact that his share of the firm's profits continued to be essentially the same as that of Fred Perkins. Perkins, by the way, became the emblem of the defects in the firm's partner compensation system—although he was totally oblivious to that unhappy reputation. It was ironic that the firm was vexed by two "Perkins matters" and that Spellman was directly involved in both of them.

It was not long after I joined the firm that Spellman asked me to side with him and a number of other partners in a concerted effort to change the compensation system. The objective, he explained, was to convert the current 10 percent merit pool to 80 percent and thereby virtually eliminate seniority as a factor in determining partnership shares. He pointed out to me that, as a partner with no seniority, I would benefit greatly by having my share of the profits determined primarily on my personal productivity. I told Spellman that, as a brand new partner in the firm, I didn't think it would be appropriate for me to become involved in a dispute over such a fundamental matter of firm policy. He called me an asshole.

Thus, I stood on the sidelines as a battle raged. On the one side were many of the firm's most able and productive partners—the men who had the charisma or the social contacts or the glowing reputations that enabled them to bring valuable clients to the firm. On the other side were the more mature partners—beneficiaries, to be sure, of the seniority system—who claimed to be more concerned with the stability of the firm, with the avoidance of internal animosities and jealousies, with the value of tradition, than with what they saw as the correction of temporary inequities. The active combatants on both sides were fewer in number than the noncombatant partners who watched the rapidly intensifying dispute with, on the one hand, anxiety about its ultimate effect on the firm and the security of their comfortable positions as partners in a thriving law firm and, on the other hand, an acute concern about whether they would come out ahead or behind as a result of the outcome of the battle.

After several weeks of impassioned arguments in the hallways, offices, and conference rooms throughout the firm, Spellman and two other partners—Jack Iverson, a young banking lawyer who brought two large banks into the firm as clients, and Douglas Schmidt, an immensely productive securities lawyer—announced in a memorandum to the partners that, "unless the seniority system is consigned to the dustbin of outmoded ideas, we are prepared to resign from the firm and organize a new firm better able to serve the major clients of Coburn & Perkins because it would not be burdened with the dead weight of partners resting on their laurels or—worse yet—on nothing more than their advanced ages."

This was too much. Even partners who supported major changes in the compensation system were appalled at the resignation threat and the insulting character of the "dead weight" comment in the memorandum from the three partners—who became known as the "Gang of Three." Paul Conway convened what he called an emergency meeting of the partners. The meeting was a spectacle. It was combative, chaotic at times; there were flashes of brilliance and moments of breathtaking stupidity. I can only remember fragments of the debate; the air was so charged with passion, anger, frustration, and sorrow that it became impossible to retain a record in my mind of what was said. Here are a few of the remarks that I have managed pull up from my memory.

Paul Conway, always dignified, always in control, opened the meeting by saying, "We have received notice from three of our partners of their intention to resign from the firm and take away with them valued clients of our firm. I would say to each of them that their resignations will be accepted without ceremony but that their effort to appropriate as their property clients who have entrusted their legal work requirements to this firm will be resisted with all the force, and all the skill, and all the power that this great law firm can muster. To that Gang of Three I say: leave if you will and good riddance."

Tom Spellman muttered that Conway misunderstood the point of the memorandum.

Warren Worthington almost screamed back at Spellman, "That piece of trash was the clearest thing you ever wrote."

Doug Schmidt called on everyone to remain calm and discuss the subject "on its merits."

Stanley Hudnut—one of our older partners—asked Schmidt, "Are you proposing that those of us resting on our advanced age should remain calm?"

There was a moment when Worthington pointed his finger at Jack Iverson and sounded like God must have sounded when he asked Job, "Where were you when I laid the foundation of the earth?" Except Worthington asked Iverson, "Where were you when we made this firm great? I'll tell you where. You were sucking milk from your mother's tits. You arrogant young whippersnapper." He really said "whippersnapper."

I confess that I was enjoying being a spectator at this spectacle.

——

How could you enjoy a meeting where everyone was yelling at each other? • I enjoyed it the way people enjoy watching a knockout in a boxing match or rubbernecking at an accident scene.

—

I have to tell you about Iverson. He was thirty-six years old, tall, slender, wavy black hair perfectly groomed atop a strikingly handsome face, a face on which luminous blue eyes framed a perfectly proportioned nose above a dazzlingly pleasing smile. He was as bright and charming as he was beautiful to look at. And he worked hard. His billable hours were among the highest in the firm. He practically created a new banking law specialty: structuring the conversion of mutual savings banks into shareholder-owned companies that made a lot of folks wealthy by merging into larger banks. He was a decent and honorable fellow, not a bomb-throwing revolutionary. Quite the contrary, he was modest, conservative, respectful and responsible. So how, you may ask, did he become part of the Gang of Three?

—

I was wondering about that. I remember you once told me that Mr. Iverson came from a very rich family, so why was he so involved in a plot to make more money? He didn't really need it, did he?

—

Of all of the people in the firm, Jack Iverson was the least likely to join a campaign about money. Although he didn't flaunt his wealth, we all knew that he and his family were extremely wealthy. He couldn't possibly have cared about a few thousand dollars, more or less, in income from the practice of law. His trust funds threw off many multiples of his income from the firm. So the question remains: Why did he become part of the Gang of Three?

Spellman is the answer. Jack Iverson was in thrall to Tom Spellman. He was absolutely captivated by Spellman's personal magnetism. Jack had spent his life among rich and powerful people, surrounded by old wealth. But no one in Jack's experience had ever displayed the dynamism that emanated from Tom Spellman. Spellman had followers, not colleagues. Jack Iverson became one of Spellman's followers and he went wherever Spellman would lead. I think Jack was thunderstruck by the vehemence of the reaction of the partners to the resignation threat from the Gang of Three. I watched him at the meeting. He looked cowed, almost frightened. He was clearly embarrassed. I remember the one thing he said at the meeting. He raised his hand, was recognized by the Presiding Partner and said, "I want to apologize to all of you for signing that memorandum and I wish to disassociate myself from it."

That one comment turned things around. As if every partner simultaneously realized that the intemperate discussion was both unseemly and dangerous to the life of the firm, the partners began a long and thoughtful discussion of the benefits and defects of the existing compensation system.

Eventually, the partners voted—almost unanimously—to change the merit pool to 25 percent of the firm's profits and to reconstitute the Compensation Committee by having its five members elected by vote of the partners. Thus the contentious issue of partner compensation was laid to rest. Seniority as a factor in the determination of partner compensation was preserved for the time being but everyone seemed to sense that its days were numbered. Echoes of that contentious partners' meeting were still reverberating during all the years that I remained at Coburn & Perkins. Animosities created because of the compensation issue never really went away. The firm was wounded but at least it was not dead.

—

Was all this really about how much a partner should be paid? Did anyone really not make enough money? • Good questions, Will. Every partner at Coburn & Perkins made a great deal of money. During this debate, one of the partners commented that, "high water raises all boats." What he meant, of course, was that if the firm prospered everyone would make more money. But he missed the point. Money became a measure, a symbol, a scorecard, of one's professional—and personal—superiority over those who were paid less money. It was always about egos and status, I'm sad to say.

NINE

Perkins did nothing to press his demand for an apology and Spellman didn't apologize. However, the subject almost seemed to be hanging in the air, always present, brooding. There was an increasing sourness in the atmosphere of our elegant offices. The usual tension that is endemic to law firms was still there; the rivalries over income, status, importance, power—these continued in a somewhat more subdued manner than usual—but something alien was present. Perkins's attack on Spellman still resounded in the hallways, the conference rooms, even in the immense library of Coburn & Perkins. Our billable hours were also depressed. The seemingly relentless month-by-month increase in billable hours and revenue paused and then declined. The partners collectively seemed to have taken a furlough from their usual frenzied pursuit of increased income. More time was spent gazing out of windows at the view of New York Harbor and the forest of giant buildings rising on all sides of our offices than doing client work or even having sociable chats. We rarely went to lunch at the Graduates Club; most of us were eating lunch at our desks.

People were thinking and—when they were sure no one was eavesdropping—talking about the Perkins matter but the subject was understood by everyone to be taboo as a matter of open conversation. I believe this was the case even outside of the offices. I hardly ever discussed it with Norah at home and she picked up on my silent signal that I just didn't feel like talking about it.

Although the subject was not being discussed, it was certainly being thought about. Gradually, but relentlessly, more and more partners seemed to be coming to the realization that this was not about Fred Perkins's hurt feelings. Barry Weinberg told me that several partners had asked him how he was bearing up. That could only have signified that people were beginning to get it. Remember, this was a Wall Street law firm, institutionally sympathetic to conservative politics. I would guess that an absolute majority of the partners intuitively felt that the Watergate scandal was something blown way out of proportion. Richard Nixon was viewed as being clumsy, tone deaf, but not evil. But no matter what one's politics might be, Nazi Germany was outside the boundaries of civilized debate.

About two months after the infamous "Perkins matter" partners' meeting, without any indication that something was in the works, Paul Conway sent the following "confidential memorandum" to all of the partners:

TO: ALL PARTNERS
FROM: PAUL G. CONWAY
SUBJECT: PERKINS/SPELLMAN

The Executive Committee of the Firm (the
"Committee") has carefully considered the issue
raised by Frederick Perkins at the June regular
meeting of the partners concerning remarks made
by Thomas Spellman at an informal luncheon at
the Graduates Club on June 6. The Committee has
interviewed all of the partners who were present at
the June 6 luncheon and has deliberated about this
matter in what I consider to have been a thorough,
thoughtful and professional manner.

The Committee concluded that the remarks made
by Mr. Spellman, although representing his perspective
on an historical event and, thus, well within the
latitude afforded by this Firm to partners to hold and
express a diversity of views, failed to take due account
of the impact of such remarks upon the sensibilities of
the listeners to his remarks, in particular Mr. Perkins.
The Committee has advised Mr. Spellman of its
conclusion and has urged Mr. Spellman to apologize
to Mr. Perkins and to have a private discussion with
Mr. Perkins in which Mr. Spellman would refine and
explain his remarks with a view to repairing his
collegial relationship with Mr. Perkins.

Mr. Spellman readily agreed with the Committee's
recommendation and has offered an apology to Mr.
Perkins and has reported to the Committee that he
and Mr. Perkins are now fully reconciled.

Mr. Spellman also authorized me to transmit the following statement to the Partners:

"In expressing my views as to the wisdom—or lack thereof—of an action taken by our country thirty years previously, I inadvertently offended Fred Perkins who participated in that action as a young and courageous officer of the U.S. military. I deeply regret the offense to Fred whom I have always held in the highest esteem as a partner of this firm since long before I joined the firm. This esteem has now been enhanced by the knowledge gained in recent weeks of his service in time of war.

I want all of my partners to understand that I had no intention to insult Fred and that I have apologized sincerely to him."

The Committee is pleased that this matter is now resolved and that we can continue to practice law together in the expert, collegial and professional manner that has made this Firm preeminent among the nation's law firms.

/s/ Paul G. Conway
Presiding Partner

So that was that. Who cares if there's a Nazi in the next room? Now let's go make more money.

The Conway memorandum appeared to have the opposite effect from that which was transparently intended. The effete formality and excessively lawyerly presentation of the firm's position and Spellman's saccharine apology combined to raise murmurings among more than a few of the partners. A few days after the circulation of the Conway memorandum, Craig Wilson, a veteran banking lawyer, mentioned to me while we were standing at the coffee machine that Spellman "reaffirmed" the views that he expressed at the luncheon—which, by this point, most of the partners could recite from memory. "The only thing he regretted was an inadvertent insult to Fred Perkins about whom everyone in New York knows he couldn't give less of a shit."

Soon after that, Henry Stevens, a young tax lawyer, came to my office—where he had never been in his life—to tell me, "I don't know whether I'm more upset by Spellman's comments or by Conway's trivialization of them." One after another, partners with whom I had virtually no working or personal relationship began to stop me in the hall or walk into my office to let me know that they were "upset" about this matter. The intensity of the "upset" varied substantially from partner to partner but it became apparent to me that more and more of them were focusing on the implications of Spellman's views rather than their effect on Perkins. It also became apparent that there was a growing feeling that I had some sort of responsibility "to do something about this." That was a responsibility that I knew I didn't want and didn't need.

"Hey," I said to Craig Wilson, "I've been a member of this firm for less than a year. I can't lead an uprising against Conway and Spellman. I'd be out on my ass before I knew what hit me."

"Yes, but . . ."

"There is no 'yes' and there is no 'but.' There is no way I'm going to touch this live wire." When Wilson said "yes, but" again, I silently took my empty coffee cup and returned to my office, closing the door behind me.

And moments later, Barry Weinberg barged into my office. I'll try to describe accurately the scene that followed. I had no way to know at that time how important it would be in the years that followed.

It wasn't immediately clear to me whether Barry was laughing or crying or raging. By the end of this encounter I realized that he was doing all three. Laughing boisterously at what he called the absurdity of Conway's memorandum. "It was as if he were doing a parody of a moron playing a lawyer in a farce." Crying, softly, for reasons that I'll tell you about in a moment. Raging at Spellman, "that fucking psychotic Nazi son of a bitch."

I tried to calm him, putting my arm around his shoulder and leading him gently to a chair.

"Get hold of yourself, Barry, and let's talk this through."

"What is there to talk about? This firm is a black comedy."

Softly, I said, "Right now I'm more concerned about you than about the firm. You're out of control and I'm afraid that you'll hurt yourself."

"Hurt? Hurt? You don't know about hurt."

"What are you talking about?"

"Conway told me to start looking for another job, that's what I'm talking about," he screamed, and then he started to sob. Tears ran down his cheeks. His weeping escalated into such an uncontrolled outpouring of grief and pain that he gasped for breath. "One month," he muttered between sobs. "One month, he gave me one fucking month to find another firm that will take me in. You know what else is scheduled in one month—Jessica's due date, our baby, our baby with an unemployed father."

"Barry, he can't do that, you know that he can't kick you out of the firm. It takes a two-thirds vote of the whole partnership."

"Mike, stop thinking like a lawyer and think like a normal human being. Wouldn't it really be great for me to stay in this firm because twelve out of thirty-five partners don't want me to be expelled? Get real, Michael, I'm done here. I'm damaged goods, my career is trashed."

"Oh, please Barry, don't get carried away."

"Go to hell," Barry interrupted. "I'm not carried away, I'm kicked out. Do you have any idea what that feels like?"

"I can only imagine what it feels like. Let's talk about it."

Barry cleared the tears from his face. He stood up, paced the floor for a few moments and then resumed his seat. He seemed to regain his composure and in measured tones he began to speak. "The first thing you have to understand is that Conway fired me because I am a Jew. I'm not much of a Jew, but in the eyes of an anti-Semite like Conway that is irrelevant. It's not about what I do or believe; it's about the blood that circulates in my veins. I am an alien element in this law firm. By reason of the fact that I am a Jew, by that fact alone, according to Conway and people like him—Spellman, for example—I cause disruption, discomfort, unrest in the firm.

"When I was offered a job in this firm, the first Jew to ever receive such an offer, I thought that I was breaking through a wall of prejudice. I was excited by the prospect of playing some small part in helping to overcome generations of bigotry and pointless animosity. I thought I could set an example in this firm, as other Jews were doing in other firms, that would lead my Christian colleagues to realize that the stereotypical images that they were brought up to hold were false, that Jews could be their teammates and even their friends.

"That dream proved to be impossible in this law firm. Because of people like Conway and Spellman, this firm will always have a toxic atmosphere for Jews. The place reeks of anti-Semitism."

I interrupted Barry at this point because I just had to ask, "Barry, am I an anti-Semite?"

"Probably not. You don't act like one but I can't see into your heart."

"I'm not sure I understand your answer. What's the presumption? Am I an anti-Semite until I prove that I'm not one?"

"Michael, anti-Semitism is one of the most persistent and pervasive pathologies of the entire human experience on this planet. I can't speak for any Jew but myself. But, because the consequences of anti-Semitism to the Jewish people have been so malignant, so lethal, I tend to think that any gentile is a prospective anti-Semite until I'm convinced otherwise."

"Wow! I thought we were friends."

"Of course we're friends. At least I hope we are. But like most gentiles, you just don't know much about what it's like to be a Jew in a gentile world."

"You're certainly right about that. Barry, I wish this were just a theoretical conversation that the Weinbergs and the Cullens were having over a glass of wine. But we're sitting in the offices of Coburn & Perkins. You've just been canned by the Presiding Partner and you've called one of the other partners a, quote, fucking psychotic Nazi. I just can't sit here and say, 'well that's an interesting state of affairs.' We have to connect this conversation to this firm, to you and me and the law firm we're part of. Let's start with Conway. Tell me, why do you think he's an anti-Semite?"

"Michael, there are all kinds of anti-Semites. Conway and Spellman are obviously different kinds of people. But the one thing they have in common is that they are in positions to hurt Jews and they sometimes do so. You have to understand that anti-Semitism is different from other kinds of ethnic prejudice. Look at it this way, Jews who are prejudiced against the Irish, for example, are not usually in a position to hurt the Irish. So big deal, a Jew thinks all Irishmen are drunks. What's he going to do about it? Not invite any Irish to his birthday party? On the other hand, an anti-Semite like Conway can turn his prejudice into something harmful to Jews by not hiring them, or by firing them for no good reason. And an anti-Semite like Spellman? There's no limit to what a shit like him would do to Jews if he had the opportunity. I'm sure you recall that he didn't think it was all that important to stop Hitler from killing all the Jews in Europe."

Barry paused for a moment, stood up and said, with emphasis, "And while I'm on the subject of people hurting people, the worst hurt that has ever been inflicted on any group of people was the Nazi Holocaust of the Jews. The Holocaust was the monster fathered by anti-Semitism. Certainly not the benign anti-Semitism of the restricted country club or law firm, but its evil twin."

By the time Barry resumed his seat and indicated that he had said what he wanted to say, I knew what I had to say. "Barry, we can't let this happen to you without some sort of response. I want the two of us to go up to Conway's office. I need to find out if he really is the person you describe. And we owe it to him, to the firm, and to ourselves to make him listen to what you've just told me."

"He won't let us into his office, no less listen to a lecture about anti-Semitism."

"Well, in that case," I said, "we will have learned a great deal about this law firm."

"I already know a great deal about this law firm. Watch your ass, Michael, he'll get you next."

"I'll take that chance." I put on my suit jacket and left my office, with Barry trailing behind me. I went to the men's room, splashed cold water on my face, and, taking Barry by the arm, walked upstairs to Conway's office.

TEN

I had no idea what I expected to accomplish with Conway, no less any idea of the words I would speak when I confronted him. But, remarkably, I wasn't nervous about the impending confrontation. I think I was strengthened by the feeling that I would be occupying the high moral ground and, no matter what happened, I would feel good about myself.

In order to enter Conway's office, one had to get past Mrs. Hadden, his long-time and utterly devoted secretary. She protected him with true concern for his well-being and happiness. There was absolutely no doubt in my mind that she loved him more than she loved Mr. Hadden.

"Does Mr. Conway have anyone with him at the moment?"

She paused to get a sense of my motives and to form a judgment as to whether a visit from two partners who were involved in the Perkins matter would disturb Mr. Conway. She guessed right, saying officiously, "He's alone in his office, but he can't be disturbed this afternoon because he is involved in an extremely urgent matter."

"Well, we need to speak with him about a more extremely urgent matter that requires his immediate attention. Please let him know that Mr. Cullen and Mr. Weinberg need ten minutes of his time."

Mrs. Hadden—who viewed herself as an extension of the status and power of the Presiding Partner—was not used to being spoken to in that matter and seemed to recoil as if she had been threatened. She sat motionless for several seconds, then gathered her strength and said, "I'll pass your message on to Mr. Conway and advise you as to his response. I suggest you return to your offices until you hear back from me."

"No. I want you to let him know that we are here waiting and that we'll remain here until he is available." It pleased me to see the distress I had caused Mrs. Hadden to experience. I have an instinctive antipathy to people whose wealth, power or status is based entirely on a relationship with another person who has wealth, power or status. I had to restrain myself from being even more aggressive with this woman standing—sitting, actually—in my way.

Mrs. Hadden picked up her phone, dialed a single number, and said sharply, "Mr. Conway, Michael Cullen is standing here insisting he and Mr. Weinberg must see you immediately about something important." After listening to whatever Conway said, she turned to me, triumphantly, and said, "Mr. Conway wants to know what it is that you want to see him about."

"I'll tell him, not you."

Into the phone, "He refuses to tell me, quite rudely I must say."

I walked past her, opened the door to Conway's office, and strode in. He looked at me in amazement, his face glaring. Barry stood in the open doorway.

"What do you mean by this intrusion?" he barked.

"I think you know full well what we're here for—your attempt to fire Barry Weinberg."

Conway remained seated behind his massive desk, the surface of which was entirely clear of papers except for one sheet that he continued to read before responding to me. After regaining his customary composure, he said in calm and measured tones, "I did not, as you put it, 'attempt to fire Barry Weinberg.' As he must have told you, I advised him that it would be in his best interests to begin to look for another law firm with which he might feel more compatible. That is all I said to him."

"Don't hand me that, Paul. Do you expect me to believe that you were just walking down the hall when you bumped into one of our star litigators and told him he would be better off in another firm?"

"Of course it didn't happen that way but I don't know why you need an instant replay of my discussion with Mr. Weinberg. I learned that he was dissatisfied with the resolution of the Perkins matter and was agitating for some sort of appeal from the decision of the Executive Committee. That did it for me."

"Stop calling it 'the Perkins matter.' This is not about Perkins."

Barry stepped forward and said, "Will both of you please stop talking about me as if I weren't here?"

"Yes," Conway continued, completely ignoring Barry, "It's not just the Perkins matter. I've been concerned for some time that Mr. Weinberg was not comfortable in this firm and that—notwithstanding his considerable skills—he was, on balance, a negative and disruptive element in the firm. Barry, is that not essentially what I told you?" Without waiting for Barry's response, Conway continued, "What you don't seem to understand is that it is my job to be concerned about such things and to act upon those concerns. Rather than taking the matter to the partnership for the expulsion vote required under our partnership agreement, I thought the decent thing to do was to give Barry the opportunity to relocate on his own motion, without the stigma of expulsion. You have the right to disagree with my judgment on this matter but that does not give you the right to barge into my office and to be rude to my secretary. That's all I have to say to you." His voice rose as he said those concluding words.

I felt sweat rolling down my back and dampening my shirt. Was I about to join Barry on the exit ramp from the firm? What was I doing here, facing off with the head of my law firm in an argument I couldn't win and risking my job, my career, my family's well-being?

With a firmness in my voice that I didn't expect to hear, I said, "Paul, there is no one in this building who is going to believe that Barry is leaving the firm on his own accord. Everyone will understand that he is being booted out because he is on the wrong side of the subject of Tom Spellman's astonishing views about the side our country chose to be on in the Second World War. Moreover—and I want you to know that I hate to have to say this—it isn't a long leap from that point to concluding that Barry has been tossed out because he's a Jew."

Conway looked aghast. A few moments later he rose from his chair, walked to the window, gazed out upon New York Harbor. He was obviously trying to compose himself. And I was willing to stand still and wait for that to happen.

ELEVEN

I'm not sure whether the correct spelling is "to the *manner* born" or "to the *manor* born."

Either way, the phrase applies to Paul Conway. He was the son of a United States senator from Indiana and the grandson of a governor of that state. There was great wealth in his family passing from generation to generation from both his father's and his mother's ancestors. He was educated at Groton, Yale, and Harvard Law School. He enlisted in the army the day after Pearl Harbor and rose to the rank of lieutenant colonel serving on the staff of General MacArthur in the Pacific theater. And, when I met him, he was a distinguished corporate lawyer and Presiding Partner of a powerful and prestigious Wall Street law firm. He seemed to know every important person in the world and he knew how to comport himself accordingly.

While I stood in his office watching him stare out of the corner window, I wondered whether he would turn around and tell me I was finished at Coburn & Perkins or whether my comments about firing Barry Weinberg hit some nerve cells in his brain that would cause some other reaction. I felt more like a spectator than a participant in this confrontation. Paul Conway was a man to be reckoned with and I had reckoned with him.

After a few moments that seemed like an hour, he turned toward me and asked Barry and me to take a seat at the small table that stood in a corner of the office. Rather than returning to his chair behind his desk, he chose a chair at the table and sat facing me directly. I waited for him to say something. Finally, in a soft, almost imploring, voice, he said, "Gentlemen, I'm not an anti-Semite. I am obliged to concede that I don't know many Jewish people; that I belong to a country club that does not admit Jewish members; that we sit around at the club and—not infrequently—tell and laugh at jokes about Jewish people. I am familiar with all of the disparaging terms that are used—sometimes by me—to refer to Jewish people. I have never had a Jewish person as a friend." He paused and filled three glasses with water from a crystal pitcher on the table, passed them to Barry and me, and took a long drink that he seemed to savor. He then resumed his remarks. They sounded like a confession and I felt like a priest must feel on the other side of the screen in the confessional booth.

"Barry, I admit that the fact that you are Jewish had a bearing on my decision to ask you to leave the firm. I hope . . ." And here he paused and closed his eyes. "I hope—with all my heart—that that decision was not a manifestation of anti-Semitism." And then he looked directly at me and actually shook his finger at me for emphasis as he continued.

"There was no hatred in my heart. I acknowledge that I was uncomfortable that Barry was a member of this firm. I projected my discomfort onto him and believed that he was as uncomfortable as I was. Beyond that, I projected my discomfort onto the entire firm and concluded that Barry had an unsettling influence on the people who make up this firm. But, gentlemen, you must believe me that there was no hatred in my heart. Can you, can you possibly, believe me when I say that?"

I sat quietly for a few moments, digesting Conway's remarks and—I admit—trying to design a response that would redound to my benefit in the firm, that would enhance my stature in Conway's eyes, or that would—at the very least—keep me out of trouble. It's not for nothing that I am a good tactician in my professional life. But I appreciated the seriousness of Conway's comments, notwithstanding the fact that they demonstrated the stunning insularity of his perspective.

"Paul, the first thing I want to say is that I am honored that you chose to share those thoughts with us. I'd like to try to respond with the same seriousness with which you just spoke to me. I claim absolutely no expertise on the subject of anti-Semitism, Jewish people, Judaism, or any related matter."

Barry held up his hand for me to stop talking. He smiled at Conway and said, "I have to say something unimportant before we continue this conversation. Paul, it's okay to use the word 'Jew.' It's not a dirty word. Jews call themselves 'Jews.' You don't have to use the term 'Jewish people' when you are referring to Jews. Just say 'Jews.' No one will find that offensive."

"Thank you," said Conway, "I don't think I was aware of that."

"You're welcome," said Barry. "Michael, I believe you were about to say something when I made the point about the Jew-word." Conway winced.

Addressing Conway, I said, "I have no problem accepting that you have—as you put it—no hatred in your heart. But I think a person can be an anti-Semite without meaning to be one. The behaviors you described—belonging to a restricted country club, telling nasty jokes about Jews—those are the sorts of things that anti-Semites do. Whether that makes you an anti-Semite depends, I suppose, on the definition of that term. I'm not sure what that definition is. As I said, I haven't given a great deal of thought to this subject. When I was a boy and my mother dragged me to church for mass, I remember the priest talking about how the Jews killed Christ. I understood that to mean that I shouldn't like Jews, but that had no great effect on my life. Other than a couple of Jewish kids in my neighborhood in the Bronx—kids I didn't hang around with—I didn't know any Jews. However, as I grew older and maybe a bit wiser, I began to think that the priest was either an idiot or a bigot and that his views were obnoxious and—more important—I got to know and actually befriend a number of . . . Jews. Funny, I almost said 'Jewish people' but Barry's lecture to you a few minutes ago came to mind and I deliberately said 'Jews' when 'Jewish people' would have been perfectly appropriate. Paul, forgive me for wandering around this subject; I'm trying to collect my thoughts as I speak."

"Please keep going. I want to hear your thoughts, no matter how they're organized."

"Okay, I'll keep going because eventually you and I are going to have to take a hard look at what triggered this whole conversation."

"I know that."

Once again, Barry signaled me to stop talking and said, "Frankly, Paul, I find it remarkable that you don't know any Jews. You live in a city that I think has more Jews in it than any city in the world. You work in a profession that is filled with Jews. To be sure, firms like this one are not exactly over-flowing with Jews—although the number has been growing rapidly in most of the other major firms. When firms like this didn't hire Jews, Jews formed their own firms—like they formed their own country clubs. But the religious segrega-tion in the legal profession has started to erode. I just don't understand how you can go through life without any mean-ingful relationship with even one Jew—except, perhaps, me whom you want to throw out of this firm. I know that folks tend to congregate with people like themselves. Certainly the Irish do that. Italians, too. And Jews of course. Brahmins like you do so and work hard to keep strangers out. So, I'm now asking myself, how does this self-imposed segregation relate to anti-Semitism?"

Conway responded, "I was just wondering whether each of these groups has the same kind of prejudice against the others that my group seems to have against Jews. See, I just said 'Jews.'"

"Good for you," said Barry. "Next thing we know you'll be joining B'nai B'rith."

"What's that?"

"Never mind. A pitiful attempt at humor," Barry replied. "I know there are Irish who still think Jews killed Christ and hate them for that reason. Probably even more so with Italians. I'm not sure. And I definitely know that Jews, when they get together, tell defamatory jokes about every other ethnic group, including yours—if the beautiful people at your country club can be called an ethnic group."

"So, if such group attitudes are so commonplace, why does it bother me so much to think that I might be an anti-Semite? Michael, are all of us anti-Semites? Are you an anti-Semite?"

"Please don't think of me as the guy who has the answer to such a questions. This is not my field of specialization," I said.

"I know that, Michael, but your insights are probably better than mine," Conway responded.

"I'll tell you why," Barry interjected. "As I told Michael before we came up here, anti-Semitism is different from other kinds of ethnic prejudice. I'll tell you exactly what I told Michael. On one level, the simplest level, Jews who are prejudiced, for example, against the Irish are not usually in a position to hurt the Irish. So big deal, a Jew thinks all Irishmen are drunks. What's he going to do about it? Not invite any Irish to his birthday party? I wouldn't join your country club even if they begged me to. In fact, I despise your entire country club set. But what does that matter to you or to them? How does that hurt you? On the other hand, gentiles like you can turn their prejudice into something harmful to Jews—or, for that matter, any group against which you are prejudiced—by not hiring them or promoting them. Or by firing them for no good reason."

"That's a low blow, Barry, I told you my reason for asking you to leave the firm."

"And you think that's a good reason? Paul, get real, the reason you wanted me out of the firm grew directly out of your prejudice against Jews. You were uncomfortable having a Jew as a partner. You projected that attitude onto all of the gentile partners in this firm. For God's sake, isn't that turning your prejudice into a weapon against the object of your prejudice? If this conversation accomplishes nothing else, I would hope it would at least get you to understand that this isn't a country club where being excluded has no real consequences. This firm is where I earn my livelihood. To kick me out because I am a Jew is to hurt me because I am a Jew. Do you get it?"

"Yes, I see your point. I have to think about what you've been saying."

It looked to me as if he was trying to bring the discussion to a close. I felt that I had escaped unscathed. But Barry wasn't ready to let it end there. For him, it was now time to come to the point. "I have no doubt, Paul, that you will think long and hard about this subject. Because when it comes to hurting people, I hope that's not who you are. But while we're on the subject of hurting, a few minutes ago you asked why it troubled you so much to think that—even inadvertently—you might be an anti-Semite. I think I know the answer. As I told Michael before we came up here and as I said a moment ago, anti-Semitism has consequences." Barry continued, using the exact words he had used when he lectured me on this subject. "One of those consequences is that it causes hurt. This is history that you have no right to ignore. The worst hurt that has ever been inflicted on any group of people was the Nazi Holocaust of the Jews. The Holocaust was the monster that was fathered by anti-Semitism. Certainly not the benign anti-Semitism of your restricted country club or law firm, but definitely its evil twin."

—

Do you think that these were remarks that Mr. Weinberg had memorized? • That's an interesting question. This was obviously a subject that Barry had talked about many times before he discussed it with me. He may well have used those words in previous conversations and he either liked the way they expressed his feelings or he may simply gotten used to saying them.

—

Barry's final comment had the impact of a rifle shot: "That's what makes Tom Spellman's presence in this firm such an abomination."

Conway stood up and walked across the room. He stopped to look at a painting on the wall. I don't remember what the painting looked like but Conway's face was ashen. There was sweat on his brow. Believe it or not, I felt sorry for him.

—

You and Mr. Weinberg were very brave. But I have to say that I think Mr. Weinberg did not make a good case connecting country club anti-Semitism with the Holocaust. I had a course on the Holocaust and Holocaust literature in school. It's a very complicated subject and Mr. Weinberg's point was—what's the word?—simplistic. • That's another interesting comment, Will. Defer judgment on the subject until you hear about what happened as a result of that meeting in Mr. Conway's office.

TWELVE

That night I told Norah all that I could remember about my long conversations with Barry Weinberg and Paul Conway. I arrived home late, almost 10 p.m. The older kids had eaten dinner and were doing homework. The little one was sound asleep and didn't stir when I kissed her gently on the forehead. Norah, knowing I'd be late, waited for me with dinner warming in the oven. I suggested we have a drink together before eating and she enthusiastically agreed.

We sat on our terrace on that warm summer evening, each with a gin and tonic, and talked into the night, ignoring the roast chicken drying out in the oven. It wasn't easy for me to reconstruct the day's memorable conversations. It was too soon for me to be able to unravel my thoughts, impressions and memory. The tension had not yet subsided. My mind was confusing things I wished I had said with things that I actually said. Nevertheless, I think I must have communicated a reasonably coherent account of what Barry and I said to Conway and a very accurate summary of Conway's "confession." Norah listened with keen interest and frequent requests that I repeat or clarify something I said. After I went back into the house to refresh our drinks and returned to the terrace with more gin and less tonic, Norah rushed toward me, knocking a tumbler from my hand and spilling the gin on my shirt sleeves. She pressed her hands firmly against my cheeks, kissed me on the lips and said, "My hero. How did you work up the courage to talk to Conway that way?" I shrugged and she continued, "Remember the time we had dinner at his home, right after you joined the firm. I found him to be unapproachable, scary even. His wife was nice but it seemed to me that he was hardly present; his mind was somewhere else. It was obvious that he and we were just participating in an obligatory ritual and that he had better things to do than talk with us. Not that he was rude or anything like that. He behaved perfectly but he was so austere, so damned sober that he made me feel like a boozer whenever I sipped some wine. I so very much did not enjoy that evening. I can't imagine giving him the dressing down that you described. I couldn't have done it."

"Yes, he's not easy to talk to. What I did was hard, but I think it may turn out to have been worthwhile," I said with excessive humility.

"Mike, I hope you realize that this story isn't over yet."

"Oh dear, I hope it is."

"No way. Tom Spellman is still a major force in the firm and we don't know how many partners are allied with him, either because he brings in so much business or because, God forbid, they endorse his politics, or, worse yet, both reasons."

As usual, Norah brought things into sharper focus. I had been so wrapped up in the struggle to confront Conway in a way that would save Barry's job and make me look good that I completely forgot to mention to Norah Barry's final comment to Conway about the Holocaust-Spellman connection.

I sighed and said, "Thank you for keeping a clear head while my muddled brain is completely exhausted. Of course, you're absolutely right. This is not about me, it's not about Conway; it's not even about Barry; it's about Spellman. I don't have even a glimmer of an idea of what to do about him—or even if there is anything that I should or can do. Help me, please."

A vertical crease formed between her eyes. I recognized it immediately as the outward evidence of a fine mind bearing down on a problem. I returned to our liquor cabinet to replenish the spilled gin and to allow Norah to gather her thoughts without any distraction from me. The late summer night was growing cooler so I also picked up a sweater to bring to her. When I stepped back on to the terrace I realized that the evaporating alcohol on my shirt was causing me to feel uncomfortably chilled. I suggested that we might go back into the house to continue our conversation. Norah demurred. "It's beautiful out here. There's a hint of autumn in the air. I'm enjoying it." She sat quietly for a few minutes, occasionally sipping some of her gin and tonic.

Finally, with a most serious look on her face, she said, "I think we should have the Weinbergs over for dinner. Before she has her baby. This weekend—Saturday, I won't be working so I'll have time to prepare a nice dinner. Does that make sense?"

"I should have thought of that. Right now we're a one-couple conspiracy. We might as well have co-conspirators."

THIRTEEN

The following morning, shortly after I arrived at my office, I was surprised—in fact I was stunned—by the appearance at my door of Paul Conway and Tom Spellman. Conway asked if I had "a bit of time" to meet with the two of them. I invited them into my office and slid out from behind my desk to sit with them at a small round table that stood in a corner of my office. I quickly collected the papers and files that cluttered that table and deposited them on my desk. I told my secretary, Patty Rogers, to hold all my calls and to bring us a pot of coffee and some mugs. Conway said to her that he would prefer tea "if that is not inconvenient for you." She assured him she could handle his request.

Conway opened the conversation by telling me he and Spellman had dinner the previous evening at Conway's home. He said that the conversation he had with me and Barry led to his invitation to Spellman and that he now wanted to "close the circle" by bringing me into their discussion. I said that I appreciated that.

Spellman—more subdued by far than his typical demeanor—began by saying that it was critically important to him that "this matter of my supposed Nazi sympathies must be addressed and resolved."

"For the good of the firm," Conway added.

Thinking that for once in my life this was a time for me to keep quiet and listen, I sat silently, not even nodding to acknowledge my agreement with the little that had been said to this point.

Spellman continued with what sounded like a prepared speech. "As I told Paul last night, in no uncertain terms, I am not a Nazi. I am not a fascist. I am not a Nazi sympathizer. I am not a fascist sympathizer. I am not an anti-Semite. I am none of those things and I never have been. What I am is a man who strongly believes in the free enterprise system, in the gravity of the threat to that system and our American way of life posed by the expansionist policies of the Soviet Union and the insidious Marxist philosophy that it espouses. The things that I am do not, in the least, equate to the things I am not. And it pains me to think that any of my colleagues in this firm could possibly believe otherwise. I might add to the things that I am,"—he said with a wry smile—"the fact that I sometimes am a jerk in the way I express my strongly held views. Case in point: my comments at the notorious D-Day lunch, comments that have been blown way out of proportion and way out of context."

I took a deep breath and said, "Well, that's certainly a clear and unequivocal statement. But I have to ask one question. Do you want me—and anyone else who's concerned about this—to understand that your remarks on D-Day do not represent your real views on what the proper alignment of the parties should have been in World War Two?"

"With all due respect, Michael, that's a simplistic question. Our only natural allies were the British and they weren't worth much militarily or strategically. Nazi Germany and Communist Russia were both what I would call our natural enemies. Both deserved to be defeated and I wish it had been possible to bring both of those powers to their knees. Obviously that wasn't possible. As a practical matter, we had no choice. Churchill was obsessed with Hitler and not bothered very much by Russia. Roosevelt's sympathies were clearly with Churchill and, for whatever it's worth, I think Roosevelt had a soft spot for Russia and Communism. For all these reasons we found ourselves aligned with Britain against Germany and, consequently, D-Day was an inevitable event in the war in which we found ourselves. It's regrettable that we handed the keys to half of Europe to the Communists when we attacked on Germany's western front. Anyone who doesn't recognize that geopolitical fact is taking a very narrow view of the event."

"And what about the Jews?"

"I would ask you, Michael, what about the Poles, the Czechs, the Hungarians, the Romanians, the Yugoslavians, the Estonians, the Latvians, the Lithuanians and everyone else who fell under Stalin's fist? Yes, what happened to the Jews was a historical tragedy. If Hitler hadn't expended so much of Germany's energy going after Jews who posed no particular strategic threat to Germany, he might have defeated the Soviet Union without our assistance. You see, Mike, it just isn't right to view this subject as a one-dimensional problem.

My mistake at the Graduates Club lunch was not really what I said but that I said anything at all. You and Paul and I could talk for hours examining the excruciatingly difficult issues that I spent twenty seconds talking about at that lunch."

Paul finished his cup of tea and looked squarely at me. "Do you think we can convince our partners that, although one might disagree with Thomas on many of his political and historical views, he has rational and defensible positions and, most important, can we squash the notion that Thomas is some sort of monster?"

"We can try," I said after a moment's reflection. "It would help if we could salvage Barry Weinberg for the firm."

—

Mr. Conway seems to have really paid attention to what you and Mr. Weinberg said to him the previous day. Were you surprised? • I think I was surprised, Will, but later, on reflection, I understood that what Mr. Conway did—I assume he read the riot act to Spellman—was very much a reflection of the kind of man he was. Also, don't overlook the fact that he was fully prepared to invite Spellman to leave the firm during the Gang of Three episode.

FOURTEEN

I spent a few hours in the office the following Saturday morning catching up on work that didn't get done while I was spending non-billable time in discussions about Spellman. I stopped in the lounge to get a mug of coffee. Tom Spellman was there. His response to my "good morning" was "yeah, right." I was certain that he and Conway had had further conversations after we finished our three-way talk.

While I was at the office, a torrential rain began to fall—a late-summer tropical downpour that had the earmarks of a hurricane. I packed my briefcase and hurried toward the subway. A strong wind turned my umbrella inside out and I was drenched by the time I reached the station. Our home in Brooklyn is three blocks from the Clark Street subway station and the walk home was an adventure. My older daughter, your Aunt Kathleen, took one look at me as I walked in the front door and quickly retrieved a blanket from the sofa and wrapped it around me. I was shivering—soaking wet to the skin and windblown into exhaustion. I announced to my family who had gathered around me that I had walked in the most ferocious hurricane ever to hit New York City. Imagine my disappointment when we learned a few minutes later from the weather person on the TV that the remnants of a tropical depression—not a hurricane—had made "a glancing blow" on the city. "Dad," said Kathleen, "you spend too much time indoors. You're not fit to deal with the elements."

I laughingly responded, "Is that right? What are my other shortcomings?"

Kathleen paused a moment, thinking, and, with a broad smile on her face, said, "You're in no condition to hear about them right now."

I hugged her and got her wet. After kissing Norah on the cheek, taking care to keep her from getting wet from my dripping clothing, I went upstairs, undressed, threw my sopping suit and shirt on the bathroom floor, and took an exceedingly enjoyable hot shower. When I returned downstairs in my pajamas, bathrobe and slippers, I was surprised to see the Weinbergs sitting in the living room talking with the kids. "Norah said this would be informal," Jessica said with a broad smile on her face, "but I had no idea it would be this informal. To think," she added, "I went to the trouble of wearing my best maternity dress."

I groped for a clever riposte but could only come up with, "Oops, I forgot."

Norah walked in from the kitchen and contributed to the fashion commentary by saying, "Mike, that outfit is perfect on you. Wear it to the office on Monday."

I was pleased to observe that Barry seemed to have emerged from the distress and tension that gripped him when I last saw him in Conway's office. He seemed to be relaxed, even cheerful, and that delighted me because I liked him so much. "Enough of this hilarity," I declared. "I am going upstairs to outfit myself appropriately for the occasion of the visit of our distinguished guests whom I hope I have amused by pretending to have forgotten our invitation for them to visit this evening."

Jessica said, "Please, Mike, don't bother to get dressed. I love seeing you in pajamas."

"All right," I replied. "If it's okay with Jessica it's okay with me. Let me be the bartender in bedclothes. What will you have to drink?"

Barry asked, "Do you have any more of that 18-year-old malt that I once got drunk on in this house?"

"Sorry," I said. "I saved the empty bottle as a souvenir of that evening but I never replaced it. How about a plain 12-year-old malt from the Isle of Skye? It's peaty with a pungent aroma that not everyone likes but I think you'll want more after you've tasted it."

"On the rocks, please," Barry replied.

"I'll join you," I said.

Norah had her accustomed gin and tonic and Jessica passed, citing her pregnancy.

Everyone, even Barry, seemed to be in a good mood. Barry, Norah and I refilled our drinks and Jessica looked on longingly, her highly protruding belly the subject of some enjoyable banter. I thought we had created the right mood for the serious conversation that was to follow.

I was wrong. Utterly wrong. As soon as I shifted the conversation to the subject of Paul Conway, Barry snapped at me, saying, "If you don't mind, I don't want to hear about him, or the firm, or Thomas Spellman, or anything having to do with them. They are not part of my or Jessica's life any longer."

I was startled, stunned.

"Barry, when we left Conway's office, I thought we had made substantial progress. By the way, your remarks to Conway seemed to have a real impact on him."

"If you think I give a flying shit about the firm of Coburn & Perkins, you are seriously mistaken. As far as the progress we made in our meeting with Conway, Michael he's still an anti-Semite. And the next generation of Conways will also be anti-Semites. Yeah, he learned a little bit from our conversation; in the future he'll be more careful about displaying his, quote, discomfort with Jews. A more accurate word would be 'dislike,' perhaps even 'hatred.' Jessica and I have discussed what happened on Thursday and we've decided that I have had it. I'm gone. I'm out of there."

"But why? You've got a great future in the firm. I love working with you. I just don't understand what happened in the last forty-eight hours."

"Mike, I'm 35 years old. If you do the math you'll figure out that I was born in 1939. My parents arrived in this country from Germany four months before I was born. If my mother didn't happen to have a brother who lived in Brooklyn, they probably wouldn't have been allowed in to this country. I would have been born in Nazi Germany on the eve of the war. I would either have starved to death in a concentration camp or I would have died in my mother's arms in a gas chamber at Treblinka or Auschwitz. My family would have been erased, murdered, turned to ashes and smoke in a furnace in a death camp in Poland. As it is, my parents lost their parents to the Nazis. They lost brothers and sisters, aunts and uncles, friends, their homes, everything that belonged to them. Because they were Jews."

"Oh, Barry, I never knew any of that. Oh my God, how awful. How awful, how terrible. How could I know you and not know that history?"

"I never talked about it. My parents never talked about it. By the way, my father was not a kosher butcher. That's something Spellman used to tease me about. My father was a broken man. He never recovered from the news of the murders of his parents and siblings. He struggled to support us with the wages and tips he made as a messenger and delivery boy in the garment district. He didn't live to see me go to college and law school. Even if I didn't know that Spellman was a Nazi, I would still hate him. He picked on me relentlessly as if I was a scab on the skin of the law firm. Someday, somehow, I will make him pay for what he's done to me and for what he is. I wish he were dead. It's utterly impossible for me to practice law with him."

Norah put her arms around Barry trying to comfort him. Jessica sat quietly on the sofa, her eyes glazing with tears. I stood looking from Norah to Barry and back to Norah, dumbfounded, helpless, without the slightest idea of what to say or do. After a couple of minutes, the paralysis that seemed to grip everyone in the room became unbearable. In a clumsy attempt to change the mood, I invited everyone to go into the dining room and enjoy the excellent dinner that Norah had prepared.

Barry looked at me for a moment as if deciding what to say and how to say it. Finally, he took a deep breath and said, "Mike, I really appreciate what you did or tried to do with

Conway. I mean that." And then, facing Norah, he continued, "Jessica and I have always valued our friendship with you and Mike but—this will sound awful—we can't have dinner here tonight and we can no longer be friends."

I almost screamed, "Barry, you can't mean that. This is crazy."

As if I hadn't said anything, Barry continued, "This afternoon, I called Ira Teitelbaum, the managing partner of the Greenberg firm. I told him I wanted to leave Coburn & Perkins. He immediately congratulated me and offered me a partnership in Greenberg's litigation department, reminding me how I whipped their ass in that trademark infringement case in February. I'm sure, Michael, that you remember that case."

"Of course I do. That was a huge win."

Barry continued, his voice and his words becoming more resonant, more confident sounding as he spoke. "I've sent a strongly worded letter to Conway resigning from Coburn. Mike, I don't want to compromise your status in the firm by continuing our social relationship. I am absolutely certain that if word got out that I had dinner with you on the day I resigned from the firm—and word will get out—you will become a pariah in the firm."

Turning to Norah, he said, "I want both of you to know that I wish Mike would leave the firm too." Then, looking me straight in the eye, "Mike, it's not a place for someone with your character. You may think you can leave your imprint on the firm's culture, but you can't. It's too deeply ingrained to be changed by an upstart lateral partner. As I said, I'd applaud if you left the firm but I want you to do it on your own terms and your own timing. Right now, I'm too much of an emotional basket case to have to deal with being responsible for getting you fired. Jessica and I feel like shit about this but we think it is the right thing, the only thing, for us to do at this point. We'll say good night now. Perhaps I'll see you in court someday."

I remember that we shook hands and said good night, but I was too stunned to be able to remember anything else that happened when the Weinbergs left. Norah and I just sat and stared at each other. Speechless.

Eventually, Norah suggested that we should eat. I said I had no appetite. She insisted that we eat the dinner she had prepared, adding with her customary insight, "It's not easy to lose a friend."

"We've both lost two friends," I said. We nibbled at the food in silence. Simultaneously, we said, "Let's go to bed." And we did.

—

I really don't understand why the Weinbergs did that. Don't you think shutting off your friendship was a huge overreaction? • That's exactly how I felt at the time and for a long time afterward. Years later, I think I understood what took place. That didn't make the lost years easier.

FIFTEEN

A lovely brightness streamed into our bedroom Sunday morning. In our funk the night before, we had neglected to draw the drapes. The previous day's storm had blown away leaving a brilliantly sunny late-summer day. Whether the storm that raged inside our home had likewise subsided remained to be seen.

I was shaving in the bathroom when Norah walked in and said, casually, "I don't know why I can't continue to be friendly with Jessica and Barry. I like them so much and I think they are hurting as much as we are."

With shaving cream on half my face and under my nose, I said, "I completely agree with you. I think it would be a good idea if you made an overture to Jessica suggesting that it would make us very happy if they'd reconsider what they did last night. There's absolutely no reason why we can't be in each other's lives. We all have lives outside of the firm. It's not the fact that Barry and I are partners—I guess I should say *were* partners—that was the reason for our friendship. I like him for who he is and what he's like as a person. Barry has been through a brutally difficult period and I think his decision to sever relations with us was an irrational reaction to the storm he's been through."

While I shaved under my nose, Norah said, "It makes sense for me to speak with Jessica. I think the two of us can work this out."

"God, I hope so."

Norah suggested that we should try to take advantage of the beautiful day. "To lighten our spirits." I jumped on that idea and proposed that we take our little one, five-year-old Jenny, to the Prospect Park zoo.

"Perfect," Norah replied, "and we can ask the big kids if they want to come with us. Then we could all have an outdoor family dinner at that barbeque place near the park."

I could feel the gloom lifting although none of the facts that brought on that gloom had changed. It's remarkable how much of the emotions we feel—joy, sorrow, fear—are driven by our internal subjective processing of the facts and not by the objective facts themselves. Why that is so is not something I understand but—whatever the reason—my mood (and Norah's) changed as we looked forward to a light and pleasant day in which the Weinbergs and the law firm were placed on a shelf to be dealt with some other time.

We had a lovely day. The older kids came with us, which gave me added pleasure because, at their age and level of independence, they rarely went on family outings. For that matter, I rarely went on family outings because of the demands of my work.

SIXTEEN

Monday was another bright and sunny day. I tried to sustain the good mood that prevailed the previous day but the joy that I felt with my wife and kids at Prospect Park was quickly crowded out as I took account of what was going on in my life. I had just lost two valued friends. My career—or at least my position in Coburn & Perkins—was almost unbearably complicated. Did I want to remain in that law firm? Could I conceive of spending the remainder of my professional life as part of an organization in which Tom Spellman—with his noxious politics—and Paul Conway—with his moral obtuseness—were commanding figures? Don't misunderstand me, I don't want to sound as if I was an exceptionally moral person. Although I occasionally dabbled in questions of right or wrong, I hadn't spent an hour of my life thinking about the Holocaust, much less connecting it to anything with real relevance to my life. I don't think I held anti-Semitic views myself but I hardly noticed whether people I knew and associated with might have hated the Barry Weinbergs of the world because they were Jews. The subject was simply not on the agenda of my life.

But now it was. However I would deal with it, I realized, might define who I was and how I would feel about myself. Why the hell was I in this position?

As soon as I arrived at the office that morning, Paul Conway phoned me and asked if I might be available to have lunch with him and Tom Spellman at noon at the Graduates Club. "Of course," I said.

"That's splendid," Conway replied.

That invitation eliminated any possibility of my doing any productive client work before lunch. I spent those hours speculating about Conway's purpose in setting up a meeting. I knew that he must have received Barry's "strongly worded" resignation letter. Was he going to use that to demonstrate to me that he was right on the mark in suggesting to Barry that he leave the firm? What possible purpose was behind Spellman's presence at this meeting? Conway didn't need Spellman to "suggest" that I find another firm in which I might be more comfortable than I appeared to be at Coburn & Perkins. I could rule out being fired as the reason for this unprecedented invitation. But the more I wrestled with the various possibilities, the further I was from understanding what was going to happen. I tried to reach Norah by phone to help me work out the purpose of this meeting. She wasn't home; no help there. Remember, this all took place in the era before cell phones.

I know that's true, Grandpa, but it's so hard to believe. Every kid in my class has a cell phone.

My phone rang. I was hoping that Norah had sensed my need to talk with her. But my secretary told me that the caller was a lawyer on the other side of a case I was working on. I asked her to tell him that I was in a meeting and would call him back. The phone rang again. This time Patty informed me that a client was on the line. I gave her the same instruction, but this time I told her to hold all of my calls except if my wife was calling. Moments later, my phone rang again. It was Mrs. Hadden, the guardian of Conway's office. Without any of the customary greetings and small talk, she informed me that she had reserved a private room at the Graduates Club—the Wilson Room—for my luncheon with Conway and Spellman "at 12 noon sharp." I thanked her but she had hung up before my thanks were out of my mouth. It tickled me that she was still steaming about my confrontation with her outside of Conway's office. But I sensed that her attitude might be a bad omen.

I didn't know there was a Wilson Room at the Club. In fact, I didn't know there were any private rooms. Was the need for privacy at this meeting another unfavorable omen? "Michael," I said silently to myself, "get a grip. You can't go into this meeting in fear and trembling." Easy to say, undoubtedly correct, but hard to do. But I tried. The minutes crept by slowly. I drank a lot of coffee, which made me need to take two trips to the men's room. I was grateful for the distraction. Finally, at 11:45 a.m., I left my office, telling my secretary that I would be at a meeting for the next couple of hours. "I might not make it back to the office today," I added. She looked at me differently than she usually did and said nothing. Another omen?

It was an especially hot August day. The humid air hung heavily on me as I walked the two blocks to the Graduates Club. Sweat was dripping from my forehead into my eyes and I feared that I might look like a wet rag by the time I reached the Club. This was the kind of day on which New Yorkers fled the city and headed to the Catskills or the beaches. Those of us who worked in nicely air-conditioned offices tried to remain indoors all day. I didn't have that option on that fateful day.

The Graduates Club occupied the 28th floor of what was otherwise an office building. It was not a place that one would stumble upon while roaming about New York City. There was no sign posted on the building indicating that there was a private club located there. On the 28th floor, the elevator opened onto a walnut-paneled lobby at the end of which a discreet brass plaque next to an elegant double door declared:

The Graduates Club
Members and Their Invited Guests Only

All of the partners of Coburn & Perkins were members. As I believe I once told you, that was a perquisite of partnership. A few years later, that policy became troublesome when the firm finally admitted a woman partner who was excluded from membership in the Club because she was the wrong gender. That issue had never entered my mind on the day of my lunch with Conway and Spellman.

Inside, the windows of the Club offered an even more magnificent view of New York Harbor and the Statue of Liberty than the impressive view from Paul Conway's office. The attractive young woman who sat at the desk near the entrance greeted me with a jaunty welcome. I asked her where to find the Wilson Room and she jumped from her chair saying, "Come with me. I'll be happy to take you there." We walked through the lounge, a room with burgundy leather armchairs and tables covered with magazines and newspapers. It was a room that always brought to my mind those classic *New Yorker* cartoons showing overly fed old men smoking cigars while sitting in such chairs commenting, as the captions might say, that the trouble with the world today was that it was different than it used to be. At a door bearing a brass plaque indicating it was the entrance to the Wilson Room, my escort knocked discreetly and then opened the door for me. I thanked her, walked into the room, and was surprised to see that Conway and Spellman were already seated at a round table in the center of the room. I was further surprised to see that the Club's sommelier—with whom I previously had had absolutely no dealings—was standing behind Conway who was peering into a leather-bound wine list slightly smaller than the Manhattan telephone directory.

Conway looked up as I entered the room. "Michael, I'm so glad you could join us today. Please sit down and help me select a proper wine to accompany our luncheon. Thomas's tastes are too rich for our budget." Spellman smiled at me and rose to shake my hand as I reached the table.

"Paul, I'm the wrong guy to consult about wine selection," I said. "Norah and I were brought up to drink beer with meals."

"Would you prefer beer today?" Conway asked in all apparent seriousness.

"Absolutely not," I countered, "I can't wait to see what wine you order so I can impress my wife this evening."

Conway smiled. "Good," he said. "Since I intend to exercise my Presiding Partner prerogative, I insist that we all select the Dover sole as our luncheon entrée and, therefore, I am going to order a Sancerre. George," he said, addressing the sommelier, "what do you recommend?" George recommended something with a French name that tasted sort of sour when I sipped it a few minutes later, pronouncing it "Delicious."

As we proceeded through the ritual of ordering appetizers and the mandatory Dover sole, I began to relax and to find the experience of dining with my two partners in the Wilson Room quite pleasant. For more than a few minutes, the table conversation was casual and comfortable. At one point, Conway went to the door and ordered a second bottle of wine. I continued to wonder what the real agenda of this meeting was about, but as each moment passed I grew less and less apprehensive. Bad things don't happen over Sancerre and Dover sole, I concluded. My only concern was when we were going to get down to business.

SEVENTEEN

It was not until the dessert and coffee (tea for Conway) had been brought to the table that Paul Conway began what clearly—to me, at least—were his prepared remarks.

"The past several days have been momentous. From my perspective, the very foundations of our law firm have been shaken. I am not referring to the recent commotion about partner compensation, which, happily, has been resolved. No thanks to you, Tom."

Spellman started to say something. Conway glared at him and Spellman waved his hand in front of him as if to say that he should be ignored.

Conway continued. "Bear with me, please, while I summarize a few facts that you both know as well as I do but which we must keep in focus as we deal with the fallout from the events of the past week. I believe it was on Wednesday—but it may have been Tuesday, it makes no difference—I circulated a memorandum to the partners setting forth the conclusions of the Executive Committee respecting what I had been calling the 'Perkins matter.' Michael made it clear to me that that was a misnomer that trivialized a far more serious matter than the hurt feelings of poor old Fred Perkins.

"I am aware that a number of partners—I don't know the number but it is more than a mere handful—reacted negatively to that memorandum. The feeling of those partners, as I understand it, was that the conclusions and the memorandum itself, together with the text of Thomas's apology to Perkins contained within the memorandum, ignored the far more serious implications of the now famous Spellman views concerning—of all things!—the decision by the government of this country to enter the Second World War as the enemy, rather than the ally, of Nazi Germany."

Spellman again began to stir and to speak at this point, but Conway placed his hand on Spellman's hand next to him on the table and said, "I think we know your position, Thomas, and I hope we will be able to discuss it with Michael, but right now I want to continue with what I understand to have been the widely held reaction of the partners.

"I did not immediately recognize what our partners were concerned about. I wrongly attributed that concern to Barry Weinberg's agitation and enmity toward Thomas. I am not proud of the fact that I was impelled toward that conclusion by what may have been—and I'll say it out loud—an attitude on my part about Mr. Weinberg and about Jews in general. On Thursday morning, I advised Mr. Weinberg that it would be in his best interests to seek a position with another firm. In plainer—and more candid—language, I fired Barry Weinberg.

"Michael did me the great service later that day of helping me to understand the deeper implications of my attitude and the action that I took regarding Barry. After my conversation with Michael and Barry, I invited Thomas to come to my home for dinner and we had a long and serious conversation about the unrest in the firm. On Friday, the three of us met in Michael's office and had what I considered to be a most constructive discussion that concluded with Michael saying that we could try to convince our partners that Thomas was not the monster that some of them thought he was. Michael concluded his comment by saying—I believe these were his exact words—'It would help if we could salvage Barry Weinberg for the firm.' I went home hopeful that ultimately all of the participants in this drama would use the weekend for thoughtful consideration of this entire unhappy situation and would try to focus on the best interests of the firm. That hope was dashed when, on Saturday morning, I received a fax of a letter from Barry Weinberg announcing his resignation from the firm. I believe you are aware of that, Michael."

"I am," I said.

"Now, Michael, I want to continue by telling you things that you don't yet know. Mr. Weinberg's letter didn't mince words. Among other things, he wrote . . ." Conway reached into his jacket pocket and took out a piece of paper from which he read: "'It occurs to me that it is entirely appropriate for an **anti-Semite** to be the Presiding Partner of a law firm that holds a **Nazi sympathizer** in high esteem. It is impossible for me and—I would think—any moral person to be a member of such a firm.'

"You can imagine—or perhaps you can't imagine—the impact that letter had on me. My first reaction was anger at his impudence, followed immediately by the realization that he was—as the saying goes—'speaking truth to power.'"

"I am not a Nazi sympathizer. That is not the truth, it's a fucking lie," Spellman declared in a raised voice.

"Please, Thomas, allow me to continue. I am almost finished with my comments and then I hope we can have a constructive discussion."

"All right," said Thomas, "but I'm going to have a lot to say."

"Oh, I'm sure you will," Conway said with a broad smile, "when have you ever not had a lot to say?" After a brief pause and a sip of lukewarm tea, Conway continued. "I paced around my study, gathering my thoughts, and reached a few important conclusions that I want to share with both of you. First, although the circumstances were tragic and my role in them was—to say the least—ill considered and clumsy, I concluded that Barry's resignation was for the best, for him and for the firm. I didn't think it was realistic for me to hope that Barry could erase the memory of the fact that I fired him. Moreover, his relationship with Thomas was irreparably damaged."

—

Grandpa, did it shock you to hear this? This sounds more like the man you have always been speaking so highly about.

• Will, it really didn't shock me, but it certainly was pleasing to hear how clearly he came to understand the situation. I privately disagreed that Barry's resignation was "for the best." It would always be a source of pain for me.

—

"Next, after considering the effect of Barry's departure on our litigation practice, I reached a couple of conclusions. Thomas, you are probably the strongest and most effective trial lawyer in New York City. Your value to the firm as a trial lawyer is beyond measure. However, you appear to give hardly any thought to your role as chairman of our litigation department. In fact, I think you regard that role to be a nuisance. With Barry gone—eventually to be replaced by one or more of the promising litigation associates we have in the firm—the department needs effective management. I believe that our friend and colleague, Michael Cullen, is the man to provide the thoughtful leadership we need if our litigation department is to continue to be a powerful asset in our practice. Gentlemen, I intend to request that the Executive Committee appoint Michael as the new chairman of the department as soon as I receive a request from Thomas to be relieved of that responsibility."

"Paul, you can consider that request to have been delivered, effective immediately," Thomas announced. "I am happy not to have that job but I would ask you to include in your announcement to the firm of this change some flowery comments about the excellence of my performance. I can help you write that." Thomas grinned.

"Now Michael," Conway continued, "I don't want you to consider this change to be in any way a negative commentary on your work as a litigator. On the contrary, I hope and expect that you will continue to do everything you have been doing since you joined the firm in January. I could make some 'flowery comments' about that performance but this is not the time or place for that. I believe you can undertake the management role on top of your client work. I'm sure you understand that this will have a significant effect on your partnership compensation as the Compensation Committee considers the additional value you bring to the firm."

———

I'll bet you weren't expecting anything like this, Grandpa.
• To this day, I find it hard to believe. Not only was my job not in danger, I suddenly found myself in one of the firm's most important positions. This was so far beyond my wildest expectations that I literally felt dizzy.

———

"I hope you're not thinking of cutting my percentage," said Spellman.

"Thomas, give me some credit for not shooting the firm in its foot. That's not a particularly elegant metaphor, but you get my meaning, I'm sure. I know without a doubt that if we cut your percentage you would grab one of the offers that our competition keeps making to you in a relentless effort to steal you away from Coburn & Perkins. Gentlemen, I'd like to hear your comments on the overly long speech I just concluded. Why don't you go first, Michael?"

I don't remember what I said. I must have said something about being honored to be named chairman of the department. I must have promised to do my best in every way possible. I must have thanked Paul for his confidence. But, frankly, I was so stunned by Paul's turnaround on the Weinberg issue, by his dominance over Spellman, and— of course—by my utterly unexpected promotion, that my emotions drowned out my memory of what I actually said in response to Conway's "overly long speech." As to Spellman's remarks, I have a hazy recollection that they were a recapitulation of his arguments at the meeting in my office. I recall him saying that he had absolutely no antagonism toward the Jewish people whom, I believe he said, he held in the highest regard for their achievements in business and the professions. He mentioned that his doctor was Jewish.

Eventually, we all shook hands and—this is no joke—we raised our wine glasses for a toast delivered by Conway "to Coburn & Perkins, the greatest law firm in the United States, and perhaps in the world." None of us returned to the office after lunch.

I arrived home while Norah was out with Jenny and the older kids were doing homework. I sat alone in my study; I might have been a bit tipsy from that wine I didn't enjoy but of which I drank at least as much as either of my colleagues. It was good that I had some time by myself so I could sort out the remarkable events of the day. I was more than pleased, I was exultant that Conway had made me chairman of the litigation department. But why had he done so? I was the most junior partner in the litigation department in terms of the length of tenure in the firm. Eight months ago I wasn't even in the firm. There were litigation partners who had been with the firm for ten years, for twenty years. Excellent lawyers, fine people. But Conway picked me. It didn't take me long to deduce that my promotion had nothing to do with my putative management skills. Conway was neutralizing me as a potential or perceived threat to the stability of the firm. With the flick of a finger, he had made me an insider, part of the management of the firm. And, coupled with that, he was giving Spellman a symbolic slap on the wrist to appease those partners who might view Spellman's political ideas as too much of a burden for the firm to have to bear. Well, so what? So I was being bought off. Conway was displaying his managerial brilliance. I would no longer be a threat and Spellman's presence in the firm was diminished. Absolutely brilliant.

I now have to share with you a few thoughts that I never imagined I would admit even to myself, no less to you or any member of our family. Deep inside of me where I keep my feelings hidden, I believe I have not been treated fairly. Despite the abundant blessings I have received—being born into a family where I was loved, gifted with superior intelligence, successful at every level of my education, having the great good fortune of meeting and marrying Norah, becoming the father of three splendid children, earning more money than anyone could possibly need—despite all of these things, I need more. I need recognition. When I was an undergraduate, I took a literature course in which we read part of Charles Dickens's *The Pickwick Papers*. In the first chapter, Samuel Pickwick, Esquire, "observed that fame was dear to the heart of every man." I'm certain that's not really true. But it certainly applies to me. I need fame. I need to be a celebrity.

Don't laugh, because this isn't funny. I once heard the term "celebrity" defined as someone who is known to a great many more people than he himself knows. The only people who know who I am are people whom I know. Why does this matter to me? It matters because deep inside where those hidden feelings reside, I need the validation that comes from widespread recognition and acclamation. Other lawyers in Coburn & Perkins—Spellman was certainly one of them—were nationally recognized people. Their opinions were sought on television interview programs; their names were in the newspapers. I worked as hard, if not harder, than my famous partners. Believe me when I tell you that I was smarter than most of them. They came to me with their problems—both legal and personal. All good, but not nearly good enough.

I once thought that getting a law degree would be enough. It was not. I once thought that passing the bar exam would do it for me. It didn't. Getting a job in a good law firm, making partner, winning cases, earning a lot of money—none of these things satisfied that craving I have for something more than that which I had achieved. Perhaps one never achieves enough or receives enough to scratch every itch of ambition and ego gratification that drives ambitious people ever onward.

That first year at Coburn & Perkins I came to the realization that the reason I felt unfulfilled was that I lacked widespread positive recognition. It may be that I will live out my life without the ultimate gratification that can only come from being a celebrity. This may be some sort of pathology. If so, I should be pitied as one would pity the victim of great misfortune or disease. Or this may be some sort of moral deficiency, a character flaw, in which case I should be scorned, not pitied. Sorry, but that's who I am. I didn't tell any of this to Norah until much later in our lives, when everything had changed.

And that is why the promotion that Conway bestowed upon me was so important to me. The fact that he did it for tactical reasons was irrelevant. I was now in a position that might enable me to move toward that elusive goal of becoming someone other than the son of a bus driver.

—

*If you hadn't told me what you just said I would never in a
million years have thought that you had those feelings. I
suppose I should feel honored that you could speak about
that subject with a kid like me, but I have to tell you, Grandpa,
that I wish you hadn't revealed so much of yourself to me.
It was almost like seeing you naked.* • Oh, my goodness,
Will, I'm sorry. I didn't realize that what I said would have
that effect on you. Believe me, I didn't intend to embarrass
you. It was my intention to give you some information about
myself that would shed some light on things that I did years
later that, even now, I have difficulty explaining to myself.
Will, I'm not a perfect person. • *Grandpa, I don't think you
need to beat up on yourself.* • You may not think that when
you hear the rest of this story.

—

By the time Norah returned home I was able to reconstruct
the remarkable events of my day for her. After telling her
about how I now had one of the most prestigious positions
in one of the most prestigious law firms on Wall Street and
how I would be making more money than we ever dreamed
about, she sat quietly, thinking, with that vertical crease
down the middle of her forehead. After a few minutes she
made a brief comment that I shall never forget: "Mike, with
all my heart I hope you are doing the right thing by staying
with the firm. We don't need tons of money to be happy. Right
now, I'm happy simply because you're happy."

I hugged her, feeling as if I was—for reasons beyond my
understanding—the most blessed person in the world. That

feeling lasted just a few seconds until Norah said, "I had a long talk with Jessica this afternoon. She told me that the problem that she and Barry have has nothing to do with me and everything to do with you—specifically, your decision to remain in Coburn & Perkins. Barry feels that that evidences a serious character flaw on your part, your insensitivity to the morally corrupt nature of that firm."

"What does she—he—mean by morally corrupt?"

"Isn't that obvious? It's the firm's willingness to tolerate having a Nazi as a partner and the accompanying atmosphere of anti-Semitism."

"Norah, that's not obvious to me and it shouldn't be obvious to Barry and Jessica, or to you, for that matter. Spellman's a nasty guy, probably holds anti-Semitic attitudes. But it's a huge leap to call him a Nazi and to paint the firm with an anti-Semitic brush. For goodness sake, you're a lawyer. Think like a lawyer. Where is the proof? What about the presumption of innocence?"

"That's what Barry sees as your character flaw—thinking like a lawyer, not a human being."

I went into my study and sulked.

PART TWO

1982

Justice, justice, you shall pursue.

—Deuteronomy 16:20

EIGHTEEN

Coburn & Perkins grew by leaps and bounds during the eight years following my appointment as chairman of its litigation department. I don't want you to think that there is a direct causal connection between my chairmanship and the rapid growth of the firm, but the two things are not entirely unrelated. I believe I managed our litigation practice effectively and its success was part of the picture that the firm presented to the world. One thing is certain: Managing a department of more than one hundred lawyers while maintaining my own substantial caseload of complex lawsuits was causing me to spend a huge number of hours in the office, in court, and traveling around the country and the world. Speaking of the world, the firm's growth included the opening of an office in London and another in Washington. Our practice took on an international dimension and our presence in D.C. added an aura of importance and influence that was valuable in attracting

clients. We now had over 300 lawyers and nearly 100 partners. Our monthly meetings were no longer held in the
main conference room but in an auditorium that was now
part of our expanded suite of offices.

My life during this period was characterized by extremely
hard work and long hours. I almost never arrived home in time
to have dinner with Norah and Jenny. My practice responsibilities preempted more weekends than not. This burdensome
and stressful existence was punctuated by moments of the
kind of lifestyle that only money could buy. I was earning a
great deal of money. Norah insisted that I carve out at least
four or five weeks every year for family time and travel. The
first foreign trip Norah and I took was to Ireland, the year
of my promotion. Since then we traveled there twice more.
Each of us met people in pubs in the West of Ireland who
claimed to be—and might well have been—distant relatives.
We've traveled to Italy, France, Hawaii (not really foreign, but
a really long trip from New York), and lots of other places in
the U.S. We took the kids to Ireland on our second trip there
and to Hawaii and on most of our trips around this country.
Except for Jenny, eventually they became too old to want to
travel with us, something that made me both happy and sad.

Although my income could pay for our lifestyle, no
amount of money could buy the quality of life Norah and I
were enjoying. Our relationship with each other grew stronger
over time. I relied on her advice about both legal questions
and the more subtle issues that entered my life from time to
time, especially about my relationships within the firm. She
ran our social life with skill and sensitivity to my formidable work schedule and the limited amount of time I had to
socialize. She was responsible for assembling the circle of

friends who enriched our lives. And, most of all, Norah had the primary responsible for raising our children while their father was slaving away in an office on Wall Street. That's not right. She didn't have the "primary" responsibility, she had virtually the sole responsibility. In this role she was masterful.

Our daughter, Kathleen—who was now 25 and very much involved with a young man—graduated with honors from Yale and was now an intern on the staff of a U.S senator. She had the poise and self-confidence that she learned from her mother and an effervescence that I think came from her Irish genes. Her brother, Kevin, was now a third-year student at Georgetown Law School.

One Sunday morning, while Kevin was home from school, he and I were the last people at the breakfast table. We were chatting casually about law school, about Georgetown, about being a lawyer. Kevin was enthusiastic about the prospect of becoming a practicing lawyer.

"But not the kind of lawyer you are, Dad. I want to be involved with 'real people' and the problems they face living under our 'system.'"

"What's wrong with our system?" I asked him, with a combination of concern and pride.

"It's unbalanced in favor of the rich and powerful—like your clients—who use it to grow more rich and more powerful at the expense of ordinary people."

"Do you see me as an instrument for the oppression of ordinary people?"

"Not like you're personally evil, Dad."

"Well, that's a relief."

"But with your skills, I think you could do more to make this a more just society."

"Where did you get these ideas from?"

"I got them from living in this house with this family," Kevin said without a hint of irony or sarcasm.

"How about you and I go camping together, without any of the females in our family? We could talk about how to fix the system. Maybe I can talk you out of becoming a lawyer."

"Why would you want to do that?"

"Son, that may well be the most important question you've ever asked me. I'll try to answer it honestly and helpfully when we are on our camping trip."

This was a conversation I had been thinking about having with Kevin for some time after he decided to go to law school. I wanted Kevin to have a balanced and realistic view of what life as a lawyer looked like. I remember well how glamorous the profession looked to me when I was his age. He needed to know about the dark side of being a lawyer—the forced compromises that you frequently have to make with your own values; the tension that arises between the duty to your client and your personal sense of right and wrong; the skewed economics of the profession which make legal skill less valued than trolling for clients; the brutally hard work that is required for both professional and financial success. I had stumbled into the profession without any hard knowledge of what life as a lawyer would be like and without a grasp of how the world outside of law school really worked. I wanted Kevin to be more fully informed about a career as a lawyer than I was. A tent in a forest on the side of a mountain would be the ideal setting for that conversation.

"Where would we go?" Kevin asked.

"You name it. You've spent a whole lot more time hiking and camping than I have."

"Could we go up to the Adirondacks? Maybe climb Mount Marcy? How does that sound?"

With genuine and rising enthusiasm, I said, "Sounds great to me. But we can't do that in the winter, can we?"

"Well, it's been done. But I don't think you're in shape for a winter backpacking trip. In fact, I'm not sure you're in shape for Mount Marcy in any season."

"I'll tell you what: I've been thinking about starting to exercise and diet and get in shape and you've just given me the motivation to get serious about that. I promise that between now and July, you'll see a new man emerge from this creaky old body."

"That'll make me very happy, Dad."

—

Uncle Kevin told me that you and he never went on the camping trip. He said he never really expected that it would take place. • You can imagine what that makes me feel like as a father. • *Grandpa, I understand—and Kevin understood—that you had to work ferociously hard at your job in the law firm and that got in the way of things you would have liked to do with the family.* • I appreciate your kindness in making an excuse for me. I was still pretty much a delinquent father. I can never recapture the opportunities I lost and my children lost because I gave precedence to being a lawyer over being a father.

NINETEEN

The Conways entertained a group of senior partners and their wives at a gala New Year's Eve party at their home on the eve of 1982. Norah and I were invited as were Anne and Tom Spellman and about eight or nine other couples, including one partner from each of our Washington and London offices and their wives. The Conway home was a duplex penthouse apartment on Park Avenue. Norah and I had been there nearly eight years previously at a dinner the ostensible purpose of which was to welcome me to the firm as a new partner. I was so tense and twitchy that evening and Conway was so cold and aloof that I barely noticed the magnificence of their home.

Both Norah and I expected the Conway home to be impressive but that word hardly begins to describe the grandeur of the place as it appeared to us when we arrived there for the New Year's Eve party. The entrance hall—larger than the largest room in our house—was paneled with some soft and warm-looking wood, perhaps cherry, and the lighting made the area look almost as if it had been burnished by the setting sun. A magnificent wood and bronze chandelier hung in the center of the ceiling. Antique tables and upholstered chairs were tastefully placed around the hall. Lovely landscape paintings adorned the walls. I could have been happy living in that hallway.

The guests all arrived at about the same time—7:00 p.m.—and were greeted by Mrs. Conway (whose name I had forgotten!) and a graceful young black woman who took our hats and coats and led us to the room where the drinks and hors d'oeuvres were available. A squad of more young black servers (would "servants" be the appropriate word?) moved unobtrusively about the room refreshing our drinks and replacing both hot and cold hors d'oeuvres as soon as we consumed their predecessors. I don't know what to call the room where the drinking, nibbling and idle chatting took place. It, too, was large and lovely with a fieldstone fireplace. I think it might have been the equivalent of what we called our den, a place of casual comfort. However, on that New Year's Eve there wasn't much furniture in the room and I suspected that it had been moved to leave space for the guests to circulate. I was never particularly adept at small talk, especially while trying to hold a martini glass in one hand and a plate of Swedish meatballs in the other. I knew that Norah would have no difficulty holding her own as the more interesting representative of the Cullen family.

———

You got that right, Grandpa. • I always suspected you felt that way about your grandmother.

———

So I left Norah and drifted to the far end of the room where Paul Conway was holding court on what to expect from the newly elected Republican majorities in both houses of Congress. A few of the partners and a couple of the wives made occasional comments on what was essentially a lecture by Conway about the importance of conservative principles and how they were responsible for the greatness of America. Suddenly, the tone of the discussion shifted as Tom Spellman pushed his way forward and began to speak in a voice that was so loud that it attracted the attention of everyone in the room.

"The greatness of America," Spellman announced, "is eroding because people who think of themselves as conservatives"—an obvious reference to Conway—"ignore one of the most fundamental of conservative principles: ethnic and racial purity."

People gasped.

Spellman continued. "When the brave people of northern Europe arrived in what is now the United States, they didn't invite the native people of this continent to join them in building a nation. They didn't extend voting rights to the Indians. They didn't pass legislation assuring the savages of equal opportunities for employment and education. They knew that a great nation had to be a nation whose people shared common values, common history, the Christian religion, and a common cultural heritage. That's what made America great and people like us have to defend those principles, and not be complicit in their erosion."

It was obvious to me that Spellman was drunk. It was absolutely remarkable how articulate Spellman could be even when delivering a drunken rant. Conway tried to intervene to stop Spellman's tirade. "That's quite enough, Thomas. This is neither the time nor the place for such a speech."

"I'm not finished, Paul. And what's true about this country is also true about law firms. Law firms are no more than a collection of people. Those people have to have the same sort of things in common that the country needs. That means there's no place in a great law firm for coloreds and, in my opinion, for Jews."

He was about to continue his drunken diatribe when Anne Spellman grabbed hold of his arm and said, "I want to apologize to everyone here, especially our gracious hosts and their wonderful staff. Something happens to Tom when he has too much to drink. I'm going to take him home now. I wish all of you a most happy New Year. Again, I apologize for Tom's comments and I'm sure he will apologize as well when he next sees you. Good night."

They left. People looked at each other blankly, at a loss for words. No one knew what to say. The room that had been throbbing with the sound of overlapping conversations fell silent and remained that way for several minutes until Mrs. Conway said, "We have a very special dinner waiting for us in the dining room. Please let's try to enjoy ourselves."

The party proceeded through a lavish dinner and the mandatory ritual of watching the televised presentation of the ball dropping in Times Square at midnight. But the Spellman outburst continued to resonate and it soured the atmosphere for the remainder of the evening.

———

He should have been thrown out of the law firm before breakfast the next morning. • Will, I wish life was that simple. By the way, if he had been thrown out as you suggest, my life would have been much simpler. • *How so?* • You'll see.

TWENTY

It's quite clear that Tom drinks too much and loses all self-control when he's drunk." This was Harry Madison talking at a luncheon table at the Graduates Club one day during the first week in January. "He is tactless, even reckless, when he's soused. He doesn't have the judgment to keep his private views private. Nevertheless, I would like to say that he is completely sincere in what he says and what he says makes a certain amount of sense."

"You can't be serious, Harry," said Warren Worthington, one of our most senior partners.

You may remember him from the meeting about partner compensation. He was no fan of Tom Spellman. "Spellman's views don't come out of a whiskey bottle. He is a right-wing racist extremist, sober or drunk. We ought to be worried about that."

"He has a right to his views, whatever they are," Madison retorted.

"Oh, for Christ's sake, Harry, how can you say it doesn't matter that the guy is a raging anti-Semite, a bigot, and—I'm sure you recall—maybe even a bit of a fan of Nazi Germany. We have a problem and it's not about free speech," Worthington replied as he slammed his hand down on the luncheon table in the Graduates Club.

There were six of us at the table, all of whom had been guests at the New Year's Eve party. Spellman's rant was the only topic of conversation at the table and, I'm reasonably certain, the principal topic of conversation throughout the entire firm. Word of Spellman's New Year's Eve tirade had spread through the firm like a brush fire during a drought.

"And to think it happened in Paul Conway's home," exclaimed Bill Scott, another senior corporate lawyer. "The man is out of control. I think he's dangerous to the firm."

Harry Madison jumped back into the conversation. "I think you're all making too big a deal out of this. I think his drinking is more of a problem—for him and for us—than his rather cockeyed political ideas."

I could see the pro- and anti-Spellman factions forming up and developing their arguments. I now knew that Harry Madison—who spent the D-Day lunch ignoring Spellman's fond remarks about Nazi Germany—was, in fact, sympathetic to Spellman's radicalism. I wondered about how many others in the firm were in that faction. There was absolutely nothing about Harry Madison that would have made me suspect that he could think that Spellman's rant on New Year's Eve "made a certain amount of sense." I decided to find out what was in Madison's mind. "Harry," I said, "a few minutes ago you said that some of what Tom said made a certain amount of sense. I'm curious about what you meant by that. To get straight to the point, do you agree with Tom that there's no room in our firm for blacks or Jews?"

This was Madison's response: "I wouldn't make that a hard and fast rule but I do think that we should be especially careful in bringing those folks into the firm and exposing them to our clients. Frankly, I'm pretty sure that none of our clients would find it acceptable to have a colored lawyer working on their cases."

"So it's about our clients, not about how we should feel about having a Jew or a black as a colleague. Is that how you view that subject?" I asked.

Warren Worthington was angry. His face reddened and his nostrils flared as he said, "Harry, that's bullshit and you know it. You never wanted Weinberg to be a partner and you seem to go out of your way to have nothing to do with the sprinkling of Jewish associates that we've hired. Don't give us that shit about concern for our clients. You and Spellman are bigots and at least he's man enough to acknowledge that. You make me sick."

As Worthington rose from his seat, either to leave or to physically approach Madison, Bill Scott reached out to him and said, softly, "Warren, try to calm down. You know this isn't good for your damaged heart. We should give Harry the benefit of the doubt about his personal views. I'd like us to get past this terribly troubling subject and remember that we are partners and that it's okay to harbor our own personal preferences and prejudices—we all have them, you know—and just get on with our work."

"Nice thought, Bill," I said, "but there's a five-hundred-pound gorilla in the room and I don't see how we can ignore it."

Worthington—who now appeared to be short of breath—sat down and said, "Michael is right. We can't ignore this. I am going to speak with Paul this afternoon because I think there is an issue here that concerns the firm and needs to be addressed. Harry, I apologize for the language I used a few minutes ago." He then rose from his seat and left the dining room. Most of us left the table in the next few moments, wondering where this was heading.

TWENTY-ONE

Several hours after we left the Graduates Club, Warren Worthington appeared in the doorway to my office, looking dreadful. He asked if he might have a word with me. I invited him to have a seat at the small conference table in my office and I sat with him. I asked Patty to bring us some coffee. Warren's face was pale, almost ashen. His hair was mussed, his tie loosened. I'd never seen this dignified senior partner look anything like this.

"Paul came down on me like a ton of bricks," he said. "Do you know what he said to me? He said 'how dare you get mixed up in the Spellman matter.' He said that he expected someone of my seniority and stature within the firm not to join the rabble-rousers. Rabble-rousers! Can you imagine that that's what he called the partners who are concerned that Spellman is a loose cannon who could wind up getting everyone in this placed tarred with the brush of bigotry that Spellman will one day . . ." Warren sputtered and sighed. "I'm getting all mixed up. I don't know what I'm trying to say. I guess I just came in here to vent. I've never been spoken to like that by anyone in this firm in the more than forty years I've been here. No less the Presiding Partner. I think it's time for me to retire."

"Absolutely not, Warren. It would be a dreadful mistake for you to retire now. First of all, you are at the top of your game as a corporate lawyer. But just as important, if the best and most principled people in this outfit start heading for the exits, Spellman wins and Coburn & Perkins loses. I implore you to drop the idea of retiring."

"Thank you, Michael. It's kind of you to say that. But if Paul is going to be Spellman's protector, if Spellman's ugly bigotry is going to circulate unabated in this firm, what will become of us? I don't want my obituary to read that I was a partner in the law firm that became known as the most restrictive, the most racist and anti-Semitic of the elite Wall Street firms."

I went to my desk, picked up the telephone and called Conway's office. Mrs. Hadden put me through to Conway without a fuss. "Paul, Warren Worthington is in my office. I think it's important for you to join us here." Conway said he be with us in a few minutes.

Following a knock on my door, Conway walked into my office and sat with Worthington and me at my conference table. Patty stuck her head in and asked, "A cup of tea, Mr. Conway?"

"Thanks, very much, I'd like one," he said.

I began immediately. "Paul, I know that you know that Warren is upset about how you talked to him. He'll get over that. I didn't ask you to stop in here to discuss the words you used in speaking with Warren. The two of you will work that out. Paul, Spellman's drunken speech at your home is sucking the air out of this law firm. Everyone's talking about it. It's being viewed as a systemic firm problem by people who are not rabble-rousers or troublemakers. The notion that Warren could be a rabble-rouser is so patently ridiculous as to be laughable."

"I know that and, Warren, please accept my apology."

Warren didn't respond so I continued to talk. "You made a gift to the firm of eight years of relative peace when you put Spellman on a leash following the D-Day thing and its aftermath. We've used that time to grow and prosper. It appears that Spellman's off his leash now. If he thinks that he can preach naked bigotry in your home without any consequences, there won't be any constraints on him, drunk or sober. The firm will get a reputation that it doesn't want and probably doesn't deserve."

"Why do you say 'probably,' Michael?"

"I used that word because Spellman has followers. I don't know how many or how committed they may be to Spellman's brand of extremist politics. I'd like to know more about that because, Paul, let me tell you, I am not going to stay with this firm if I find out that it's a neo-Nazi hotbed."

"Me, neither," said Warren.

"Don't you think you're overstating the scope of the problem, Michael?"

"Yes, I do think I'm overstating it. I'd just like to be sure that we have a sense of how many of the partners share Spellman's desire to turn the firm into a white gentile ghetto."

"You can't be thinking about asking the partners for a declaration of their political views, or circulating a questionnaire, or anything like that," Conway said.

"Give me a little credit for not being a total jerk, Paul. But I do think we can sort out the issue of what to do about Spellman's disturbing comments—and his evident drinking problem—and get a sense of what the mood is in the firm."

"Do you have something in mind?"

"At this moment, only a few ideas but nothing concrete," I replied.

"Well I have a very concrete idea," Worthington interjected. "I strongly recommend, Paul, that you persuade the Executive Committee to propose that the Partnership Agreement be amended to state that the policy of restricting the firm to white Christian lawyers, as advocated by Spellman—something that every partner, every associate, every secretary, every file clerk, everyone in this firm, without exception, is fully aware of—is a policy that is contrary to the fundamental moral and ethical principles of Coburn & Perkins. I will be happy to draft the appropriate contract language to be inserted into the Partnership Agreement. That will require a vote of the partners. When that vote is taken we will know who in this firm is aligned with Spellman."

"Hey Warren," I said, "I can see why you are such an effective deal maker. That is a brilliant solution, an elegant solution. The Partnership Agreement ought to read that way not just because it's right, but as a means of getting the partners to go on record as to where they stand on the matter of institutionalized bigotry. It's absolutely inspired. I wish I'd thought of that. Paul, say something."

Conway looked troubled. "Amending the Partnership Agreement is not something that can be done casually. It's a big deal and it can be divisive. The firm could break apart over it. I recognize that we have a problem but I'm hesitant about pursuing a solution that could be worse than the problem."

Worthington raised his normally calm and gentle voice and said, "Paul, I am as politically and personally conservative as you are. And I think I care about this firm as much as you do. After all, it has been my professional home for my entire career. But, goddammit, if we find out that this firm is—as Michael put it—a neo-Nazi hotbed—then, goddammit, it doesn't deserve to exist. Do you hesitate to follow my proposal because you're afraid it might reveal how pervasive Spellman's bigotry is in these handsome offices? I don't share that fear. I don't think this place is contaminated by people I am ashamed to be associated with. But, if Thomas Spellman thinks that spouting hateful remarks at a gathering of partners and their wives in the home of the Presiding Partner is something that can be done without consequences, we might as well put something in our firm recruiting brochure that we circulate at the law schools that says 'no blacks or Jews need apply.' By the way, that policy is illegal."

I watched the pained expression on Conway's face as he digested and analyzed Worthington's comment. I could see the issue moving in the right direction. Paul Conway was inherently a good man, an instinctively cautious man, but a good one. Finally, after several minutes of silence, he said, "Warren, draft the proposed amendment and then let's meet to discuss it."

TWENTY-TWO

The circulation among the partners of what came to be known as the Worthington amendment caused much less excitement than I expected and Conway feared. Most of the partners seemed to view it as a routine effort to align the firm's partnership agreement with the fair employment laws that had been enacted more than ten years previously. The linkage of the Worthington amendment to Spellman's New Year's Eve outburst was apparent to most of the partners I spoke with, but that seemed like a secondary consideration. The Worthington amendment was about non-discrimination in employment and not about Spellman, *per se*.

The Worthington amendment was on the agenda of the February partners' meeting. The discussion was perfunctory. When Worthington moved the approval of the amendment, it was unanimously adopted. Tom Spellman seconded the motion! We now had an improved partnership agreement but we knew no more about the extent of entrenched bigotry within the firm than we did before the amendment was approved.

Several weeks passed and life at Coburn & Perkins seemed to return to its normal level of stress, tension and brutally hard work. The nature of my position in the firm made it necessary for me to be in frequent contact with Tom Spellman and actually to collaborate on a particularly important and complex case.

Tom Spellman and I never became close. For that matter, we never even began to like each other. But we did develop some sort of *modus vivendi* that enabled us to work together on the biggest and hardest cases. Both of us had the good judgment to stay away from discussing politics and we each treated the D-Day episode of 1974 and the New Year's Eve spectacle as if each was a poisonous snake. Which they were.

———

You must have hated working with him. • I understand why you would think that, Will, but somehow I managed to compartmentalize. I put my feelings about Spellman as a person in one box and my feelings about him as a lawyer in another box. • *Grandpa, I don't think I would be able to do that. And I also don't think it is an honest way to deal with a subject as important as that.* • Well, then, Will, what would you have done in my place? • *I would have quit the firm—or better yet, I would have said to Mr. Conway: Either Spellman goes or I go.* • Will, I wish I had done that.

———

Each passing year, actually each passing month, I noticed changes in Spellman's level of enthusiasm for the legal work we were doing. Thinking back, I realized that Conway's decision to replace Spellman with me as chairman of the firm's litigation department was a blow to Spellman. It was not that he attached any great importance to the chairmanship—in fact he thought it was a nuisance. As Conway observed back in 1974, Spellman gave little attention to the responsibilities of the chairmanship. For him—I now realized—it was just a status symbol. And during the years I was chairman, it was a symbol he could no longer wear. Had I been more discerning, I would have understood immediately that Spellman considered his removal from the job to be a symbolic demotion that, over time, lessened the pleasure he derived from his involvement with the firm and the practice of law. I don't think he held it against me or anyone else. He recognized the merit of Conway's decision. Nevertheless, it hurt. And it gradually diminished him, in his own eyes, as an iconic figure in Coburn & Perkins.

"What's bothering you, Tom?" I finally asked him one day when he showed up in the office after 11 o'clock one morning. "You're not acting right. I know something's wrong."

"Nothing's wrong."

"Good. Try not to miss another settlement conference."

"Don't lecture me, Michael. You know what's wrong? You're what's wrong. You strut around this place like you own it."

I restrained myself from continuing this schoolyard bickering. "Tom, I'm sorry if there's something I've done that's upset you. I certainly didn't intend to do whatever it was. Frankly, I'm concerned about you. I know that the kind of work we do can wear you out. At least six times a week I say to myself that it's not worth it. This job, this profession, can eat you up alive."

"There was a time when I loved this work, when I loved this firm. That's history now," Tom said. "Now every day is either boring or upsetting or degrading or—think of another sloppy adjective; it will apply as well. I get absolutely no satisfaction from all this. That case that we tried together last month, the case that fell apart when our brilliant Jew client was caught lying like the snake that he is and ruined our case. Do I need that shit?"

"Tom, I hope I didn't hear you right. Did you really say 'Jew client'?"

"It slipped out. Don't let it get under your skin." He turned and walked away, saying, "I'm going out. I'll probably see you tomorrow."

I had hoped that Worthington and Conway had successfully managed to isolate, perhaps to neutralize, Spellman's odious prejudices. I had put the Barry Weinberg affair in a vault that I hoped would never be opened. The whole miserable issue of Spellman's politics came flooding back when Spellman mentioned our "Jew client." There was no escaping the fact that we had a confirmed, committed bigot as a partner. Eight years earlier I had wondered if I might have a Nazi sympathizer as a partner. That question never went away.

⁓

"Is bigotry an incurable disease?" I asked Norah that evening as we discussed my conversation with Spellman.

"Depends on the bigot, I would think," she responded after a moment's thought.

TWENTY-THREE

February 1982

Several months after I replaced Spellman as litigation chairman, two of my favorite partners—Craig Wilson and Henry Stevens—had a conversation with me at the Graduates Club.

"Conway seems to have drawn a red line around Spellman and his clique of right-wing fellow travelers," Wilson observed.

Stevens then added, "And he gave them to understand that it would not be acceptable for them to step over that line."

"If that's what he did," I said, "he did the firm a great service. How do you think Tom is dealing with that?"

"About as well as Napoleon dealt with being exiled to Elba," Stevens quipped.

"Napoleon escaped from Elba," Wilson noted.

Stevens replied, "Yes, and he restarted his war if I remember correctly. I'm still waiting for Tom to try a coup d'état. I should say a 'coup de firm.'"

I said, "I don't think Tom will try anything like that. He'll sulk and grumble but, frankly, I don't think he cares enough about the firm or people like us to go to the trouble of trying to oust Conway. I think he'll eventually find another forum in which to spout his vile ideas."

We all agreed that it would be a good idea to keep an eye on Tom Spellman.

It turned out that I was right about Spellman. The firm enjoyed eight years of stability and success. The dark side of Tom Spellman was kept in a closet until his New Year's Eve eruption and even that seemed to have been subdued by the Worthington amendment.

I want to tell you about Craig Wilson and Henry Stevens. Knowing about them may give you a better impression of the firm than I think I may have given you up to this point.

—

You're right about that, Grandpa. My impression of the firm is that it's more like a zoo than a professional organization.

—

Craig Wilson was probably in his sixties at the time I'm describing. He had spent his entire career with Coburn & Perkins. He represented a number of large banks, making sure they complied with the morass of regulations to which they were subject. I thought that that must be boring work but Craig seemed to thrive on it. As a senior banking lawyer in a Wall Street law firm, it was almost inevitable that he would be personally conservative in his lifestyle and politics. In those days it was possible to be conservative in the manner of Craig Wilson and yet not be ideologically rigid. Craig was a supporter of Ronald Reagan and yet he thought Reagan's "Evil Empire" description of the Soviet Union was a reckless and dangerous policy. Craig was the only partner in the firm to have a beard, making him not only unique but idiosyncratic. He was also among the most literate of the partners. I prided myself on my liberal education but I don't think there was a serious work of literature, history, or biography that I had read that Craig had not also read.

Craig lost his wife to breast cancer a few years before the conversation I just described. He made no secret of the fact that he continued to grieve over that loss and expected to do so for the rest of his life. Nonetheless, he was charming and entertaining company. Norah and I invited him to dinner in our home shortly after his wife died. Despite his profound grief, he proved to be charming company and he became a frequent guest at out dinner table. He could talk knowledge-ably about any subject that Norah, Jenny, or I could have any interest in. I suggested to him that he ought to wear his gray hair in a ponytail. He took this suggestion seriously and finally approached me with his decision. "Michael," he said to me one day, "I think a ponytail would be making a statement that I am not prepared to make. It could be understood to mean that I am trying to make myself attractive to younger women and I can't possibly do that. Thank you, nonetheless, for the interesting suggestion." I treasure him as a partner.

On a surface level, Henry was as different from Craig as it was possible to be. He was in his early forties but he had already established himself as a potent figure in the firm. Although he was a tax specialist, he had a broad and astute perspective on the firm and the world in which the firm operated. He was actually interested in the workings of the law firm as a business. Although he held Tom Spellman in the lowest imaginable level of esteem, he had allied himself years earlier with the movement for radical change in the partnership compensation system led by Spellman. Whereas Craig Wilson was calm and sedate, Henry Stevens was dynamic. He had an electric personality that could occasionally be irritating but was much more often exciting and exhilarating. I enjoyed being with him. He, too, along with his extremely attractive wife, was often a guest at our dinner table.

Craig and Henry made my life in Coburn & Perkins far more enjoyable than it might otherwise have been.

Two important things happened during the week following my unpleasant conversation with Tom Spellman in which he used the expression "our Jew client."

Spellman asked for a leave of absence from the firm so he could seek the Republican nomination to run for Congress. It was widely expected that the incumbent Democrat in the Third Congressional District on Long Island would retire at the end of his current term; the election in November would be to determine who would fill the open seat. In view of Spellman's increasingly obvious dissatisfaction with his professional life, it was hardly surprising to me that he would look for something else to do. However, I didn't expect him to run for elective office. On reflection, I concluded that there was a certain logic in Spellman's decision. The Reagan presidency had stimulated a drift to the political right in the country and Spellman might just have the wind at his back in the 1982 mid-term election. He certainly had the conservative credentials if that's what the voters in the Third District were looking for. The first thought that occurred to me was that I was glad I didn't live in that district so I wouldn't have to tell my partner that no power on earth could make me vote for him. After all these years, I was still intimidated by him.

—

Does this mean that Mr. Spellman was gone from the firm? • Not necessarily. He could certainly return if he lost the election and I'm not sure whether he could remain "on leave of absence" if he was serving in Congress. I must say, however, that I strongly doubted that he would ever be back in Coburn & Perkins. As I'm sure you imagine, Will, I was not brokenhearted at the prospect of never being Tom Spellman's partner again.

—

The other major event of the week was the announcement by Paul Conway that he intended to retire from the practice at the end of the year. This was entirely unexpected—by me and by most of the partners. I wasn't personally close to Conway. Although we were on excellent terms in a formal sense and he told me on several occasions that he appreciated my performance as chairman of the department, I can't say that we were personal friends. Except for the conversation with Warren Worthington about Spellman's infamous remarks at the New Year's Eve party, he had never shared any personal thoughts with me since the discussion about anti-Semitism we had had eight years earlier at the time of the Barry Weinberg episode. I had no idea whether he still belonged to that restricted country club that he had told me about in that conversation. His personal life was a virtual unknown to me.

I was sorry that Conway would be leaving. He was undoubtedly a good leader of the firm. He commanded the respect—even admiration—of the great majority of the partners. Somehow, using skills that I didn't possess or even understand, he had managed to contain the damage resulting from Barry Weinberg's resignation—which many partners perceived as having been forced by Conway. He seemed to have limited the fallout from Spellman's New Year's Eve speech. And he also subdued the discontent of those partners who viewed Spellman's blatant bigotry as raising fundamental questions about the firm's moral principles. I like to believe—and I really do believe—that Conway's ability to deal with those issues was enhanced by the raised awareness that he had acquired through my discussion with him about anti-Semitism and the implications of Spellman's D-Day remarks.

I stopped by Conway's office a few days after his announcement. I wanted to discuss with him his reasons for his retirement decision. By the way, the fearsome Mrs. Hadden now granted me virtually free access to Conway's office. I'd come a long way since those unsettling days of the "Perkins matter."

Conway greeted me warmly and invited me to sit with him at the same intimate table where we had sat with Barry Weinberg and discussed anti-Semitism eight years earlier. Mrs. Hadden brought me a cup of coffee and Conway had his usual cup of tea. "I suppose you want to know why I've decided to retire," said Conway.

"I hope you have a very good reason," I said. "Otherwise I'm going to try to talk you out of it."

"That's most gracious of you, Michael. I do have a very good reason and you will not be able to change my decision. You've had a great influence on me, you know, and have changed my mind about many things over the years. But this is one thing about which my mind is made up. As you are no doubt aware, the partners recently voted to again amend the partnership agreement, this time to eliminate seniority entirely as a factor in the determination of partnership shares in the firm's profits. I think that was an extremely ill-advised decision, a decision that carries with it the danger that this will become a different type of law firm, much like many of our competitors. We will be driven far more by the aim of maximization of income and less by the traditional values of our profession. The quality of life of the lawyers in this firm will be diminished. Family lives will become secondary to work lives. Ten years from now, Coburn & Perkins will be unrecognizable. Partners will become 'free agents' like star athletes moving from firm to firm, following the money."

"I moved here from another firm eight years ago."

"Best thing that ever happened to us. But, decidedly, an exception to the rule. In any event, I don't want to be, simply cannot be, a partner in a firm whose values I don't share."

"Paul, I understand completely. Don't be surprised if one of these days I follow you out the door."

"Michael, it would mean a great deal to me if we could sustain our personal relationship."

"I can't think of any reason why we couldn't do that. In fact, Norah and I would very much like to see more of you and Mrs. Conway."

"Her name is Beverly. She and I will see to it that we remain in close touch with you and Norah."

We shook hands and as we did so he placed his left hand firmly on my right shoulder—a sign of a degree of intimacy for which there was no precedent in our relationship.

TWENTY-FOUR

June 1982

Tom Spellman received the Republican congressional nomination for the Third District. After some initial stirring about by several other potential candidates they all eventually dropped out, leaving Spellman the only one standing.

The race for the Democratic nomination was much more vigorously contested. The Democrats held four highly publicized debates that inflicted damage on all of the contenders and seemed to make a Republican victory in November more than likely. The Democratic nominee was a guy named Arthur Landauer, a veteran Long Island politician with a vaguely unsavory reputation. Although I didn't know what Landauer's personal foibles may have been, I was quite certain that Tom Spellman would try to exploit them, probably successfully. Henry Stevens cleverly summed up the prospects for the

Third District election by saying, "Coburn & Perkins's gain will be the nation's loss."

Paul Conway, in his characteristic, excessively formal style, wrote the following memorandum to the partners:

> Gentlemen [still no women partners, although we had a couple of female associates]: This firm is honored to have one of its senior partners—currently on leave—as a candidate for a seat in our nation's House of Representatives. Coburn & Perkins has never been a "political" law firm, by which I mean we have never attempted to use political influence to advance the interests of the firm or of its clients.
>
> That certainly does not signify, however, that we have been indifferent to or uninformed about the great issues of our time. We have been called upon time and again by governmental officials of both parties from Presidents of the United States down to the local aldermen and councilmen in the communities in which we reside, to provide advice and counsel on the issues of greatest concern to them.
>
> Thomas Spellman has taken that tradition one step further and has put himself on the front line of the debate over the great problems and concerns of this country by offering to sacrifice his prestigious and lucrative position in this firm in order to serve as the Congressman from the congressional district in which he was born and raised and in which he continues to reside.
>
> Whether we agree or disagree with all or any Thomas Spellman's political positions is of no

moment. What matters is that one of us has entered the fray and we, as his partners and friends, can do no less than wish him well in this great undertaking and to let him know that he makes us proud to call him our partner.

Paul Conway
Presiding Partner

The first thought that jumped into my mind was that Conway certainly had a knack for writing embarrassing memos. This was followed immediately by vivid memories of his missive on the "Perkins matter" written eight years earlier. Even men who were not partners in 1974 knew all about that memorandum. It was part of the folk history of Coburn & Perkins.

I didn't think this memorandum would trigger a backlash similar to that following the 1974 message. That was no laughing matter. This was. I took the memo home to show it to Norah and the kids. Kevin, who was home for the summer working as a summer associate for the Legal Aid Society, thought it was intended to be funny, a thought that hadn't occurred to me. "No, that can't be right, Kevin. Mr. Conway doesn't believe in jokes," I responded after mulling the point for a few moments.

"Then why did he write it, Dad? It is so pointless, so immature," Kevin persisted.

At this point Norah was laughing so uproariously that she nearly fell on the floor.

"Immature? Paul Conway? No way. He was not even immature before he reached puberty! It's too bad Kathleen isn't here to enjoy this with us."

Kevin, getting with the flow, suggested, "Mom and Dad, do you think she can get to be Spellman's chief of staff if he's elected?"

"I think it's a very nice note," said Jenny, age 13.

"Jenny, you are the only kind person in this family," said Norah.

"No. Kathleen's kind too."

I had a trial scheduled for the next morning and needed to get some sleep. Otherwise I could have kept this conversation going all night.

TWENTY-FIVE

It was an ugly campaign with insults flying back and forth between the two men, neither of whom made the slightest effort to conceal his disdain for the other. The theme of Landauer's campaign was that Spellman was born into great wealth and had spent his adult life adding to that wealth by representing the interests of the powerful and the greedy. He contended that Spellman was an elitist, out of touch with—even contemptuous of—the average citizens of the Third District. Landauer even stooped to reminding the voters of the scandalous divorce proceeding of Spellman's parents decades earlier, as if Spellman was somehow complicit in his parents' misconduct.

Spellman characterized Landauer as a "tax-and-spend liberal," a man with a shady background of political and personal corruption. He called Landauer a "moron lacking the necessary intelligence to serve the interests of the voters." "Even if Landauer wanted to go to Congress to serve your interests," Spellman asserted in a speech that received a lot of attention, "he lacks the brains to figure out how to do so." The ferocity of Spellman's ad hominem attacks on Landauer surprised me. In court, although he often sliced opposing witnesses to pieces, he did it with a scalpel, not an axe.

It was clear to me that Landauer was getting under Spellman's skin, that Tom was losing control of himself and that his famous temper was rising to the surface. I actually phoned him to warn him against appearing to be a raving maniac, advice for which he thanked me graciously, and somewhat sardonically. He asked me if I would review the text of his speeches to make sure they had the appropriate tone. I equivocated, claiming to be unusually busy due, in part, to his absence from the firm. He said that he understood. "But if you could find some time, I'd be grateful," he concluded.

My feelings about the election were decidedly mixed. I could not possibly support Tom's candidacy. He was much too far to the political right for my tastes. On the other hand—I'm ashamed to admit—Spellman in Congress meant that there would be no Spellman in Coburn & Perkins. That seemed like a decidedly pleasant prospect.

On Tuesday morning, September 21—a date I'll never forget—while I was seated at my desk, Patty came into my office with the day's mail. She typically opened and sorted my mail and she did so that morning. Among the usual assortment of letters and legal periodicals there was one unopened large envelope marked "Personal and Confidential: Deliver **ONLY** to Michael Cullen." The return address was that of Greenberg,

Gordon & Kantor, the law firm that Barry Weinberg joined when he left Coburn & Perkins in 1974.

My life changed when I opened the envelope, pulled out a plain manila file folder, and looked at its contents.

On top of a sheaf of what looked like a collection of letters and photos was a handwritten note that reading, "Landauer has this. BW."

The first piece of paper I looked at was a copy of a letter dated August 27, 1967, addressed to Matt Starr, "Deputy Commander, National Socialist White People's Party." It was handwritten and read as follows:

> Dear Matt,
>
> I learned of the murder of our beloved Commander, George Lincoln Rockwell, yesterday on the radio. I am heartbroken as I'm sure you are too. I understand that they caught the bastard who shot the Commander but the report didn't say whether or not he was a Jew.
>
> My sincere sympathy goes out to you and the entire leadership of the Party. We always knew that there would be setbacks. I know we will continue the struggle. You will have my full support.
>
> Sieg Heil,
> Thomas Spellman

—

Who was George Lincoln Rockwell? • He was the founder of the American Nazi Party and the author of books on the subject. • *Grandpa, did you know that when you saw his name in the letter?* • Yes, I did. You know, Will, the remarkable thing is that I wasn't really surprised to see Rockwell's name in Spellman's letter.

—

It looked like Tom's signature but it didn't sound like him. "Sieg Heil?" It was impossible that Tom could have written that. And yet, and yet . . . I could not let go of the breathtaking notion that Tom Spellman could indeed have written it. I turned the page and looked at the next document in the file, typewritten on the stationery of The National Socialist White People's Party in Arlington, Virginia. The stationery had a logo in the upper left corner in the form of a shield with an American flag motif in the center of which was a swastika. The brief letter, dated September 10, 1967, read as follows:

Dear Fellow Aryan:

On behalf of the governing council of The National Socialist White People's Party, I thank you for your kind words and pledge of support for our Party as we mourn the tragic death of our leader, George Lincoln Rockwell, founder of the American Nazi Party.

Sieg Heil,
Matt Starr
Acting Commander

Next came the following, dated January 18, 1968, again on the swastika-adorned stationery of The National Socialist White People's Party:

Dear Tom:

I am so glad you could join us for the rally in Cincinnati. Although the number of our fellow storm troopers who were able to attend the rally was disappointingly low, those of you who did participate brought new energy into our movement at a time when we are still reeling from the loss of our beloved founder and comrade.

We must remember that Adolf Hitler himself suffered disappointments and setbacks before he succeeded in establishing Nazism in Germany and throughout Europe. I agree with you that if it were not for the intervention of the U.S. caused by the jew Roosevelt, Nazism would now be a world-wide movement and the U.S. would be a racially pure country.

The niggers are acting up. I am hopeful that our new President will put them in their place. Stay strong in your actions and beliefs. The movement needs you.

Sieg Heil,
Matt

The folder contained three other pieces of correspondence along the same lines together with two photos of

Tom Spellman and three other men whose identity I didn't know, all wearing swastika armbands. Spellman looked both younger and thinner than he was now.

The last letter in the pile, dated August 29, 1974, was the most interesting to me. In it, Matt Starr wrote the following to Tom Spellman:

> I am terribly sorry to hear about your difficulties in your law firm. The prevailing climate in America at this time is not disposed to hearing the truth about how the niggers and the jews have taken over this country. Believe me when I tell you that the tide will shift and white Americans will rise up and take their country back.

I sat frozen at my desk, confused, dumbfounded. This was unbelievable, but it seemed as if I had no alternative but to believe that Spellman—at least at one point in his life—was actually a Nazi, not a Nazi sympathizer but an active, affiliated Nazi.

No, I thought, I did not have to believe this. These materials had to be forgeries. This was too grotesque to be real. Someone must have fabricated these papers and photos. There had to be ways to do this, although I had no idea how it could be done. There was someone out there determined to destroy Tom Spellman. Someone so filled with hatred for Spellman that he produced this set of obscenities. Someone, perhaps, who had something to gain by sabotaging Spellman's election campaign. Worse than that, someone who wanted to shatter his career and lay waste to his reputation and his life.

Barry Weinberg. He sent those papers to me. Where did he get them? How? Why are they now on my desk? Was it he who sent them to Landauer?

In the eight years since the evening when he and his wife left our house and said what turned out to be a final good-bye, I had had virtually no contact with Barry. Norah maintained a warm relationship with Jessica Weinberg and, to a lesser extent, with Barry. She frequently had lunch with Jessica in the neighborhood. It's possible that she saw Barry from time to time but I'm not sure of that. I was glad that Jessica and Norah were seeing each other because it kept alive my hope that someday Barry would come to his senses and we would be able to rekindle our friendship. I truly liked Barry. He was bright, funny, gentle, decent, modest, and honest. I never stopped missing him. A couple of times we bumped into each other in the federal courthouse in Foley Square. Each time, I greeted him and made some innocuous friendly remark intended to spark a conversation. He only nodded curtly and walked away. I knew that he felt that I had deserted him. The fact that I remained at Coburn & Perkins and, worse yet, rose in its ranks confirmed to him that I was on the wrong side in a clash of fundamental principles. In his eyes, I had allied myself with the dark side. I felt injured, aggrieved by his attitude toward me. Yes, of course, there were serious problems inside Coburn & Perkins. But I truly believed that I made it a better place, that Barry's understandable grievances against the firm were based on conditions that had been addressed and, if not totally remedied, they had at least been mitigated. I often wished that Barry would give me the opportunity to discuss this subject—but on the day I received Barry's package about Spellman, that was clearly a discussion that would have to wait for another time.

"Landauer has this. BW." The implications of that note were frightening. I had to do something. But what? I don't think I ever felt so befuddled, so impotent. I simply had not the slightest idea what to do with the bombshell that landed on my desk. Was it possible for me to do nothing? Could I treat the letters I had just read as mere junk mail, not requiring any response on my part? Doing nothing simply seemed impossible. Driven by a sense of some vague and unfocused responsibility, I decided that I needed to act, thereby stepping into a maelstrom that could possibly change the course of my life.

I decided to phone Barry. I had to know the source of the damning letters and photos before I could possibly confront Tom Spellman—if I were to confront Spellman, not a sure thing at all.

Barry's secretary answered the phone. We went through the annoying ritual in which I was required to identify myself, disclose the nature of my relationship to Mr. Weinberg, and indicate the purpose of my call, all before I was told that "Mr. Weinberg is in a meeting and cannot be disturbed."

"It would be a very good thing for Mr. Weinberg to be 'disturbed' within the next thirty seconds or I will come to your office and really disturb him," I shouted, my patience having run out even before the end of my cross-examination by Barry's secretary.

"Are you threatening me, or Mr. Weinberg?" she replied.

"You might say so."

"Well I'm going to tell him that a very angry and rude man is threatening me and him on the telephone and that he should call the police."

"Look, madam . . ."

"It's 'Miss.'"

"Look, Miss whatever-the-hell-your-name-is, I know it's your job to protect Attorney Weinberg from people you don't know, but he knows me very well and he knows what I'm calling about, and he will be very angry with you if you don't get him out of his meeting—if he's really at a meeting, which I don't believe—and connect me to him." I paused for a beat and then yelled, "Now!"

"One moment please."

There must be something wrong with me. Every important confrontation I have seems to involve a fight with an officious secretary as a prelude.

"Hello, Michael, I was waiting for you to call. How are Norah and your kids?"

I certainly wasn't expecting that kind of an opening from Barry. This was the same Barry Weinberg who refused to speak with me for eight years.

"My family is healthy and doing well. I hope the same is true with you and Jessica and whatever number and gender of kids you now have."

"All's well at this end. I assume you received my package."

"We probably should talk about that in person rather than on the phone. Just one thing, first. I have to know if it was you who sent that stuff to Landauer, or did he send it to you?"

"I sent it to him at the same time I sent it to you."

"Do you know what he's going to do with it?"

"I don't know."

"That's ridiculous, Barry. You sent a goddamn bombshell to Tom's opponent and you don't know what he's going to do with it? You're a goddamn bomb thrower. Are you out of your mind? Why the hell did you send that shit to me?"

"I thought you might be interested to learn something about your law partner."

"I'll be at your office in thirty minutes. Tell your secretary not to get in my way." I hung up.

TWENTY-SIX

stuffed the Nazi papers back into the file folder. I put on my jacket and rushed out of my office, telling Patty that I'd be out for the rest of the day. Out on the street, I watched one occupied taxi after another pass by my frantically waving arm. Finally, a taxi pulled up in front of my building and a passenger squirmed out. As I was about to jump into the cab, I realized that I had left the Nazi file on my desk. I turned and ran back into the building, waited what seemed like an eternity for the elevator, travelled up to the 49th floor and zoomed into the firm's offices and back into my office while my secretary gaped at me trying to figure out what could possibly have been going on. When I entered my office, my desk was neat and clear. "Patty," I yelled, "where is everything I left on my desk?"

"You said you'd be gone for the day, so I straightened up your desk and filed everything that was on it. Was that wrong?"

"No, it wasn't wrong but where did you file the large envelope from Greenberg, Gordon?"

"I kept it on my desk since I didn't know where to file it."

"Did you look at what was in it?" I asked, in trepidation.

"Of course not. It said clearly to deliver it 'only' to you."

"Patty, you're the greatest. See you tomorrow." I took the envelope and rushed out of the office.

I knew that I was behaving in a frenzied manner and that I needed to gain control of myself. But how could I be in control when I didn't know where I was heading, what my objectives were, what role I was playing, whose side I was on, what outcome I should desire? The brief phone conversation I had had with Barry did nothing to help me answer these questions. It only added to my disorientation.

An hour after I ended that phone conversation, I arrived at Greenberg, Gordon & Kantor on Madison Avenue in midtown Manhattan. I was told that "Mr. Weinberg left for the day about an hour ago."

"Where did he go?"

"He didn't say."

"Do you happen to have the phone number of his car phone or mobile phone?"

"I don't think he has one of those."

Remember, this was 1982. Mobile phones were not in widespread use and there was no way to contact someone who didn't want to be contacted. I was spinning around in a circle making no progress. I was very much afraid that time was running out and whatever chance I might have to avoid the destruction of Spellman's life was quickly disappearing.

—

Grandpa, why did you think it was your responsibility to save Spellman? It looks to me that he really was a Nazi and that he deserved whatever bad things might happen to him if that became public information. • You know, Will, it's easier to see things clearly from a distance than when you're right in the middle of those things. • *That may be so, but I don't understand why you were in the middle. It seems to me that you jumped right into the frying pan when you didn't have to do that.* • Looking back on what I did that day, I realize—more than you can possibly know—that my reaction to the materials that Barry Weinberg sent me was reckless, unnecessary, stupid, dangerous—add any other words you think apply. But I did what I did and the consequences are what this story is about. • *I think you were looking for trouble.* • That may be true, Will. But lawyers thrive on trouble. • *Oh, Grandpa, I don't buy that as an explanation of what you did.* • Do you have a better explanation? • *No, I don't.* • Well then, let me get on with the story and maybe we can both try to make sense of my actions.

—

While standing in the waiting room of Greenberg, Gordon, I suddenly had an idea. I asked the receptionist if Sam Teitelbaum was in the office. She looked at her attendance sheet, said that he was, and asked if I wanted to see him.

"I would very much like to see him if that's at all possible. I don't have an appointment."

"Who should I say is in our waiting room?"

"Please tell him that Michael Cullen would like a brief word with him about a rather urgent matter. He knows who I am."

Moments later, a short, chubby, gray-haired man with a big smile on his face came bounding into the waiting room.

"Mike, it's great to see you! It's been a long time. What brings you here?"

"It has been a long time. Neither of us gets to court as often as we used to. I hope all is well with you."

"Things are great here, especially since I stole Barry Weinberg away from that powerhouse law firm of yours," he said with a friendly grin, as he led me by the arm into his corner office. The brightly lit room was furnished with glass and chrome that immediately evoked an impression of importance and individuality. Sam was an outstanding lawyer with an excellent reputation for skill, judgment and integrity. He had sparked the growth of Greenberg, Gordon from a small group of lawyers into one of New York's preeminent firms. It was no longer just a "Jewish" firm, although it would probably never shake the reputation—by no means a negative one—that it was the place that outstanding Jewish lawyers were drawn to in the era when the white-shoe gentile firms wouldn't give them a second look.

"As it happens, it's Barry that I'd like to talk to you about," I said in a serious voice.

"Is there a problem with Barry?"

"We had a rather unpleasant phone conversation earlier today and I came up here to see if we could straighten things out. But he's not here and no one knows where he is. I was hoping you might help me contact him."

"I have no idea where he is. Did you try his home? You know Jessica, his wife, don't you?"

"Good idea. Could I use your phone? I used to know his home number but I haven't used it in years. Do you have it?"

Sam handed me his phone and dialed the Weinberg home. Jessica answered the call and was obviously surprised to hear that it was Mike Cullen on the phone. After a moment in which neither of us said anything, Jessica asked how Norah was. I said she was fine and continued, "I haven't given up that someday Barry will see his way clear to understand why I stayed at Coburn & Perkins when he left, and forgive me. Jessica, do you know how I can get in touch with Barry? I really need to speak with him."

"Barry came home early today. He's here. Let me call him to the phone."

"Please do."

Minutes passed. I heard indistinct voices in the background. Jessica and Barry were talking but I couldn't catch a word.

Finally, Barry came to the phone and said, "You frightened me when we talked this morning."

"I didn't mean to frighten you. You must have realized I was upset. Barry, you have a lot of things to explain to me."

"I thought those materials speak for themselves."

"Yeah, if they're genuine, they sure do. At least they tell us that at some point in his life, Spellman was so far to the right that he fell off the edge. But that doesn't explain how you got hold of that stuff, or what you hoped to accomplish by sending it to Landauer and me. You owe me an explanation."

"OK. If you promise not to scream at me, come to my house and we can talk."

"I'm in Sam Teitelbaum's office right now. It'll take me at least 45 minutes to get to your house."

"What are you doing in Sam's office? You didn't tell him about this, did you?"

"Of course not. I'll be at your house as soon as I can get there."

I thanked Sam Teitelbaum for his help and turned abruptly to leave. "What's this about?" he asked.

"I hope you never know," I said, as I rushed from his office leaving a much-bemused Teitelbaum staring at me as if I had lost my mind. I may well have lost my mind.

I rushed to the nearest subway station for a trip to Brooklyn Heights.

TWENTY-SEVEN

Unbeknownst to me, the Weinbergs had moved from Brooklyn Heights to Scarsdale several years after they severed their relationship with us. I felt a certain troubling disappointment that Norah had never mentioned this fact to me, although she undoubtedly had learned it from Jessica. When I arrived at the Weinbergs' former home in Brooklyn, the nice people who had purchased the house three years earlier told me that they had moved to Scarsdale. They thought they had the Weinbergs' new address and, after rummaging through a desk drawer, they found it and gave it to me, together with their best wishes for good luck in finding our old friends.

Barry probably thought that Brooklyn Heights was too close to Michael Cullen for comfort. I know that's an utterly unfounded statement but by the time I had unraveled their new address from their old one and managed to transport myself from midtown Manhattan to Brooklyn Heights and from there to Westchester, it was evening and I was fuming. I managed to phone Norah and tell her that I wouldn't be home for dinner and that I might be quite late. She had been married to a lawyer for enough years to know not to ask for a reason and only to express the wish that I wasn't working too hard. In any event, this mission to Westchester was not something I could discuss with her from a phone booth.

When I finally arrived at the beautiful brick and stone English Tudor–style house on a leafy street in Scarsdale after an $85 cab ride from Brooklyn, my first words to Barry Weinberg were, "You bastard. Would it have killed you to let me know that you had moved thirty miles from your last known address when you knew I was heading toward your house in Brooklyn? What is this game you're playing?"

Jessica, noting my flushed face, stepped between us saving me from the mistake of punching Barry in the face. "Please try to calm down, Michael," she pleaded, "it was an oversight on our part not to tell you we'd moved but we had no idea that Norah didn't tell you about it. I've saved dinner so the three of us could eat together—perhaps not the way we used to years ago but I hope in a civil manner. Barry's told me what you came to discuss."

"Good grief, Barry," I exclaimed, "is there anyone in New York you haven't told about Spellman?"

"Jessica and I have no secrets from each other."

"Jesus Christ! Do your clients know that all of their con-fidential information goes directly to Jessica?"

—

Grandpa, you really sound as if you were completely

unhinged. I never saw you so out of control. • So now you know that your grandfather is not the perfect person you thought he was.

———

Again, Jessica intervened. "Michael, you know better than that. Please stop looking for reasons to have a fight. Barry told me about the Spellman documents for the same reason he sent the documents to you. It was too heavy a burden for him to carry alone. Come, let's sit down in the dining room."

As Barry and I followed Jessica toward the dining room, I couldn't help but notice how tastefully the house was furnished. Norah would love this, I thought. Then I thought she must have already been here but decided not to tell me about it. That thought didn't improve my mood.

The table was set for three. I was the first to take a seat. Barry, still standing, said, "I would really like to have an aperitif. How about you, Mike?"

"You might like an aperitif but I'm from the Bronx where an aperitif is called a drink. And I need a drink." I thought that was a clever remark and I intended it to try to defrost the icy tension that enveloped the three of us. It failed utterly.

"You want scotch? That's what I'm going to have," Barry said.

"Perfect. Neat, please," I replied, followed by "Me too" from Jessica.

Barry brought a bottle of 18-year-old Balvenie to the table with three tumblers and a small pitcher of water. "Ice, anyone?" he asked and Jessica and I declined. Barry dropped a couple of cubes in his glass, sat down and passed the bottle to me. I poured a generous splash into my glass and passed the bottle to Jessica. We sat back and, as we sipped the splendid whisky, Barry began to speak, addressing me directly.

"You know I never liked Tom Spellman. 'Hate' might not be too strong a word. From the day I arrived at Coburn & Perkins, I sensed an animosity from him. It manifested itself in what seemed to me almost to be an obsession with the fact that I am Jewish. Sometimes his remarks were taunting." Imitating Spellman's voice, he continued, "'I understand that kosher butchers, like your old man, make lots of money. That's ironic, isn't it. A Jew getting rich off of other Jews.' I told him time and again that my father wasn't a kosher butcher—or any kind of butcher—but he never let go of that idea. On other occasions, he feigned a serious interest in Judaism, asking about obscure practices and customs, most of which I knew nothing about. He suggested that I consider converting to Christianity, becoming what he liked to call an 'apostate Jew.'"

I jumped in and said, "I actually heard him discussing that subject with you. That's when I asked him whether he considered himself 'an apostate Episcopalian.'"

"I remember that," Barry said. "I thought it was hilarious to see how startled he looked when you said that. I've told you, Mike, that it was apparent to me that the guy was an outright anti-Semite. But I was reconciled to the fact that as a Jew breaking through the wall around a gentile law firm, I had to endure the fact that there would be some anti-Semites in the mix. But guys like you and Craig Wilson and Henry Stevens and others proved to me that far from the entire firm being a nest of Jew haters, there were lots of folks who were warm and welcoming to me, without an anti-Semitic bone in their bodies. Spellman was the gold standard of the firm's anti-Semites. Really, no one else came close to making me as uncomfortable as he did. Unfortunately, as a litigator, I had to work with him—and under him—as chairman of the department.

"And then there came the famous D-Day speech. I knew Spellman was rabid when it came to Jews but it knocked my socks off hearing him becoming an advocate for Nazi Germany. When I gave him the 'final solution' cue and he embraced it, that was it for me. I knew he was a Nazi, for real, a Nazi. You tried to downplay the importance of this. I knew you were doing that for my own good, to preserve my place in the firm. But that just didn't work. After that ridiculous partners' meeting when that doofus Perkins rose up and distracted everyone from the real meaning of Spellman's D-Day remarks, I felt compelled to try to deal with the situation. I talked to one partner after another, including guys I hardly knew. I must have discussed Spellman, his D-Day comments and his anti-Semitism with at least twenty partners. There were two, maybe three, strong Spellman defenders: Porter, Kohler, and I'm not sure about Brown. Porter and Kohler actually told me that they agreed with Spellman's D-Day remarks. Then there were a small handful of guys, maybe four or five, who still didn't get it, who seemed to wonder what it was that I was concerned about. After all, Spellman apologized to Perkins. The remainder of the partners I talked to were supportive in that, to one degree or another, they expressed concern about having a partner who held such obnoxious views.

"After these conversations—all of which took place over three days—I decided that I could remain at Coburn & Perkins, Spellman notwithstanding. I knew I was in bed with an enemy, an enemy who had some allies, but I thought I had the resiliency to deal with that problem. And this thought was reinforced by the knowledge that there were good people in the firm who would protect me from Spellman, if the need arose for such protection. My conclusion was that Spellman was not a life-threatening enemy. Of course, you know what happened after that. It turned out that I wasn't as safe as I thought because I didn't factor Conway into my analysis. I know you thought our meeting in his office had a positive outcome. But for me, Conway's own description of his personal anti-Semitism confirmed what I had believed about him. When he showed his anti-Semitic stripes, I couldn't get out of there fast enough. I left Spellman and his poison behind in your law firm."

Barry refilled his glass with more excellent whisky, nibbled on some pretzels, drained his glass and filled it again. I sat and sipped silently, waiting for Barry to tell me something I didn't already know. It wasn't long before he broke the silence.

"Years went by and I hardly ever thought about Spellman. But when I learned this past February—I don't remember from whom I heard it—that Spellman was going to run for Congress, I thought that was simply intolerable. The idea of having a Nazi sympathizer in the Congress of the United States set my blood boiling. I felt that I had a special, personal, moral responsibility to do whatever I could to cause that bastard to lose the election. It was one thing for Spellman to contaminate a law firm with his obscene views. It was quite another thing for him to be in a position to infect our entire country.

"I contacted Landauer—whom I didn't know—and told him what I knew and believed about Spellman. He said it was interesting but that he really couldn't use that information unless it was supported by something more than my limited experience with Spellman and my personal opinions. It was obvious to me that he was right. I decided to try to find supporting evidence of Spellman's Nazi sympathies. I spent evenings doing research in the New York Public Library and learned that there actually was an American Nazi Party. I dug deeper seeking membership information. That proved to be impossible to find. I guess the Nazis were sensitive about the risks of maintaining a membership list. However, I did find some names in newspapers and other periodicals. I read and re-read George Lincoln Rockwell's autobiography and all of his filthy essays on 'National Socialism.' I read all of that pornography I could get my hands on and I compiled a list of names mentioned in those writings. Then I tried to contact people whose names were on my list. They were hard to find. When I did manage to contact someone on my list, the usual response was antagonistic and completely uncooperative. I didn't use my real name in making these contacts. Instead, I chose a name that didn't sound Jewish."

"What name did you use?" I asked.

"Cullen."

"You have to be kidding."

"I'm not kidding about any of this. Eventually, I found a guy—who made me commit to never disclosing his name—who had been a member of what was then called 'The National Socialist White People's Party'—successor to the American Nazi Party. This guy—I'll call him Mr. X—dropped out of the party after a dispute over the wording of some publication. He remained angry with the leadership and seemed willing to help me 'gather information' for a book

I was writing. He said he thought he knew Spellman and that he might have some materials that mention his name."

"You told him you were interested in Spellman particularly?"

"Not just Spellman; I told him I was researching the party and its membership. But, yes, I did mention Spellman and my experience as his partner in Coburn & Perkins. Mr. X suggested that we meet at his home in Texas. I remember saying that I'd be there the next day but he said he would be traveling for the next ten days. So we made a date for two weeks later. I could hardly wait.

"Mr. X's home is about 75 miles from Dallas. I booked a flight and a hotel room in Dallas for the night before our meeting. I also booked a car rental and studied road maps for the drive from Dallas to his house. Finally, sitting at a table in his kitchen, I asked if he was able to find anything about Thomas Spellman. He said he had met Spellman two or three times in the 1950s and '60s. You can imagine how this discovery took my breath away."

Barry paused again to refill his whisky glass and take a long swig.

"I hope I'm not boring you with this long story," he said, knowing that I was captivated by his narrative. "Mr. X had an old wooden filing cabinet in his shabby kitchen. I can't tell you too much about where or how he lived because—as I said—I am obliged to protect his identity.

"He opened the bottom drawer of that cabinet and leafed through a bunch of file folders. Eventually, he pulled four or five folders from the drawer and spread them on the table. They each bore a label that read 'NSWPP' and various dates in the 1950s. He looked through the papers in these folders and then said that he was wrong about when he knew Spellman. He said that he probably didn't know about Spellman in the 1950s, that it must have been the 1960s. He returned the folders to the cabinet and pulled out some different folders. While leafing through the papers in those folders he finally looked up and said 'Aha, I got something for you.' At that point he showed me one of the letters that was in the package I sent you. He continued to pull papers from the folders until he had assembled all of the papers and photos that I eventually sent you. 'How much are these worth to you?' he asked.

"I hadn't been at all prepared for that question. It never occurred to me that he expected to get paid. I asked him how much he wanted. I remember his exact response. 'That stuff ain't worth shit to me but it's worth a lot to you. You can have it for $10,000.' I equivocated and said something about having to test the authenticity of the documents before I could agree to pay anything for them. Again, I can remember his exact response. 'In that case, sonny boy, you can get the fuck out of my house. I ain't got nothin' that ain't authentic.' He said something about being insulted by my authentication comment. Then, 'The price just went up to $15,000.' I wrote him a check in that amount and he said, 'Cash, sonny boy, your paper ain't no good here, Jew boy.' He had seen my real name on the check.

"I told him I would have to arrange to get $15,000 in cash. 'I can wait, Jew boy.' I told him I'd be back in two or three days. I drove to Dallas and flew back to New York. I called my private banker and told him I needed $15,000 in cash. He said I could pick it up at the bank the next morning. That's what I did. I phoned Mr. X and told him I would be arriving that evening. I flew to Dallas on the first available flight, rented a car and drove to Mr. X's house. I handed him the money and he turned over the documents. It was too late to get a flight back to New York so I stayed in a hotel in Dallas where I made two sets of photocopies of the documents. I flew back to New York the next morning and sent a set of copies to you and to Landauer. Does that answer your questions?"

"I still don't know why you sent me that stuff. What do you want me to do with it?"

"That's for you to figure out, Michael."

I now had Barry's story. To say that it strained credibility would be an understatement. The only thing that prevented me from concluding that the story of Mr. X and the Nazi Party was some sort of deranged invention by Barry was the physical evidence—the letters and photos themselves. They looked real.

And then there was Barry himself. Everything I knew about him was inconsistent with him behaving like a maniac. I needed to confront Spellman.

TWENTY-EIGHT

left the Weinbergs' house without having dinner—there being a precedent in our relationship for such a thing—and took another expensive taxi ride home. I was at a loss to account for the hostility that Barry displayed toward me. It had been eight years since he and Jessica abruptly terminated their relationship with me, ostensibly to protect me from the repercussions of his resignation from Coburn & Perkins. That rationale had long since lost its credibility. At this point something else was eating at Barry. I could only speculate as to what that might be. But while sitting in that taxi, I had no time for such speculation.

I decided en route that it was essential that I confront Spellman with the letters and pictures as soon as possible, before Landauer went public with them. Tom's reaction was impossible to predict. It was not inconceivable that he would react violently but I hoped he would be rational and perhaps even be forthcoming about those horrible documents. I also had a vague and formless hope that he might deny the authenticity of those materials. But if he couldn't do that, perhaps he could claim that they represent a misguided episode in his life that he had renounced long ago. After running through the possibilities, I still had no clear vision as to what Tom would say or do when I showed him the Nazi file. I looked at my watch and noticed that it was after 9:00 p.m. I asked the driver to take me to my office rather than home to Brooklyn. It was nearly ten o'clock when I entered the building, was cleared by the security guard and, finally, settled behind my desk—a place where I usually do my best thinking. I looked up Spellman's home phone number and called it. Anne answered.

"Sorry to disturb you so late but I need to speak with Tom."

"Are you kidding, Mike, we're running for Congress. This is still the middle of the day," Anne quipped. "How are you and Norah? Long time no see."

"Is Tom home by any chance?"

"Believe it or not, he is home."

"May I please speak with him?"

"Mike, is something wrong? I don't like the sound of your voice," said Anne.

"Nothing's wrong, but I really have to talk to Tom."

Moments later, Tom came to the phone. "What's up, Mike, Anne said it sounded urgent?"

"It is urgent. I need to see you tonight, if possible."

"Mike, I'm utterly exhausted. This campaigning stuff is harder than trying a case."

"I'll come to your house. I can get there in less than an hour."

"If it's that important, I'll wait up for you. I must say you've got me worried."

I hung up and called the firm's limousine service. I was on my way to Great Neck within a few minutes, carrying Weinberg's bombshell in my briefcase. I tried to work out how to approach Spellman and concluded that there was no gentle way to do this.

Tom and Anne were waiting at the front door of their home when I arrived. We proceeded immediately to their kitchen where Anne had a pot of coffee waiting. No one said a word as she poured the coffee for all three of us. I quickly concluded that Anne's presence at this meeting would be useful. I also felt that she had a right to know what my late-night urgent visit was about. She put a pitcher of milk and a bowl of sugar on the table, sat down and stared at me. Tom looked fatigued. His hair was tousled. He wore jeans and a white tee shirt.

I took a deep breath, opened my briefcase, removed the folder, and said, "You both should look at this."

Anne stood up so she could look over Tom's shoulder. I kept my gaze squarely on Tom's face. Anne appeared aghast as Tom carefully and slowly turned over one document after another. His face was surprisingly serene. As he reached the last photo in the folder, he turned to Anne and said, "Were you able to see everything?" She nodded and flopped back onto her chair, ashen.

In a perfectly calm voice, Tom asked, "Mike, where did you get this stuff?"

"We can discuss that later. First, I need to hear your comments about these materials."

"That's easy. Everything in that folder is a forgery. Now where did you get it?"

"I can understand how the letters could be forged but what about the photos? I don't know how a picture can be forged."

"There are lots of ways to do that," Tom said. "I'm not an expert on photo forgery but I know it can be done. Someone had to get hold of some early pictures of me—the guy in the photos has a 20-year-old Tom Spellman face. That face," Tom said with a broad grin, "was pretty good-looking, wasn't it?" He paused. "Now tell me where this came from."

I had no choice but to answer Tom's question. "It arrived at my office in this morning's mail in a Greenberg, Gordon & Kantor envelope with a handwritten note with Barry Weinberg's initials saying that Landauer has a copy. I have spent the last twelve hours chasing after Barry and you to find out what this is all about."

Tom smiled. "I wondered when something like this might happen. He hates me, you know. That's partially my fault. It may even be mainly my fault. I teased him, mostly for my personal amusement, but—to be perfectly candid—mainly because I am genetically an anti-Semite. I say 'genetically' because my father was a real hot-blooded Jew hater and I think I received his genes. But that's all ancient history. I don't think I've had any contact with Barry since he left our firm. I can only marvel at the persistence of his hatred."

This was the first time in all these years that I had witnessed this very different side of Tom Spellman. He continued his comments as I listened intently. "Like most bullies, I picked up the scent of a likely victim when I interviewed Barry for the firm. I sensed a certain vulnerability and I quickly perceived that it involved the fact that he was a Jew in a completely gentile environment. After that incident about D-Day, I knew that he went bananas and wanted the partners to gang up on me. Perkins came to my rescue with that absurd demand for an apology because I insulted his heroism at Omaha Beach. But that was only a temporary respite so I went to see Conway and recommended that he fire Barry. Paul did what I asked but then you jumped in and you know what happened after that. Barry was gone but I was the big loser. I don't think you ever fully realized how much a blow to my enormous ego it was to be removed as department chairman. Over the past several years, whenever I thought about Barry and what I did to him, a wave of guilt, of contrition would sweep over me. If I were a better person, I would have sought him out and asked for forgiveness. But I'm not that good a person and now I'm facing what may be an entirely just form of retribution."

I was experiencing Spellman being humble, introspective, candid. He was the opposite of the swaggering, overbearing, egotistical person I had worked with for eight years. Could this have been the real Spellman? Was it possible for me to dismiss the D-Day incident, the speech at Conway's home, the "Jew client" remark, and everything that Weinberg had told me about his treatment by Spellman? And yet, there was something so convincing, so genuine about the calm and contrite Spellman who was sitting next to me, baring his soul. Against all the objective evidence, I found myself inclining to believe his contention that the Nazi stuff was phony.

He continued by saying, "But that is all in the past. As one Roman Catholic to another, it almost feels as if I have just been to confession and you have been my confessor. I don't suppose you can grant me absolution for my sins but I hope you can tell me that you believe what I've said about those disgusting forgeries."

"Tom, I think it's possible that I do believe you."

"That means everything to me."

"And to me," Anne added. I had almost forgotten that she was present through all of this and that she was profoundly invested in Tom's truthfulness—which I had now endorsed.

"The question now is," Tom announced, "what the hell do we do about this? I'd bet my house that Landauer will hold on to that stuff until right before the election and then spring an October surprise bombshell. That will completely trash my election prospects, unless," he added with a wink and a smile, "my constituency is further to the right than I am."

"Tom, it's nearly midnight and I have to get home and try to have a night's sleep."

"You have no transportation. I'll drive you home. We can talk on the way."

"I'll come along," Anne said.

We didn't talk on the ride from Great Neck to Brooklyn. I slept. I assume that Tom drove without incident since we arrived safely in my driveway and I was gently awakened by Anne.

TWENTY-NINE

All was quiet in my house. Norah and Jenny were both sound asleep. I realized that I hadn't eaten anything since breakfast many hours earlier and I was hungry. I found a container of chocolate ice cream in our kitchen freezer and I devoured it.

I tiptoed into our bedroom and tried to get into bed without disturbing Norah but she awoke anyway. "What time is it?" she asked, her voice hoarse and slurred with the remnants of sleep.

"It's nearly two in the morning, darling, go back to sleep."

"Where have you been?"

"Well, the last place I've been today was the Spellman home in Great Neck. It's a long story."

"The Spellmans? What on earth were you doing there? I thought he was running for Congress."

"I told you, it's a long story. I'll tell you about it in the morning."

"No, now. I'm wide awake now and I want to know what you were doing in Great Neck, of all places."

So, in the darkness of our bedroom in the middle of the night, I told Norah the whole story of Barry, Mr. X, the Nazi file, and Tom Spellman.

Norah turned on the lamp on her nightstand. She looked at me curiously, almost warily. A minute or two passed and then she said, "Barry didn't forge those letters and pictures. That's simply not something he would do. I don't believe he did that. I can't accept that."

"I have to tell you that I am inclined to believe Tom. I think you would believe him too if you had heard him—and seen him—when he insisted that the stuff was a forgery motivated by Barry's hatred of him, a hatred for which Tom feels responsible."

"Why responsible?"

"Because of the torment that Tom inflicted on Barry while he was in the firm. Tom actually told me that he was motivated by anti-Semitism which—to my amazement—Tom openly, fully and contritely acknowledged. Tom wasn't angry, he was remorseful."

"Michael, he was bullshitting you. He is an actor. He can step from one personality to another whenever it serves his purposes. Just as he does in court . . ."

"Norah, please, stop. You don't know what you're talking about."

"I don't want you to be involved with Tom Spellman. He will use you to save his career, his reputation, maybe a seat in Congress, whatever he wants."

"But I am involved with Tom. Barry got me involved by sending that Nazi file to me. Do you think I enjoy being the man in the middle of this situation?"

"I certainly hope you don't enjoy it. But you don't need to be the 'man in the middle.' Just walk away. You delivered the Nazi file to Tom. That's it. Enough. Above and beyond the call of duty."

"Okay. He hasn't asked me to do anything for him. I'll tell him I'm too busy to help him with the situation."

"Good. The thought of you working with that Nazi appalls me."

"Norah, he's not a Nazi. Do you realize what will happen to him if that's the label that he has to carry for the rest of his life?"

"Whatever happens to him will be something that he brought upon himself."

"Oh, God. Norah, he confessed to me, one Catholic to another, as if I were a priest."

Norah left the room without saying another word. I followed her downstairs to the kitchen. "Leave me alone," she said. "For the first time in twenty-six years, you're suddenly a Catholic again."

This day had become altogether too much to bear. I went into my study and went to sleep on the sofa.

THIRTY

I awoke at 9:30 a.m., the latest I had slept in my adult life. No one was in the house.

Norah had not left any note letting me know where she had gone. The phone rang. It was Spellman. He had been trying frantically to reach me all morning. He had tried my office and had called our home phone four times without anyone answering.

"I need to see you as soon as possible," Spellman said, with an anxious tone in his voice.

"I can't see you today."

"Why not? You know the urgency."

"You're not the only problem in my life, Tom. There are other things I need to deal with."

"Well, when can I see you?"

"Maybe tomorrow. I'll phone you."

"Please, Mike, as soon as possible."

I said again that I'd call him and then abruptly ended

the conversation. The silence made me realize that I had rarely been alone in my house. That realization added to my sense that things were spinning out of control, that my life was different from what it had been in ways that I couldn't yet fully identify. I told myself that I had to try thinking like a lawyer, whatever the hell that means. I think it means systematically, something that I was hardly equipped to do in my unsettled state of mind.

What were my choices? That's the first question I needed to address. It seemed to me that there were three choices, all hard.

I could simply leave the battlefield. I had no obligation to judge whether Weinberg or Spellman was the liar.

I could jump in on Spellman's side, as I was so strongly inclined to do when he drove me home the previous night. I really did believe that Spellman was telling me the truth—at least I did believe that before I had the middle-of-the-night conversation with Norah. Spellman faced a profoundly difficult uphill battle to overcome the damning contents of the Nazi file. This was, for me, the most professionally challenging alternative. It was a temptation, perhaps for that reason alone

Finally, I could listen to Norah—who was almost always right on the hard questions. This meant aligning myself with Barry Weinberg—and, incidentally, with the disagreeable and unlikable Arthur Landauer, Spellman's election opponent. It was unclear to me whether this alternative actually presented me with a role to play. The Nazi file seemed to speak for itself. It didn't need an advocate. Spellman would be condemned the instant the contents of that file were exposed.

I wished I knew where Norah was. I needed to talk with her. I needed to repair the damage that suddenly occurred last night when I tried to explain why I thought Spellman was not a Nazi. I was so besotted with Spellman's "confession" and repudiation of the Nazi file that I failed to recognize that to defend Spellman meant to condemn Weinberg for a hideous act of malice and deceit. It was not hard to understand that it was impossible for Norah to accept that conclusion. However, last night I just didn't get it. Her anger was entirely justified. I had to fix that before I did anything else. But to do that I had to find her.

I phoned the law firm where she worked part-time. They told me that she had not been there for several days but they expected her on Friday. I phoned some friends and neighbors and no one had seen her that day. Norah had an aged mother who lived in a retirement community in Queens. The retirement community was, in reality, a nursing home. Norah's mother was failing, both physically and mentally. Her memory was spotty. There were occasions when we visited her and she didn't know who we were. I feared that I might upset her if I called her. I hesitated to contact her about—of all things—locating her missing daughter. But I nevertheless decided to phone her for want of any other place to look for Norah. That was a mistake; she thought I was a crank caller and she hung up the phone. I got the bright idea to phone Kathleen at her office in Washington. That too was a mistake. After Kathleen told me she had not heard from her mom that day, she naturally wanted to know why I asked. I couldn't tell her so I made up some feeble and unbelievable story. As a result, on top of my other concerns, I now had a daughter who was worried about her missing mother.

It was now early afternoon. I had exhausted every possibility I could think of to locate Norah. I was sitting in our kitchen in my pajamas and it occurred to me that I hadn't told my secretary that I would be out of the office today. I called her and told her that. She said she thought I might not be in after noting my frantic departure the day before. She asked if there was anything she could do to help me with whatever it was that I was working on in connection with the file that was sent to me from the Greenberg office. I thanked her and suggested she take the rest of the day off.

With nothing better to do, I returned to analyzing the Spellman problem. I knew he was waiting for a call from me. It was possible he had something new to report on his situation and I was wondering what that might be. I called Spellman's home. Anne answered and immediately called Tom to the phone.

In an agitated voice, he said, "Landauer announced that he was calling an important press conference at 6:00 p.m. today. That has to be about Weinberg's stuff. We need to discuss my response. Can I see you at your office?"

"I'm not in the office, I'm at home."

"I'm on my way to your house." He hung up. I immediately called back and told him it was impossible for me to meet him at my home and that I would drive to his house. That pleased him.

Moments later, the phone rang and it was Norah.

As soon as I heard her voice, I said, "Norah, my dear, I've been searching for you all morning. I'm so sorry about last night. I've been worried sick about you and about us. Are you all right? Where are you?"

"I'm with Jessica Weinberg. She called early this morning to tell me that Barry was in a terrible state and that she needed to meet with me. I took the Honda and drove to their house in Scarsdale. I've been talking with Jessica for two hours. I haven't seen Barry. He's in bed and won't leave their bedroom. You should come here. Right away."

"I have to get dressed. I'll come as soon as I can."

"Please hurry."

I phoned Spellman and told him that I needed to deal with a family emergency and that I couldn't drive to Great Neck. I said I'd phone him when I could but I didn't know when that might be. He said something but I wasn't listening and the conversation ended.

I was truly the man in the middle.

———

Hey, Will, have you fallen asleep? You haven't said anything in quite a while. • *I have definitely not been sleeping. I just don't know what to say. I've been trying to get a sense of what you were feeling. It's such a weird situation. Please go on with the story. I need to know the ending.* • Will, we're a long way from an ending.

THIRTY-ONE

The storm in my head began to subside as I drove across the Triborough Bridge. It was a brilliantly clear early autumn day. The scuzzy waters of the East River glistened brightly under the midday sun. I had time to think.

Heading toward Scarsdale and the Weinberg home, I tried to account for what Norah called Barry's "terrible state." I thought I knew the answer. He had "let slip the dogs of war" but had neither the strength nor the appetite to deal with the consequences. Richard III? No, Julius Caesar. Barry was an intellectual, a humanist, a sensitive soul. He was anything but a bomb thrower, yet he had thrown a bomb. Small wonder that he was curled up in bed, hiding from the havoc he had created.

As I drove through the South Bronx—derelict, decaying neighborhoods, made worse by the intrusion of the interstate highway on which I was driving—I thought about what Tom Spellman must be going through at that very moment. He knew that in just a few hours he would be labeled publicly as a Nazi. Only he knew with certainty whether that label was justified.

Spellman had no choice other than to fight to clear his name. If the Nazi label stuck to him, he was finished. Not only would he lose the election in a romp, he would be washed up as a lawyer. I can't imagine that Coburn & Perkins would let its carefully cherished reputation be sullied by having a partner who was publicly exposed as a Nazi—even a former Nazi. The psychological damage to Tom would be incalculable. There were two outcomes that could be fairly described as "worst." If the accusation stuck because it was true, or if the accusation stuck even if it were untrue. As I thought about these two worst outcomes it became clear to me that the second of these was truly the worst of the worst. If Spellman had to carry the Nazi label for the rest of his life notwithstanding the fact that it was untrue and unjust—that would be too much for him to bear. That prideful, arrogant, self-important, egotistical, overbearing bastard—he would be destroyed.

With the stakes as high as they were, it was clear that Spellman needed and was absolutely entitled to the best legal representation he could obtain. There was no question about that. The Constitution guaranteed him that right. The questions I had to answer were whether I was the lawyer Spellman should have and whether it made sense for me to take on that representation. Although it was obvious that some sort of litigation was inevitable if Spellman were ever going to be able to erase "the Nazi" as his new middle name, it was not at all clear what shape that litigation would take. I had a few random thoughts but, as I drove toward Scarsdale,

I just didn't know what the representation of Spellman would entail—professionally or personally.

I had enough self-confidence—perhaps too much—to conclude that I was as qualified to design and implement a litigation strategy as any lawyer I knew. It was the personal issues that were most troublesome. I knew Norah would react negatively to my representation of Spellman. But she has always been supportive of whatever I thought it was necessary for me to do as a practicing lawyer and I was confident that she would defer to my judgment on this matter.

The more I thought about the opportunity to represent Spellman, the more appealing that opportunity seemed. This was a case that was going to be in the headlines. How often does a major party candidate for Congress get labeled as a card-carrying Nazi? If somehow I could clear Spellman of that label, I might finally get the recognition that I have long thought I was entitled to but never seemed to obtain. Merely being engaged by Spellman in a case like this would, in itself, give me more public visibility than I had ever had in my entire career. I needed to seize the opportunity. I took a deep breath and decided that I would try to help Tom Spellman refute the evidence in the Nazi file. That's what I was thinking as I pulled into the Weinberg driveway.

—

No, Grandpa, I strongly disagree. You didn't need to seize anything, other than your own self-interests! You were thinking irrationally. This is really upsetting. • It's so easy for you to sit in judgment of my thinking and my actions. You're a million miles away from what was happening to me in real time. This was no hypothetical situation; this was real life whirling around me. • *That's all the more reason for you not to be rushing wildly into a decision that had consequences beyond the fate of that man Spellman who— even if he wasn't a Nazi, which seems improbable—was definitely an anti-Semite. Grandpa, I don't want to hear any more about this.* • Oh no, Will, it's now time you gave me my day in court. You wanted to hear about this and I must insist that you hear this story to its conclusion. Please bring me a glass of water. • *Are you enjoying this?* • I'm telling you about the most difficult and—in its own way—the most exciting professional experience of my life. So, yes, I am enjoying this. • *I'll be right back with the water.*

THIRTY-TWO

One of the Weinberg children opened the door when I rang the bell and showed me into the living room where Norah and Jessica were sitting together on a sofa with cups of tea or coffee on a table in front of them. Jessica thanked me for coming. Norah appeared cold and distant.

"What's happening with Barry?" I asked.

Jessica responded, "This morning, when he heard that Arthur Landauer was calling a press conference for later today, undoubtedly to disclose the Nazi letters that Barry sent to him, Barry seemed to have some sort of seizure. He turned pale, was sweating profusely, said he felt cold and faint. He went into the bedroom and got into bed. He's been there all day. I know he's not sleeping but he doesn't answer when I talk to him. I was hoping he might respond to you if you go upstairs and speak to him. Please, Mike, I'm so worried about Barry."

"I don't think I can do that, Jessica. In fact, I know I can't do that."

"I don't understand."

"Barry is likely to be called as a witness in a lawsuit that I may have to bring against Landauer if he . . ."

Norah erupted in a furious rage. She stood and ran toward me, shouting, "I don't fucking believe this! You're going to represent that goddamn Nazi. You son of a bitch, how can you do that? I hate you."

I had to grab both of her wrists to stop her from hitting me. She was screaming obscenities, weeping uncontrollably. Jessica tried to pull her away from me and eventually forced Norah back down onto the sofa.

"Well, Jessica, it looks like you now have two hysterical people to look after. I can't do anything for Barry and I can't deal with Norah in her present state. Barry forced me into an impossible situation. You and he should know it's a situation that's causing me pain and it seems it's now endangering my marriage. I'm trying not to feel sorry for myself but I wish someone would try to understand the no-win situation I'm in. Barry did the stupidest thing he ever has done in his life. Tom Spellman is an insufferable human being. And I find myself in the cross fire between them. I'm getting out of here before I lose my temper. Before I lose my mind."

The two women were weeping. As I was leaving the house, I saw Barry at the top of the stairs.

———

I hate this story. I don't want to hear any more. • Oh no, not again Will, you asked for it and now you're going to have to hear it through to the end. • *Please, Grandpa, it's so upsetting.* • Well, I'm not going to tie you to a chair and force you to listen to the rest of the story. But I'll tell you this—if you think this is too hard to take, imagine how I felt. This was happening to me. You will never really know who your grandfather is unless you know the whole story of the Spellman case. It's the story of my life. • *In a way then, I guess it's part of the story of my life, isn't it Grandpa?* • I think so. Please stay and listen. • *I will.*

THIRTY-THREE

Anne Spellman answered the phone when I called their home. I asked her to tell Tom to meet me in my office in 45 minutes. She said he was in the house and I could talk with him. I said that I'd rather talk in person.

An hour later Spellman bounded into my office with such exuberance one would think we were going to a party together. He smiled broadly, telling me—before he sat down—that he believed he had a solution to Landauer's expected announcement about the Nazi file.

"It's so simple," he said. "Landauer is screwing up. He doesn't have the brains to hold on to Weinberg's stuff—as I thought he would—and release it just before the election when I wouldn't have the time to counteract it. But now, I can have my staff launch a full-scale investigation of Landauer's cloudy background and pull together what I expect will be tons of tawdry details of corruption and misconduct. We'll fight fire with fire. People will say 'a plague on both their houses' and the Nazi stuff will be neutralized. Don't you love it?"

I didn't respond immediately. When I did, I told him I thought it was a stupid idea. "You don't seem to have a real appreciation of the enormity of the Nazi accusation. Nothing you can come up with about the routine bad stuff that voters expect goes on with politicians can come close to stinking like the Nazi file."

Tom's face clouded over. I continued, "Besides you're focused only on the election. Frankly, I don't give a shit about the election. I'm concerned—as you should be—about what people will think about you for the rest of your life. There isn't enough deodorant in the world to rid you of the stench of being associated with Nazism. You know what just popped into my head? A line from Shakespeare: Macbeth asked, 'Will all great Neptune's oceans wash this blood clean from my hands?' And, of course, the answer was 'No.' There are some things that can't be washed away. The stain of being a Nazi is one of them."

"Oh, God, how could I be so dense? What you're saying is that I'm doomed, that I'm ruined."

"That's exactly what I'm saying—unless we can prove that you're not and never were a Nazi." I looked at Spellman. He seemed sunken, defeated. "Tom, for us to succeed—and it won't be easy—it has to be true that the Nazi file is a forgery and, beyond that, I need you to be vigorous and aggressive. I need you to be the Tom Spellman of eight years ago—the best litigator in the city. So stop moping and listen carefully."

His face brightened a bit but he still appeared frightened and dispirited. In a soft, almost imploring voice, he asked, "What do you want me to do?"

"Before anything else, I want you to swear to me, before God and on the heads of your wife and children, that the Nazi file is a forgery."

Spellman stood up, put his hands on my desk, looked directly at my face, and said—in his courtroom voice—"Michael, I swear to you, before God and on the heads of my beloved wife and children, that everything in that file is a forgery. I mean that from the depths of my soul."

"Good. It matters to me that you are a practicing Catholic. Not because I am—which I decidedly am not—but because I know that what you have just said has a meaning—an importance—to you that it would not have if I had said it. Does that make sense to you?"

"Of course it does."

"Okay, let me tell you what I have in mind. As soon as Landauer releases the materials in the Nazi file, we are going to sue him for libel. We need to get the best, toughest, smartest litigator in New York to represent you."

"Wait a minute," Spellman interrupted. "I don't want anyone to represent me other than you." I then presented to Spellman a list of reasons why I thought it was inadvisable for me to be his trial counsel. I didn't tell him that among those reasons was my desire not to further imperil my marriage. Perhaps if I had told him that he wouldn't have persisted so intensely in imploring me to handle the case. In any event, I eventually relented and agreed, subject to the approval of the firm's Executive Committee, that I would lead the team of litigators from the firm who would be plaintiff's counsel in the case of *Spellman v. Landauer*.

I was now in so deep, I felt I was drowning.

———

Grandpa, I hope you don't resent my saying this. You may have felt like you were in over your head, "drowning" as you said. But I don't think you were forced into this. I think you wanted to be exactly where you were—Spellman's lawyer in a highly visible case. • Will, I think you may have inherited your mother's brains and intuition. I don't resent what you just said. You may very well be right. I can't count the number of times I replayed these events in my head. I still don't know with certainty what led me down the path I took. Your theory may be a partial answer. But if it is, it still doesn't fully explain why I wanted to be Spellman's lawyer.

THIRTY-FOUR

We went into the law firm's lounge where there was a television set. A number of lawyers had already gathered to watch the Landauer press conference. Among them was Paul Conway. I pulled him aside and said that it would be good if Tom and I could watch this without anyone else in the room—other than Conway. He grasped instantly that Tom didn't need an audience to hear what lousy things his opponent was going to say about him. Conway ushered everyone out of the room and posted himself by the door to prevent anyone else from entering.

There was a long introductory session in which reporters and commentators discussed what they called "the most bitterly fought congressional election in memory." Then Landauer appeared, looking serious, almost somber. I seriously expected him to say something like, "It hurts me to have to do what I am about to do, but the interests of our district and our country demand that I bring to your attention information that I have concerning my opponent in this election."

In fact his opening sentence was virtually what I expected. Reading from a prepared statement, he went on to announce that "in the past half hour I have released to all of the major news services, television and radio networks, and all of the newspapers that circulate in the greater New York area copies of a file of letters and photographs that prove beyond a shadow of a doubt that Thomas Spellman was—and may still be—a member and supporter of the American Nazi Party." He paused to let that bombshell reverberate throughout the room. He then read excerpts from several of the letters, emphasizing the "Sieg Heil" closings in all of the letters, and he held up each of the photographs of Tom wearing a swastika armband so the television cameras could zoom in. He continued his remarks. "With these facts now available to the public, it would be an insult and a disgrace for Mr. Spellman to continue to seek to represent the Third Congressional District in the Congress of the United States of America. I call upon Mr. Spellman to withdraw from the race. I'll take a few questions at this point."

A chorus of shouts from the reporters ensued, all asking where these items came from.

Landauer's answer: "They were sent to me by Attorney Barry Weinberg, a former law partner of Mr. Spellman, who is now a distinguished and highly respected partner in a major New York City law firm. I will defer revealing anything further about the source of these materials until I've had a chance to discuss them with Mr. Weinberg. I have been trying all day to contact him but thus far he has not been available. I decided to release this information almost as soon as I saw it because the nature of these facts is so significant, so momentous, that I thought the public had a right to know about it without delay."

The volley of reporters' questions continued for several more minutes without any new information emerging. Paul Conway looked as if he had been physically assaulted. He said to Spellman, "I expect to receive your resignation from the firm before you leave our offices today." He stormed out of the room.

I said to Tom, "I'm afraid I'm going to have my hands full with him."

THIRTY-FIVE

Spellman and I returned to my office. Landauer's premature disclosure of the Nazi file gave me an opportunity to file a lawsuit in which Spellman would be seeking to salvage his reputation. It was my hope that the story of the forgery of the Nazi file would be at least as captivating as the contents of the file itself. To capture the moment, we needed to launch the lawsuit without delay. I summoned Brenda McGovern to my office. Brenda was a fourth-year litigation associate, smarter by far than any other junior lawyer in the firm. I wanted her to draft our complaint and file it on my behalf tomorrow at which time I would issue a press release to announce the commencement of the lawsuit against Landauer.

—

You see, Grandpa, you immediately seized the opportunity to become the star of the show. • Yes, I see. But this had to be done.

—

I had no time to spend trying to persuade Paul Conway to authorize me to represent Spellman.

As soon as Brenda knocked on my door and came into my office, I began to outline—for her and Spellman—the theory of our case and the complex legal issues that would swirl around it. I asked Brenda to draft a complaint alleging that Landauer had made public statements about Thomas Spellman that were untrue, defamatory, and clearly intended to destroy the plaintiff's reputation and career, and that the statements were made with reckless disregard for their truth or falsity. The complaint should allege that Landauer publicly distributed forged documents and pictures, the content of which was defamatory, without making any effort whatsoever to ascertain the authenticity of such documents and pictures. "Brenda," I said, "use all the adjectives you can think of to paint Landauer as someone bent on the destruction of Spellman's life and career. Finally, claim ten million dollars in compensatory and punitive damages. I want to be able to announce the filing of this lawsuit by 10:00 a.m. tomorrow." Brenda returned to her office to draft the complaint.

Spellman said, "It's a hard case, isn't it?"

"You bet it is. You're a 'public figure,' which raises the bar that we have to clear to win the case. We have to prove that Landauer's statements were made with, quote, actual malice, which means that he knew the stuff was forged or he distributed it with, quote, reckless disregard for its truth or falsity."

"You have to get Barry Weinberg to admit he forged the letters and pictures. That'll be hard to do, but you can do it. You know him. You know his weak points, his vulnerability. You can shake him up and squeeze the truth out of him."

"Tom, if Barry stood in Times Square tomorrow and announced that he paid a professional forger a lot of money to prepare those forged letters and pictures and told us how, when and where it was done, and says he did it because he hates your guts, we still don't win the case."

"Why not?"

"You know, you always were a lousy lawyer. You just don't get it, do you? Schmuck, Weinberg's not the defendant, Landauer is. To beat Landauer we have to prove that he had doubts that the Nazi file was authentic but made no effort to find out the truth about it. We don't have a chance in hell to be able to do that."

Looking utterly confused, Spellman barked, "So what are we wasting our time for?"

"Tom, I don't understand why I care about your reputation more than you do. I don't even like you. Listen, asshole, this is not about winning a case against Landauer. It's about neutralizing the effect of the Nazi file—either by getting Barry Weinberg to acknowledge that it's a forgery or by creating sufficient doubt about the authenticity of that crap to make it possible for people to believe that you're really not a Nazi. The lawsuit is the vehicle to try to accomplish one of those objectives."

"I think I get it."

"Good. Now go home and don't call me; I'll call you if and when I need you. Don't make any public comments or appearances. And don't resign from the firm."

"Hey, Mike. Don't forget I'm running for Congress."

"No you're not. You're running for your life."

He didn't say another word. He left me alone in my office. I presumed he went home. I wondered what would happen when I went home.

THIRTY-SIX

I t wasn't long before Brenda McGovern showed up with a draft of the complaint. It was perfect—better, in fact, than I could have written. I told her to arrange to have a marshal serve the complaint immediately. I wrote a press release and asked Patty to see to its distribution to all the appropriate news organizations.

I wanted to present my Presiding Partner with a fait accompli. With the lawsuit document in the hands of a marshal and a press release announcing that Spellman was suing Landauer, Conway's options had been reduced to the choice between firing me or supporting me in the prosecution of the lawsuit. He knew that I knew that he really had no choice.

Conway walked into my office without knocking on the closed door. "You are a clever son-of-a-bitch, Michael," he said with a hint of a smile on his face. "I wish you luck with that cockamamie lawsuit. You'll be doing our firm a great service if you can erase the swastika from Spellman's forehead." An interesting allusion, I thought. The Black and Scarlet Letter.

I had spent two long and exceptionally hard days on the Spellman case. I was exhausted. It seemed as if this day had begun a week ago. It was now time to go home, time to face Norah, time to try to make peace.

For the first time ever, before heading home I stopped for a drink at the bar in the Graduates Club. The bar was located in a dimly lit, wood-paneled room that was intended to evoke the atmosphere of a cozy pub. In one corner of the room, there was a large round table that bore the scars of decades of use—initials carved in the heavy wood, scrapes and burns—all giving the table an antique appearance that imparted to it a value much cherished by its regular users. The table could accommodate eight or ten people and was famous for being the after-work refuge for men whose divorces were pending or final and who had effectively been kicked out of their homes. They were affectionately called the "Homeless Rich Men." They typically nursed their drinks slowly to defer the moment when they needed to return to their cheerless hotel rooms or empty apartments. Very little conversation took place among the Homeless Rich Men but there was an occasional card game. Usually they just watched television. A baseball game if there was one. That night's game had been rained out.

That evening, I vowed to myself that I would not become one of the Homeless Rich Men. I stood at the bar, alone, ordered a martini. The bartender was an elderly black man whom I knew from his years of waiting on tables at lunchtime. I could almost swear that he said, "Yes, Massa Cullen," when I ordered my drink. I had long ago found the obsequious, servile nature of the serving people at the Club to be an embarrassment and I wondered why I continued to patronize the place. I was thinking that thought when several men joined me at the bar. I knew them by sight but not by names that I could remember. I was sure they were all lawyers from one or more of the firms in the Wall Street area.

"Well, if it isn't the famous Michael Cullen whose name is in the paper for having sued a candidate for Congress," said one of these men.

Another said, "I think he's famous for representing a Nazi. That takes guts."

To which another responded, "It takes more than guts, it takes lunacy."

"That makes Mr. Cullen a courageous lunatic."

"Gentlemen," I said, "if you're going to talk about me while standing next to me, I wish you would not refer to me in the third person, as if I wasn't here."

"Sorry, Michael. We're all a little tipsy. What's with the lawsuit?"

"It's quite straightforward. Even in a race for Congress, you can't call someone a Nazi if it isn't true," I responded.

"But what about the letters and pictures?"

"Forgeries."

"Forged by Barry Weinberg? Why?"

"The heart has its reasons," I responded cryptically. "Sorry, guys, I have work to do."

"I think you've got a lot of work to do," one of them re-marked as I left the bar.

It was raining when I reached the street. I didn't feel like walking to the subway. Back inside the club, I phoned my firm's car service and asked that a car pick me up at the Graduates Club. Knowing that it would be at least half an hour before the car arrived, I went back into the bar and ordered another martini—ordinarily something that guaranteed a headache the following morning. I was alone, sipping my drink, when a young man—whom I didn't recognize—approached me at the bar. He introduced himself as Lou Galliano, a lawyer in the Hadley, Jenkins firm. He was a pleasant fellow who said he knew who I was and had overheard the earlier conversation about my now notorious case. He said that a partner in his firm was likely to be retained by Arthur Landauer and that he—Galliano—was going to be his associate on the case.

"Welcome to the war, Lou," I said with a smile.

He responded by saying, "I don't know much about the case at this point but it sounds like it raises a bunch of really interesting issues." I agreed with him and asked if, by any chance, he knew which judge would be assigned to the case. "As it happens, I do a lot of work in the Nassau County Supreme Court and the judge who takes on the complex cases is almost always Anthony Santangelo," he responded.

"What's he like?" I asked.

"Very smart. Very sharp. No nonsense, but if you're prepared and respectful, he's a pleasure to deal with. But don't try to put anything over on him. If he thinks you're doing that, you'll be sorry."

"That's good to know. If you know anything about me, you know that I'm a straight shooter."

"That's what I've heard. I really look forward to being at war with you," he said with a smile. "We're probably going to file a bunch of motions as soon as the case is on the docket and I'll get to argue at least one of them—the summary judgment motion."

"So, who's the general in your army?"

"Bill Schofield. This is the first case I've had with him."

Damn, I thought to myself. Schofield is a slimy, slippery son of a bitch. I've had cases with him and I wouldn't trust him as far as I could spit. I liked the young man I'd been chatting with but I wouldn't want any of my associates to be quite so forthcoming while standing at a bar with opposing counsel.

"Well, my car is probably here so I'll say good-bye. It's been nice chatting with you and, as they say, I'll see you in court." We shook hands.

THIRTY-SEVEN

The house was dark when I arrived home. It was after midnight. I needed to sleep. I was in no condition to have a serious conversation—much less an argument—with Norah so I decided to sleep in Kathleen's vacant room. It had a more comfortable bed than the sofa in my study where I had slept the night before. I couldn't help wondering whether I would ever be back in my bed next to Norah. The last time I had seen her—hours earlier, at the Weinbergs' home—she was trying to beat me up and calling me every dirty name in the book. Dear God, I said to myself, don't make me become one of the Homeless Rich Men.

Jenny woke me at 8:00 a.m. "Mom wants to see you in the kitchen before she leaves the house."

"Where is she going?"

"I think she said she was going to be with Mrs. Weinberg."

This wasn't starting out right. I realized I had slept in the clothes I was wearing the day before. I was groggy. I needed to wash my face and brush my teeth. I just wasn't ready to confront Norah. I peeked into our bedroom. Norah wasn't there so I walked into our bathroom and did a quick wash and brush.

She was waiting in the kitchen, dressed in business clothing, looking severe. She said, "I want to apologize for the way I behaved yesterday at the Weinbergs. I lost my temper and I behaved abominably. I will try never to behave that way again."

"I certainly accept your apology. Believe me, I understand what triggered what happened."

"I don't think you begin to understand what happened," Norah said. "We didn't just have a little spat so now all is forgiven. Michael, nothing is forgiven. Nothing. You have messed up something at the very core of our relationship. Your values are not my values. Your principles are not my principles. You are not the person I always believed you were."

"Just wait a minute, Norah. Don't you think you're overly dramatizing this thing?"

"How is it possible to over dramatize the fact that my husband has chosen, of his own free will, to ally himself with an admitted Nazi, a vicious anti-Semite, a cruel and hateful man, and that my husband has done this after I pleaded with him not to do that? How is it possible to over-dramatize the fact that my husband has taken on a case that will require him to attack and attempt to destroy the reputation and career of the husband of one of my dearest friends? How is it possible to over-dramatize the fact that my husband has betrayed me and the principles that, for our entire lives, we shared with each other? Michael, I'm trying hard not to lose it again. I'm going out now. It's impossible for me to talk to you. I want the house and the children. You can keep everything else."

"I don't believe what you're saying. We need to talk. You can't just throw away the last twenty-six years of our lives like this."

"Good-bye."

"Don't go, please!"

She left without another word.

I ran upstairs to look for Jenny, forgetting that she was on her way to school. That day, Thursday, September 23, 1982, is a vacancy in my mind and memory. During the entire day the words "I want the house and the children" thundered in my head. I think I slept that night in the home of one of my partners, but I can't remember which partner or where his house is. I think we got drunk.

THIRTY-EIGHT

Friday, September 25, 1982

Still wearing the same suit, shirt, tie, socks and underwear that I was wearing on Wednesday, I remember getting into my car and driving to Wall Street to go to my office. I left the car in a parking garage several blocks from the office and gradually shook off the headache that had plagued me all night. My head cleared and my problems came sharply into focus as I walked to the office. It was a fresh and clear autumn day. I had a lot to do and I had neither the mind nor the spirit needed to do it.

Patty greeted me as I walked toward my office. "Are you all right, Michael? I've been worried about you."

"That's really sweet of you, Patty. I'm fine. It's just that I have a lot on my mind."

"Just let me know whatever you need from me. I want to help you—just like Norah must be helping you," she said, oblivious to the irony of that comment.

My press release didn't get quite as much visibility as Landauer's explosive announcement the day before but it did stimulate a front-page headline in the *New York Post* that read, "Accused Nazi Sues Opponent." Not exactly the headline I was hoping for but the battle had been joined, the issues were framed, and we now had to sharpen our weapons. I asked Brenda McGovern to come to my office. I described to her my analysis of the case. "We need to clear two hurdles to win the case. One, we have to prove that the Nazi file is a forgery and, if we get past that huge hurdle, we have to prove—in some way that I've not yet come close to figuring out—that Landauer must have suspected that something was fishy but chose to ignore that suspicion and recklessly let loose with his bombshell announcement."

"Will the judge give us the opportunity to attempt to prove those two points?" Brenda asked.

"Good question. I think he has to let us try to prove the forgery claim. After all, he has to believe that it's at least theoretically possible that that stuff is a forgery. The other issue, I just don't know. He would be within his rights if he asked us to indicate what evidence we have that Landauer suspected there might have been a forgery. I want you to lock yourself in a quiet room and do some hard thinking about how to answer that question. I have a few ideas but, at the moment, your mind is clearer than mine and I'd like to hear what you come up with. I don't think we have to lay out our evidence but I think Judge Santangelo will expect us to outline our theory as to Landauer's recklessness. Please, Brenda, I really need your help on this. Let's plan to have dinner tonight to talk about it."

"Great," she said. "You can count on me to do the very best I can."

So, now I had a dinner date with a bright, attractive female lawyer who reminded me a lot of what Norah was like thirty years ago when she was the brightest, most attractive female law student at Georgetown. When I fell in love with her.

Patty buzzed me to tell me that a lawyer named Brad Silverman was calling. I thought I recognized the name but I wasn't sure. "Mr. Cullen, this is Brad Silverman of Greenberg Kantor. How are you?"

"I'm fine, a bit harried, but fine. What can I do for you?"

"I wanted you to know that I'll be representing my colleague, Barry Weinberg, in the lawsuit that you just started on behalf of Thomas Spellman."

"Thanks for telling me that, but Barry isn't a party to that action."

"That's technically true. But I assume he'll be called as a witness to testify about some sensitive facts. He wants me to look out for his interests."

"Well, Brad, this is America and everyone's entitled to a lawyer but, if there's a trial, don't expect me to allow you to say a word."

"We'll see about that. But what do you mean 'if there's a trial'? You don't think there's going to be a settlement, do you?"

"I have reason to believe that Landauer's going to sue for peace."

"That's news to me," Silverman said, as if I'd taken his breath away.

"I would think that Barry would think that'd be a good development."

"I'll have to discuss that with him. I'll get back to you."

"Don't hesitate, Brad."

Cullen, you've been a lawyer too long. Lying has become a reflex.

Another buzz from Patty announced that the clerk of the Nassau County Supreme Court was on the line. "Hello, this is Michael Cullen."

"Mr. Cullen, Judge Santangelo will be handling the case of *Spellman v. Landauer*. He would like to have a chambers meeting with you and defendant's counsel, William Schofield, regarding that case. Is next Tuesday convenient for you?"

"Let me check my calendar." I paused for a couple of minutes. "I have a pretty heavy schedule that day. Let me see if I can rearrange things. What time did the judge have in mind?"

"He was hoping to meet at the end of the court day, say, at 5:30 p.m."

"I'll try to get back to you before the end of the day today. Is Bill Schofield available on Tuesday?"

"Yes he is."

"I'll get back to you as soon as I can."

"Thanks."

More lies. Cullen, you have nothing on your calendar on Tuesday or any other day that week. Remember, Michael, when you used to be lily white? I wanted the judge to think I was going out of my way to accommodate him. So I lied about my availability. That made me wonder what kind of a person I had become after twenty-five years as a lawyer. An important question, but I had no time for such questions. I had to prepare to meet with the judge and I had to try to save my marriage. I told Patty to wait about an hour and then call the clerk to tell him I had arranged my schedule to be available for a meeting with the judge on Tuesday.

———

I don't know what you gained by lying to that lawyer and the court clerk. • Well, Will, now that you raise the question, I gained nothing. But at least I didn't hurt anybody with my lies. • *If that gives you comfort, Grandpa, I guess that's okay. But if that's what lawyers do all the time, I think that's a shame.* • Hey Will, you're getting unbearably judgmental. • *What can you expect, Grandpa, when you drag me into the middle of this awful story?*

———

I phoned our house. No one answered. I asked Patty to find the Weinbergs' home phone number in Scarsdale "Michael," she asked, "can you tell me what you're going to do with that number?"

I sighed deeply. "I'm going to call it, of course. Patty, Norah and I are having a bit of a problem. I can't seem to be able to get in touch with her. I think I might be able to reach her at the Weinbergs' home."

"Let me do that for you. I'll let you know when I get Norah on the line. I'll explain that I was calling because you were very busy but that it was important for you to speak with her."

"Thank you so much. You are a dear."

Brenda knocked on my door, walked in carrying a load of law books and file folders, deposited everything on my desk, and sat down. "I want to give you a preview of what I've found. This is a mind-blowing case."

"Mind blowing? Is that a legal term?"

"Sort of," she replied. "It means a case that's all questions and no answers."

"I have to meet with the judge in chambers on Tuesday. I'll tell him what you just said. May I attribute that comment to you?"

"I'd be honored."

Brenda McGovern had a magical ability to make me relax, even at the tensest, most stressful moments. I mentioned that to her and, believe it or not, she blushed.

Patty appeared at my door. She said, "I spoke with Mrs. Weinberg but she said that Norah wasn't there."

"Did you ask where she was?"

"I did. She said she didn't know. Brenda, could I have a few minutes with Michael, privately." Brenda looked at me and I asked her to leave the room.

Patty is about sixty years old. She's never been married. She looks unhealthy—gaunt, skinny, pale, wrinkled—but she never misses a day of work. She's been a legal secretary for many years, most them working for me. Her desk was right outside my office and I have more contact with her than with any other person in the firm. We had never had a conversation that I would describe as personal. Her request for a private conversation was unprecedented.

"Michael, what the heck is going on between you and Norah? You may be too old to be my son but that's how I look at you. Right now I am seriously worried about you. There's something very wrong."

I started to cry. I actually wept, I wept sitting at my desk. I fell apart. Patty shot up from her seat, checked to make sure the door to my office was shut tight, and then came around behind me and wrapped her bony arms around my chest. I wept even harder as she embraced me. My face was sopping wet from a cascade of tears that would not stop flowing from my eyes. I heard my own wailing and it was the sound of my misery, rising from the depths of my being. Even now, it embarrasses me to describe that scene.

As my tears subsided, Patty went to the door and mentioned to Brenda that I was not feeling well. I heard Brenda say that we were supposed to have dinner that evening to discuss the Spellman case. Patty said that that would have to be postponed. I was immensely grateful that Patty was my comforter. I told her that.

Eventually, I told her about Norah and me, and about Spellman and Weinberg. Telling her about my problems was helpful. It was as if my real mother was listening to me, showering me with love when I was hurting badly. The hurt was still there but she made me stronger.

Only Norah mattered. I had to talk to her. I asked Patty to get me the Weinberg's phone number, which she did. I asked her to leave me alone while I made some phone calls. I hugged Patty, feeling deep and genuine affection for her. She told me to be strong and I said I would be as strong as I possibly could.

I phoned Jessica Weinberg. "I'm so glad you called, Michael; I couldn't really talk to your secretary. I'm terribly concerned about you and Norah. She came here this morning, looking terrible, distraught, angry. She started to cry the minute she walked into my house. She said she decided to get a divorce." Then Jessica started to cry. "Michael, what are we going to do? This is horrible. Why is this happening? It's all Barry's fault."

"Jessica, stop, please stop. It's not all Barry's fault. But you're right, it is horrible. I need to talk with Norah. Do you know where she is?"

"She's lying down on the sofa in our living room."

"You told my secretary that you didn't know where she was."

"I was afraid to tell her. I didn't want to tell her that you had your secretary call me. That was stupid of you. It would have made things worse."

"Forgive me, Jess. My mind is a muddle. Please tell Norah that I'm coming to see her."

"Good. She needs you."

I retrieved my car and headed toward Scarsdale. I remember nothing about the drive except that I got lost and wandered around the town, stopping to ask people on the streets if they knew where Oak Grove Road was. Several said they never heard of it, but finally a young man with a back pack said he knew the street and that it was right on the way to where he was going and he would appreciate a lift in my car. I finally arrived at the Weinberg home and my navigator jumped out and continued walking to wherever he was going. I envied him because he knew where he was going. I wished I knew where I was going.

Jessica greeted me at the door. She appeared much calmer than she was when we spoke on the phone an hour or so earlier. She showed me into the room where Norah had had that terrible angry eruption earlier that week. "I think it would be best if I left the two of you alone," Jessica said, as she left the room.

Norah was sitting on the sofa, her hands folded on her lap. She did not seem pleased to see me but at least she was calm. She said nothing, not even "hello." I walked up to her and bent down to kiss her on the cheek. She abruptly turned her face away from me and said, "Why did you come here?"

Still standing, I said, "Norah, please. I desperately need to discuss where we are, as a husband and wife."

"I thought I made that quite clear yesterday. I'll say it again now. Please don't stand there. Sit down." Her voice was that of a stranger. I remained standing.

She took a deep breath, straightened in her seat and continued. "You have done something that I find incomprehensible and despicable. For reasons that I find impossible to understand, you have undertaken to do something that violates my trust in you. I thought I knew you. I thought I knew what your values are. I thought you and I—when it came to fundamentally important things—shared those values. I was wrong. You have chosen to represent someone we have both despised for a long time. Now, when we have every reason to despise him even more than ever, you became his ally. I know lawyers often have to represent real scumbags. I can even understand—in theory at least—that a lawyer can even represent a Nazi." She paused, and looked up at the ceiling. "God, that very word sticks in my throat."

Another pause, with her eyes closed. "But to choose to represent a Nazi in a case that will require you to turn on someone, to attack someone who was once a dear friend, someone who is a decent, gentle, honorable person, someone who is the very antithesis of that piece of shit who is now your client—that is something that is so far outside the bounds of decency that I don't see how it can be possible for me to continue to share my life with you."

"Norah, I don't want to lose you," I exclaimed. Tears streamed down my face. "I adore you. I can't conceive of life without you." I gasped for breath. I struggled as I exhaled each word. "I need you to stay with me, to help me, to love me. Please, please, don't leave me."

"Then drop the Spellman case."

"I can't."

"Then we are finished. And if you think that's the outcome I want, you are so wrong, so very, very, very wrong."

I tried to collect myself, to gain control of my thoughts. My mind was in disarray. I was overwhelmed by the realization that this could be the most important moment of my life.

"Norah, I implore you, I beg you, listen to me, please. Twenty-six years. Don't throw them away without giving me a chance to explain what I'm doing and why I'm doing it."

"I already know what you're doing. *Why* you're doing it is a mystery to me. Go ahead. Explain the inexplicable." Norah snapped at me as she said this.

I began the most critically important argument of my life. Here is what I said: "I don't know whether the horrible stuff in the Nazi file is authentic or a forgery. I pressed Barry to tell me how he obtained it. He told me how he found a guy in Texas—a former member of the American Nazi Party—who said he knew Spellman and that he had a file of papers relating to Spellman and the Nazi movement. He said he paid the guy $15,000 for the file. He told me that he sent it to Landauer because the thought of Spellman being in Congress was morally insupportable. On the other hand, Spellman swore that it is all a forgery. I didn't know which of them was telling the truth and which of them was lying. Or, in Barry's case, whether the guy in Texas sold him forged documents. I had to allow for that possibility.

"What I do know is this: If that Nazi label sticks to Spellman—and it definitely will stick if no action is taken to prevent that—he is destroyed, he is ruined. His career is over. Conway has already demanded his resignation from the firm. I don't know what will happen between him and Anne, but I know it won't be good. His life will be a shambles. If he really is a Nazi—or even if he just dabbled with being a Nazi—he deserves to be ruined. But if the Nazi file is a forgery and Spellman is nevertheless destroyed by it, then a terrible injustice will have occurred. This may sound corny, but justice still means something important to me.

"I hope you don't think that I am oblivious to Barry's interests. But Barry set this whole thing in motion. He had to be fully aware of the implications of what he was doing. He had to know that Spellman was virtually certain to claim that the Nazi file was a forgery. If Barry is able to sustain his story of how he came into possession of it, he will not only *not* get hurt, he will be a hero to everyone other than right-wing fanatics. But—Norah, please listen carefully to this—if it turns out that Barry's Nazi documents are a forgery, a forgery intended to ruin another human being, then doesn't he deserve to be exposed as someone who did an awful thing? There will probably be those who will still think he's a hero, but I won't be one of them—and I don't think you will either."

I must have looked terrible. Wearing three-day-old wrinkled clothes, my face damp with tears. I didn't remember when I had last shaved or showered.

I made one further remark. "By the way, right or wrong, Barry has already accomplished his objective. There's not a chance in hell that Spellman will win the election." I slumped into a chair. There was nothing more I could say.

After several minutes in which we just stared at each other, Norah—having gathered her thoughts—said, "Michael, you have always had a talent for making a powerful argument in favor

of an unworthy cause. You just told me—in your typically elo-
quent manner—why Spellman is entitled to a lawyer. Did you
think I didn't know that? For Christ's sake, Adolph Eichmann
was entitled to a lawyer. But you didn't say a single word to
convince me why Spellman was entitled to have you as his
lawyer. You're chairman of the litigation department of Coburn
& Perkins. You can assign any one or more of your hot-shot
litigators to represent Spellman. Why does it have to be you?"

"I tried to tell Spellman that I didn't think I should represent him, but he insisted that I be his lawyer."

"And whatever Spellman wants, Spellman gets. Is that it?
Well that's not how the system works, and you know it. I'll
tell you why Spellman wants you as his lawyer. It's not because of your great legal talent; it's because he thinks you are
uniquely equipped to tear Barry Weinberg to shreds. You have
to know that that's what this is about. If, in your excitement
about handling a high-visibility case, you somehow missed
that point—now you know it. If you insist on representing
Spellman, you should know that you are choosing Thomas
Spellman over your wife and children. Now please leave. I
don't want to be with you."

The temptation to say that I would drop out of the case
was overwhelming. But something held me back. I rose to
leave and said to Norah, "I'll be in touch with you."

"Don't bother. You will hear from my lawyer, after I've
chosen one."

THIRTY-NINE

Saturday, September 25, 1982

I went home and stuffed a suitcase as full as possible with all the things I thought I would need during an indefinite time living in a hotel. Then I checked into the nicest hotel I could find in the Wall Street area and went to sleep while it was still light outside. In my first moments of consciousness when I awoke Saturday morning, the realization struck me that I was now in a very different place in my life. Instead of trying to get a grasp on my situation, all I did was feel sorry for myself.

Norah was unreasonable. She was indifferent to the pain she was causing me. What right did she have to cause an honest disagreement about a difficult decision I made to become the reason for banishing me to this lousy hotel?

Spellman had absolutely no right to force me into this position. His insistence that I represent him—with no thought given to the consequences to me—was typical of his selfishness. He never did anything for me. Our relationship from its first day until now was a one-way street. I served his interests and received nothing in return, not gratitude, not friendship, not even courtesy, nothing.

And then I thought about Barry. It was impudent and infantile, absolutely inexcusable of Barry Weinberg to have sent the Nazi file to me. That was an unprovoked act of aggression on his part.

Jessica Weinberg poisoned Norah against me. I saw them sitting together when Norah turned on me for not consoling Barry as he suffered the awful realization of the storm he had incited. That wimp—he throws a stink bomb and then curls up in bed in a fetal position because he can't stand the smell. Norah kicks me out of her life because of concern for that coward. She accuses me of choosing Spellman over my wife. How about her? She chose that gutless weakling over her husband.

Then there is the audacity of Barry and Jessica. They abandoned me for eight years and then, suddenly, they pulled me into the whirlpool of their lives—that was absolutely unforgivable.

I felt angry, misused, victimized by all of those people.

I spent the entire day playing and replaying these thoughts, sinking deeper and deeper into a dark place I didn't recognize. I had to escape, but I didn't know how.

I phoned our house and, to my amazement, Kathleen answered the phone.

She asked if I was all right and I lied—again—and said I was fine. She said that she knew that Norah and I were having a problem. In fact, she told me, the reason she had come home was that Norah had phoned her in Washington and told her about the problem.

"I need help, Kathy darling, I really need help," I said.

"I'd like to help you, and Mom, but I don't know what to do. Mom wants you to get out of that case and you refused. I agree with Mom. I don't understand why you can't give that case to one of your partners."

"Kathy, I have a client who needs me and wants me."

"But you're not the only lawyer in the world. You're not even the only lawyer in your firm."

"But he wants me, no one but me."

"I don't know whether you are being stubborn or egotistical or both."

"Kathy, I'm being a lawyer. That's who I am, that's what I do."

"I don't get it, I just don't get it."

"Tell Mom that I love her." That was the end of the conversation.

Egotistical? Yes, probably. Stubborn? Undoubtedly.

Cullen, I said to myself, you're an egotistical stubborn jerk. That's who you are and that's why you, Michael Cullen, are such a great lawyer. Go to work on the Spellman case, save Spellman's lousy life, be true to your calling, and everything will work out in the end. In the one phone conversation with my first child—now an adult, but still only a child—I went from feeling sorry for myself to feeling Pollyannaish.

I took a shower, got dressed—jeans and a sweatshirt—and walked the six blocks from the hotel to my office.

It was after 7 p.m. when I arrived at the office. I was ravenously hungry, not having eaten a thing all day. I called Brenda McGovern's number on the off chance that she might be in the office. To my delight, she answered the phone.

"You still want to have dinner with me?" I asked.

"Sure. I've already eaten but I'll be happy to watch you eat. And I can tell you my ideas about the Spellman case."

"I'll meet you in the lobby."

Coburn & Perkins was never closed. We had a nighttime staff and a weekend staff. The billable hours just kept on grinding and the cash register kept ringing. I asked our receptionist to book a table for two at Delmonico's. "Tell them it's for Michael Cullen."

Brenda was obviously excited about the prospect of dinner with the head of the litigation department. I had stopped feeling sorry for myself and devoured a porterhouse steak that was large enough for two hungry people. Brenda talked nonstop. Her ideas were thoughtful, even creative, and I thoroughly enjoyed listening to her. The focus of her comments was Barry Weinberg's explanation of how he obtained the Nazi file. The nameless "Mr. X," the undisclosed location in Texas, the fact that everything in the file was a photocopy. Where were the original documents? Did Barry send the originals to Landauer, or did our defendant go public with nothing but photocopies? Astute questions. Brenda had already located several experts who could explain how the photographs could have been doctored. She said it would help the expert if we had the originals.

I asked Brenda to research cases in which the defendant had published (that's the technical term for libelous disclosure) defamatory materials that were furnished to the defendant by a third party. I reminded her of our conversation on Friday in which I indicated that this issue presented the most difficult hurdle that we had to overcome to win the case.

I decided that I would like to bring Brenda with me to the meeting with the judge on Tuesday. I remarked about how extraordinary it was for a judge to call for a meeting with counsel just a couple of days after a complaint had been filed.

"Why do you think he wants to have that meeting?" Brenda asked.

"It could simply have to do with procedure. He's obviously aware of the election and he may just want to tell us that it is procedurally impossible for the case to be scheduled before election day."

"We don't care about that, do we?"

"No, not at all. But the judge really doesn't have to have a chambers meeting to deliver that message. I think there's more to it. He may want me to drop the case because we have such an uphill battle on our hands."

"He can't make you do that, can he?" Brenda asked.

"He can't force me to drop it but he certainly can deliver a strong message that he thinks I'm wasting the court's time. But, Brenda, whatever he says, we have to prosecute the case as vigorously as we can because that's the only way we can save Tom Spellman from going through the rest of his life as, quote, that convicted Nazi."

"We will be doing him a great service if we can accomplish that." Brenda paused briefly, looked up at the ceiling and then, with an embarrassed look on her face, she asked, "I'm not sure I should ask you this but, Mike, are you having marital problems? Don't answer if you think that is an improper question."

I chuckled and said, "It's a hugely improper question. If this was a trial, the judge would sustain an objection to that question. But the answer is yes, we're having a problem but

I think we'll work it out. I don't believe you've met Norah, have you?"

"I haven't. In fact I don't think I even knew that Norah is her name."

"You would like her. She's the smartest person I've ever known."

"I'll tell her you said that if I ever meet her."

"Please do. I need to collect some Brownie points with her. Let's go back to the office."

There was a note from Patty on my desk that Tom Spellman had called four times after I left the office. Good, I thought, let him suffer a bit. I read cases on the law of libel until after midnight. As far as I knew, Brenda was still working when I left the office.

FORTY

After a good night's sleep—was I growing used to living in a hotel?—and a hearty breakfast in a nearby coffee shop, I decided to take the day off. It was a bright, crisp early autumn day. Although my home had been in New York City every day of my forty-nine years, I had never been to the Statue of Liberty. I had never taken the boat trip around Manhattan Island. I had never been a tourist in my city. That Sunday was a perfect day to spend as a tourist.

Although the nonstop spiel of the tour guide on the boat was annoying, the two-and-a-half-hour voyage around Manhattan was far more enjoyable than I expected. Manhattan is indeed a magical place, at least when viewed on a clear day from the rivers that encircle it. Its aptly named skyscrapers, the seemingly solid block of man-made structures filling the island from end to end, the apartment buildings—homes to millions of people, people like the family I came from—all of these things impressed me at least as much as they did the gaping tourists from the Midwest. Standing next to me at the railing of the boat as it passed the Wall Street area was a man from Iowa. I kid you not; he really was from Iowa. Pointing to the skyscrapers at the southern tip of Manhattan, I said to him, "That's where I work." He asked what kind of work I did and I told him I was a lawyer.

He looked at me, disgust written on his leathery face, and said, "So you're a Wall Street lawyer. I grow corn." He and his wife moved away to a different spot on the railing. He obviously had little interest in city's native fauna.

I wasn't going to let that rude farmer ruin my day. I was tempted to tell him that I was risking my marriage to save the reputation of a person I didn't even like. But he would never have understood. I had trouble understanding myself.

After the boat trip, I treated myself to an excellent dinner at an Italian restaurant in Greenwich Village. The bottle of Chianti Classico with which I washed down my veal marsala was empty when I rose from the table. I was feeling mellow.

I had hardly thought about Spellman; I thought about Norah five hundred times.

—

That boat ride was the most sensible thing you'd done since you got the Nazi file in the mail. • I couldn't agree more.

FORTY-ONE

Tuesday, September 28, 1982

After spending a good part of Monday working with Brenda, this was the day of the chambers meeting with Judge Santangelo. I also spent much of Monday hoping to hear from Norah or Kathleen. I even thought it was possible that Kevin might come into the picture of the Cullen family crisis. But there was nothing but silence from any of them.

We arrived at the judge's chambers at the Nassau County Courthouse in Mineola. This was my first visit to that courthouse and to Mineola. The same was true for Brenda. We were immediately ushered into the plush office of Judge Anthony Santangelo. The American flag and the New York State flag flanked the judge's high-backed leather chair which stood empty when we entered the room. Landauer's lawyers—Bill Schofield and Lou Galliano, the nice young man I had met at the Graduates Club the previous week—were already seated. They rose to shake hands with us and I introduced Brenda to them.

Moments later the judge, wearing his robes, entered the room accompanied by a short gray-haired man carrying one of those devices that court stenographers use to transcribe the proceedings. The judge thanked us for coming. Everyone was introduced to him. He mentioned that he thought it would be a good idea to have this meeting "on the record." Schofield and I agreed; we could hardly do otherwise. The judge began to speak, saying how this case immediately caught his attention because of the election and the fact that he lived in the Third District.

He had barely said ten words when Bill Schofield interrupted and said, "Your Honor, before we go any further I think it is my duty to inform you and Mr. Cullen that I believe Mr. Cullen should withdraw as counsel for the plaintiff because of a serious conflict of interest."

"If you don't mind, Mr. Schofield, I'd like to defer consideration of that point until later in this meeting," said the judge, with what I thought was unnecessary politeness. Schofield was attempting a preemptive attack, a typical Schofield tactic, and the judge was correct in ignoring it. "Of course, Your Honor, as you wish," said Schofield—as if he had a choice.

—

What exactly is a conflict of interest? • It's usually a situation in which a lawyer may owe a duty to different parties whose interests are adverse to one another. • *Were you worried that you might have such a conflict in this case?* • Not really. I assumed that Barry Weinberg would somehow be involved in Schofield's claim but I didn't think I had any professional obligations to Barry, even if—on a personal level—I didn't want him to be harmed. The real conflict of interest I had was one that Schofield knew nothing about—the conflict that raged within me between this case and my marriage and family.

———

"Thank you," the judge continued. "I have done a great deal of thinking about this case since I first read the complaint last week, and especially over this past weekend. I must say it is a fascinating case, presenting complex legal and factual issues. I have no idea what the facts are but they certainly seem to be uncommonly dramatic. Right in the midst of a nasty election campaign, things got to be about as nasty as anyone could imagine. One of the candidates may be a Nazi. Imagine that. On the other hand, the other candidate may be guilty of outrageous defamation of character. Imagine that. I have some thoughts that I want to share with you about how this case may be managed. Mr. Cullen, I'm sure you realize that there is no possibility of this case being heard and decided before election day. Is that correct?"

"Absolutely correct, Your Honor. My client fully under-stands that the voters of the Third District will be going to the polls on election day with the Nazi accusation ringing in their ears."

"Good. This case will not decide the election but it may ultimately have a great bearing on the plaintiff's personal reputation," said the judge. "I hope you understand, Mr. Cullen, that I am going to hold as a matter of law that your client is a 'public figure' and that according to the U.S. Supreme Court public figures have got to have a pretty thick hide because the law of libel gives them very limited, if any, protection."

"I've explained that to Mr. Spellman and he fully understands that point."

"That brings me to the idea that I have about how to handle this case. It's an idea that requires a stipulation by counsel—I'd like your help in formulating the language of that stipulation—but I think we can streamline this case and focus all of our attention on the single issue that will be decisive of the outcome of the case. What if we agreed to assume that the materials published by the defendant are actually forgeries . . ."

Schofield erupted as if the judge had insulted his mother. "No way, judge," Schofield hollered, "those materials are genuine. And the burden of proof is entirely on the plaintiff to prove that they're false. No way will I allow my client to agree that he published false statements. Forget about it."

"If you had allowed me to finish the point I was making, Mr. Schofield, perhaps you might not have reacted so vehemently. If I may continue what I was saying, I was proposing for the consideration of all counsel the following approach. My suggestion is that if we assume, hypothetically—*hypothetically*, Mr. Schofield—that the materials published by the defendant are forgeries, that would bring us to the most decisive issue in the case: whether the disclosure of those materials by the defendant was done with actual malice and with knowledge of their falsity, or with reckless disregard of whether they were authentic or false. That is my understanding of the standard as to which the plaintiff has the burden of proof in a defamation case where the plaintiff is a public figure. Mr. Cullen, do you agree that that is a fair statement of the applicable standard?"

"I do, Your Honor."

"So you see, Mr. Schofield, if the plaintiff, Spellman, is unable to satisfy his burden of proof that your client acted in violation of that standard, you win the case. If I find—or the jury finds, as the case may be—that Spellman has succeeded in proving actual malice on the part of Mr.—what's his name, the defendant?—Landsman . . ."

"It's Landauer, Your Honor," said Schofield.

"Whatever," continued the judge, "then, and only then, we go to the issue of the truth or falsity of the defendant's statements, the other issue on which Mr. Cullen also has a tough burden of proof. You see, Mr. Schofield, I'm trying to make it easier for you to defend the case by making the plaintiff have to satisfy the more difficult burden of proof as the first order of business, or the case is over. Mr. Cullen or Miss McGovern, I'd like to hear your reaction to my suggestion. Perhaps you'd like to take a short break to talk between yourselves?"

"That won't be necessary, Your Honor. I appreciate the thoughtfulness of your analysis and the suggestion you made. If this case were simply about who wins and who loses, the procedure you outlined would be a creative approach to reaching a legally sustainable outcome as efficiently as possible. However, as you very perceptively noted a few minutes ago . . ." I paused to look at my notes. "I believe Your Honor said, quote, this case will not decide the election but it may ultimately have a great bearing on the plaintiff's personal reputation. The paramount issue in this case is the plaintiff's reputation. He has been accused of membership in the

American Nazi Party. A mere hypothetical assumption that that accusation is false won't clear my client of the stench of that accusation. Could any of us agree to live the rest of our lives known as someone who is only hypothetically not a Nazi? I know that I could not do so. My client needs to have the burden—which he gladly accepts as an opportunity—of proving that the stuff that Landauer threw at him was nothing but a vile forgery. Therefore, Your Honor, I must respectfully reject your proposal. I would be grateful if the case could be scheduled for trial at the earliest practicable date."

"You know, Mr. Cullen, for a lawyer who's almost certain to lose a case, you are approaching it with more enthusiasm than I would have thought possible."

"I'll take that as a compliment, Your Honor."

"You should," said the judge.

"Your Honor," Schofield said, standing between me and the judge, "can we now deal with the issue that I raised at the beginning of this meeting, Mr. Cullen's conflict of interest?"

The judge responded by addressing me. "Mr. Cullen, do you believe you may have a conflict of interest in this case?"

"Your Honor, I don't have the slightest idea what Mr. Schofield is talking about."

"Mr. Schofield, what are you talking about?"

"Your Honor, in order to prove the alleged inauthenticity of the letters and pictures that show the plaintiff's involvement with the American Nazi Party, Mr. Cullen will have to attack the credibility of his former law partner, Barry Weinberg of the firm of Greenberg, Gordon & Kantor, a highly respected partner in a leading New York law firm."

"So?" asked the judge.

"I intend to call several of Mr. Cullen's partners to testify as to Mr. Weinberg's flawless reputation for integrity and credibility. These are people who have actually practiced law with Weinberg."

"Do you want me to disqualify Mr. Cullen because you—not he, but you—intend to call some of his partners, making them witnesses adverse to his client?"

"Exactly, Your Honor. But, moreover, I intend to show that Mr. Cullen interviewed Mr. Weinberg before filing the complaint in this case without disclosing to Mr. Weinberg that he was representing Spellman."

"I have to say, Mr. Schofield, that those are some of the lamest arguments I have heard in my more than fifteen years on the bench. Imagine: You want to disqualify a lawyer for interviewing a witness before filing a lawsuit? I never heard of such a thing. You can file a motion at the appropriate time if you wish to pursue those points. I think we can conclude this meeting. Thank you all for coming here today."

We rose as the judge left the room. "I'll see you in court, Bill. Brenda, let's get back to the office."

———

That seemed to go well for you, Grandpa. • I suppose it did, but it did nothing to solve the enormous problem of how we were going to prove that the Nazi file was a forgery.

FORTY-TWO

October 1982

My separation from Norah—and, apparently, from my children—had taken on a seemingly permanent character. At my request, Patty found a suitable small "bachelor" apartment for me just west of Washington Square and, in mid-October, I moved in.

As I expected, there was a great deal of chatter among the lawyers and staff of Coburn & Perkins about the Spellman *cause célèbre*. I received a phone call from one of our partners in London who had read about the case in both the *Times* and the *Guardian*. He said the London office of the firm would be following the case closely. He also asked whether he was correct in his belief that Spellman had long been a troublesome partner. I had to acknowledge that Tom had "an interesting history in the firm."

Henry Stevens expressed concern that my involvement in the Spellman case "might be more trouble than it's worth. The man is dangerous. The reason the materials that Barry Weinberg produced are so credible to me, I must say, is that they are so clearly consistent with Spellman's past behavior. And, Michael, I've heard about your separation from Norah."

"It would be more accurate to say Norah's separation from me."

"All right, her separation from you. Frankly, Michael, it simply cannot be that Tom Spellman is more important to you than that absolutely wonderful woman to whom you are married."

"Do you think I don't know that, Henry?"

"Then why the hell are you in that case—I might say that hopeless case?"

"I know you're speaking to me as a friend. But, Henry, you're not being helpful to me. I may be in the midst of making the worst mistake of my life. But that's where I am and I would like you to be supportive of me."

"How can I be supportive when I can't comprehend why you're doing what you're doing?"

"Just be my friend and wish me luck—with the case and with my marriage."

"I love you, Michael, and I want only good things for you."

"Thanks, pal," I said, and I hugged him.

Word reached me that there were people in the firm who thought I might be having an affair with Brenda McGovern. Taking a step back and looking at my situation objectively, it wasn't hard to understand how people could think that.

—

Grandpa, I have to tell you that I've been thinking that.
- Oh, that hurts, Will. I swear to you that I've never been unfaithful to your grandmother and there has never been a moment when I haven't loved her with all my heart.

—

I needed to do something to squelch the rumor about Brenda and me. But I wasn't sure how to go about doing that. A mere denial was impossible because no one would think of initiating a conversation on the subject and I obviously could not spontaneously say something stupid like, "You know, Brenda and I are not sleeping together." I could understand where the rumor was coming from. I was separated from Norah, living in a "bachelor" apartment. Brenda was single, attractive, and obviously enthusiastic about working closely with me. We spent hours every day in each other's presence preparing the Spellman case for trial, often working well into the evening, and leaving the office together at the end of the day, occasionally after midnight.

The subject came to a head when Patty Rogers came into my office, closed the door behind her, and said, "Michael, you must know that everyone is talking about you and Brenda having an affair. I know it's none of my business but I can't ignore what people are saying and I can't help wondering if it's true. You may fire me for this, but I simply must ask you if what people are saying is true."

I laughed. "My dear Patty, I wouldn't fire you if you embezzled a year's revenue from the firm and set fire to my office. Despite what it looks like, Brenda and I are not having an affair. I may be separated from Norah, but I still love her and hope that when this Spellman thing is over we will overcome our differences and resume our lives together. I know what people are thinking and saying about Brenda and me. They are as wrong as wrong can be but I'm at a loss as to what to do about it."

"I am so happy to hear that. Leave it to me to take care of the rumors."

"Oh Patty, you are so good to me. But I can't let you take the responsibility for squelching the rumors about Brenda and me. I've got to do that myself when I figure out how to do it. I'm going to make that a priority starting right now."

"How?"

"Watch me."

I immediately placed calls to Paul Conway, Warren Worthington, Henry Stevens, Craig Wilson, and Jack Iverson (the former member of the infamous Gang of Three), asking each of them to meet me in Conference Room Six, near my office, "to discuss an urgent personal matter." Remarkably, each one of these very busy people said he was available that afternoon. We agreed upon 4:00 p.m. as the time to meet.

"Patty, I want you at that meeting." She winced at that request; secretaries did not attend meetings with senior partners at Coburn & Perkins unless they were assigned to record the discussion. "I need you there, Patty, for moral support."

I had about an hour and a half to gather my thoughts and decide how to approach this delicate subject.

FORTY-THREE

On the dot of 4:00 p.m., six partners and Patty Rogers assembled in Conference Room Six. It was a relatively small room with a mahogany table and eight leather chairs on wheels.

There was one window affording a view of neighboring buildings. Two of the walls were adorned with cartoonish lithograph prints showing wigged and robed barristers at work arguing cases. It was an intimate place, ideal for this meeting. I took a seat at the head of the table and Patty sat in the chair nearest to me on my left.

"Gents, and Patty," I began as soon as everyone was seated, "I've asked you to meet me here because I think of all of you as my friends. I'm grateful to you for coming. This is about the rumor that appears to be spreading around the firm that Brenda McGovern and I are having a romantic or, worse yet, a merely sexual affair. I can understand how such a rumor got started and how it has obtained traction. Brenda and I are working together—I might almost say working night and day together—on the Spellman case. Brenda is a spirited and exceptionally attractive young woman. My wife and I are currently living apart. I live in an apartment in Greenwich Village. Our separation was triggered by Norah's strenuous opposition to my representation of Tom Spellman.

"If I were not me but someone else in the firm fitting into the facts I've just outlined, I would probably share the belief, or suspicion, that something's going on between that someone and Brenda. I want to tell you—as I told Patty earlier today—that, despite appearances, the rumor is utterly untrue. I hope, I pray, that all of you will believe me and help me to squelch that rumor. Personally, I can live with anything anyone in this firm thinks about my behavior, my morality, or anything else having to do with my character. I know who I am and I know what I have done and what I've not done. But Brenda McGovern is in a different position. She is young. She is unknown personally to most of the lawyers in this very large law firm. She is vulnerable to having her career, her reputation, and even her life irrevocably damaged if she is perceived to be sleeping with a married partner. I cannot live with the responsibility of having brought that damage upon her.

"Please believe me as I look each of you in the eye and swear to you that there is nothing between Brenda McGovern and me other than a professional relationship and mutual admiration for each other's legal talent. I have a daughter who is not much younger than Brenda. If I have any feelings about Brenda, they involve the wish that my daughters, both of them, grow into as excellent a young woman as Brenda is. Please help me to end this rumor and save Brenda from being hurt by it."

The room was silent for what was probably no more than thirty seconds but the silence seemed to last much longer than that. Jack Iverson finally spoke up. What he said affected me profoundly.

"Michael, you opened this meeting by saying that all of us were your friends. I wish that were the case. But frankly, I've not had enough contact with you in or out of the office to call you a friend. But I gladly accept the invitation to be your friend and intend to aggressively step into that role. I absolutely accept, without any reservation, your denial of any impropriety between you and Brenda McGovern. I accept it because of what I know of your character and—and I expect that no one here knows of this—because I have had the pleasure of several dates—chaste dates, I hasten to say—with the remarkable Brenda McGovern. Brenda and I have been discreet about this social relationship because, frankly, I don't know what the policy of the firm is concerning such relationships."

I noticed broad smiles on the faces of everyone around the table.

"There is no policy," said Paul Conway.

"I'm happy to hear that," responded Iverson. "I haven't given up on my prospects of successfully wooing Brenda. But with specific reference to the subject matter of this meeting, I think it would not be a betrayal of confidence for me to report that Brenda has mentioned to me several times that she is working with Michael, that she admires him greatly, and that she is deeply concerned about the fact that his involvement in the Spellman case has caused a disruption in his marriage. Unless I am completely obtuse, I have not perceived the slightest evidence of a romantic relationship between Michael and Brenda and I intend to broadcast that fact throughout our firm."

Henry Stevens spoke up at this point. "I am Michael's friend. I am also Norah Cullen's friend. Jack's statement should remove any doubt about the falsity of the rumor that caused Mike to call this meeting. I think it is incumbent upon all of us to do everything we can to put an end to that rumor, promptly and decisively. Jack, I think you should tell Brenda about this meeting and what Michael said about her. And, by the way, best of luck in your wooing."

Craig Wilson summed things up. "Don't worry, Michael, we will kill this thing dead. Let's go back to work."

"We all agree," Conway and Worthington said simultaneously.

—

You handled that very well, Grandpa. • Well, Will, I hope even you are convinced of my good conduct.
• *Oh, Grandpa, you know I never doubted you.*

FORTY-FOUR

S pellman lost the election in a landslide. Landauer received more than 70 percent of the votes.

In fairness, Spellman virtually abandoned his campaign after we started our lawsuit and spent most of his time aimlessly wandering through the law of libel. Brenda's research was immensely more productive and useful than Spellman's.

My separation from Norah was becoming increasingly painful. I had, for all intents and purposes, become one of the Homeless Rich Men. My apartment in Greenwich Village was anything but a home. I did manage, however, to avoid hanging out at the round table in the bar of the Graduates Club. The Spellman case gave me enough to do every day so that time did not weigh heavily on me. I could fill up the days and the evenings with serious legal work.

I sent money to Norah every week. She always sent it back. I wrote her a rather harsh letter about her responsibility to maintain Kevin's and Jenny's quality of life and to use the money I sent her for that purpose. If she wanted to subsist on her salary from a part-time job in a small law firm, that would be up to her. But her grievance against me was not a valid reason to deprive our children of the quality of life that my earnings could support. I continued to pay the mortgage on the house; Norah apparently had no objection to that. All of this had created an atmosphere of constant sadness that weighed on me and, in private moments, moved me to tears. I worked hard to distract myself from that sadness but it never went away.

Thus far, Norah had not taken any legal action—no divorce or legal separation papers had been served on me—and I derived a measure of hope from that. But the more time passed in that silent war, the more the light of that hope dimmed.

Spellman v. Landauer had been scheduled for trial starting on November 23. Schofield tried to delay the trial on the grounds of congressional immunity. His motion was denied for two reasons that should have been obvious to anyone: Landauer wouldn't become a member of Congress until January and, moreover, there is no such thing as congressional immunity except for actions based on statements made in Congress. Motions to dismiss and for summary judgment were all denied by Judge Santangelo. Brenda McGovern argued all of these motions and Spellman remarked, "she's a terrific lawyer."

I decided not to take Barry Weinberg's deposition. I wanted his first exposure to my cross-examination to occur in open court before a judge and jury, an environment that I thought would be more conducive to him telling the truth. I still didn't know what the truth was and I wasn't even sure I knew what I wanted the truth to look like. The idea that Barry might be a forger, a liar, and a perjurer was so fantastic that I could not develop a trial strategy that would be based on that idea. Yet Barry's recent behavior was so erratic, so driven by emotion and righteous indignation, that I could not completely dismiss the notion that his mind was disordered. But the possibility that Spellman was a Nazi was something that never completely left my mind after the D-Day anniversary luncheon in 1974.

I did file a motion seeking to compel Weinberg to disclose the name of Mr. X. Judge Santangelo denied the motion, giving me the right to refile it during the trial. He would then be in a position to assess the relevance of that information. I think the judge erred in that ruling.

FORTY-FIVE

I was discussing with Brenda whether there was a risk in calling Spellman as a witness.

"He's a loose cannon, you know," Brenda remarked. I said I was fully aware of all of Spellman's personal attributes. "I know," she said, "but he's still a loose cannon and he won't let you guide him through his testimony. He thinks he's smarter than you, than anyone."

In the middle of this discussion, my phone rang. It was Patty telling me that Paul Conway was on the line and wanted to speak with me. "Hello, Paul, what can I do for you?"

Sounding annoyed, Conway said, "You can spend a bit of your time serving as chairman of the litigation department."

"Other than the fact that we could use another four or five capable associates, the department is in great shape. Paul, what is it that you need me to do?"

"I need you to help me try to untangle a personnel issue that you probably know nothing about. It has to do with

Gregory Crosetti and Simon Turner. Can you come up to my office? I really need your help and I need it now."

Conway's tone was at maximum authority level and I realized that I needed to interrupt my work on the Spellman case and meet with the Presiding Partner immediately. Conway was wrong about my not knowing of the Crosetti and Turner issue. Turner had stopped in to see me in my office a couple of evenings earlier and told me what was obviously his side of a troubling story.

I have to tell you that Simon Turner was one of my least favorite partners. He was a corporate lawyer with a good professional reputation for representing corporations that were targets for hostile takeovers. On a number of occasions I was called upon to collaborate with him since litigation was often both a strategy and a consequence of an attempted hostile takeover.

——

I don't have the slightest idea what a hostile takeover is.
- Of course you don't, Will. I shouldn't have used the term without explaining it to you. A hostile takeover usually involves a publicly owned corporation with numerous shareholders, each owning tiny percentages of the outstanding stock. It also usually involves another company, or a very rich person, or a group of people with money to burn who start to buy up a large chunk of the stock of what we call the "target company." We also call the folks who are buying up the stock the "raiders." The raiders usually make a demand on the management of the corporation either to

sell the company or to break it into pieces and sell some of the pieces or some similar demand the purpose of which is—according to the raiders—to drive up the market value of the stock. The raiders almost always claim that the stock is undervalued because management isn't pursuing the right strategies for increasing the value. Management of the target company typically rejects these demands and comes running to Coburn & Perkins to defend against the efforts of the raiders to mobilize the shareholders of the company to support the raiders' demands. The takeover effort often leads to a proxy fight in which the raiders attempt to replace the target company's board of directors with new directors nominated by the raiders. • *Sounds to me, Grandpa, like a really complicated fight. Do the raiders ever win?* • Once in a while they do but management usually prevails. The problem between Crosetti and Turner was one of the rare cases where our client—the target company's management—lost the fight and got kicked out.

———

Let me tell you a few things about Simon Turner. He was about forty-five years old at the time of the incident I'm going to tell you about. He was bright, knowledgeable, and exceptionally hard working. He had an excellent record of successful outcomes in take-over cases. But more than anything else, he was ambitious—ambitious for recognition, ambitious for an increasing share of the firm's profits, and especially ambitious to become the highest compensated partner at his level of seniority in the firm. Greg Crosetti became a partner in the firm on the same day as Simon Turner.

Not only that, they were in the same class at Harvard Law School where Turner ranked fifth in the class and Crosetti ranked tenth. In a more perfect world, they would have been ideal collaborators. Not so at Coburn & Perkins. Not so because of Simon Turner.

Turner never missed an opportunity to point out inadequacies in Crosetti's work. The unsuccessful defense of our client, Primary Metals Corporation, against a group of raiders was such an opportunity. Primary Metals was at one time a leading producer of alloyed metal parts for the defense and automotive industries. But its failure to keep up with technological changes coupled with the burden of maintaining its sprawling and increasingly obsolete manufacturing facilities led to declining revenues, profits and stock prices. It was the ideal target for investors with a well-developed plan to sell off the profitable components of the company and discontinue the unprofitable operations. Turner was the lead corporate strategist and expert in Delaware corporate law and Crosetti was the first-chair litigator when the Primary Metals case went before the Delaware Chancery Court on our motion to enjoin the raiders' takeover efforts. When the judge ruled against us—which he did orally from the bench—the game was over and Primary Metals was destined to disappear.

Turner and Crosetti returned from Wilmington having suffered the most stunning defeat in the history of Coburn & Perkins's vaunted anti-takeover career. They probably had not been back in our Wall Street offices for more than ten minutes before Turner barged into my office, where Brenda McGovern and I were discussing an interesting decision in a libel case recently reported by the California Supreme Court. Addressing Brenda, he said, "Young woman, I need to have a word with Michael immediately, in private." Brenda turned to me with a bemused look on her face obviously seeking guidance as to what to do.

I said to Turner, "Simon this 'young woman' has a name that you should know. It's Brenda McGovern. She may well be the most promising litigator that we've had in this firm since Barry Weinberg left. She is helping me on a critically important case and I need her to be with me now."

"Sorry, Mike . . . and Miss McGovern. I didn't mean to be rude. But I need to have a few minutes alone with Mike."

"I know what happened in Wilmington, Simon. Let's talk later this afternoon. I'll call you when I'm available."

"Please, Mike, just ten minutes and I'll get out of your way."

Brenda came to his rescue and said, "I need a few minutes to make some phone calls. This would be a good time for us to take a break." She gracefully left the room, shutting the door behind her.

"You know what I've always said, Mike. There hasn't been a good Italian lawyer in the world since Cicero died. Crosetti's performance at the Primary Metals trial proves that, if any proof were needed."

"Is that tasteless and stupid remark why you needed to break up my preparation for the trial of the Spellman case? I have no reason to have this conversation before I discuss the case with Greg. Leave the door open, please." I picked up my phone and called Brenda before he left my office. That was the day before Conway summoned me to his office.

The Presiding Partner was looking out at New York Harbor when I entered his office. I didn't like the way he looked when he turned around to greet me. His face appeared drawn and tired. He sighed and said, "Michael, I can't wait to get out of here and leave this impossible job behind."

"I'm truly sorry to hear that. Is that because of the Turner and Crosetti problem?"

"That problem is merely a symptom of a much larger problem. I'm sure you recall our discussion several months ago about my decision to retire. I said then that the action taken by the partners on the subject of partner compensation would eventually turn this firm into something unrecognizable. I believe I said that would happen in ten years. It hasn't taken ten months. The partners have begun to look at one another as adversaries in a zero-sum game of who wins and who loses in the division of firm profits. Simon Turner came to my office yesterday to tell me that Gregory Crosetti caused us to lose the Primary Metals case in the Delaware Chancery Court. You wouldn't believe what he said about Crosetti."

"Let me guess. He said Crosetti was proof of the claim that there hasn't been a good Italian lawyer since Cicero died."

"How on earth did you know that?"

"He came to my office and said that to me."

"Michael, Michael. What's happening to us? The partners have begun to eat each other alive. I should have resisted the changes in the compensation system more vigorously. People like Turner view the system as an invitation to attack and defame one another. The law of the jungle has invaded this place."

"Paul, Turner isn't representative of the partners as a whole."

"I know that. But I do believe he is representative of his generation and soon that generation will be in charge here, as it is throughout our profession. By the way, did Crosetti really screw up in the Primary Metals case?"

"I'm not sure. I don't know all the details. I think they both messed up. Turner certainly overlooked the provision in the bylaws giving two directors authority to call a shareholders' meeting and he seems to have forgotten that the raiders succeeded in electing two directors at last year's annual meeting. Crosetti appears to have asked a witness a question that proved fatal to the injunction claim."

"What was that question?"

"I don't know the question but the answer was that a shareholder vote would not have any legal weight; it would be merely advisory. And so the judge concluded—correctly— that there would be no irreparable harm to the corporation in permitting the vote to take place."

———

Why was that so important, Grandpa? • Because, Will, you can only get an injunction if it is necessary to avoid "irreparable harm."

———

"But, Michael, wouldn't the judge have raised that question himself?"

"Probably. No, not probably—certainly."

"Whose decision was it to seek an injunction?"

"Turner's."

"Well, in that case, I am going to bring to the attention of the compensation committee the fact that Simon Turner made a grievous legal error in the representation of an important client. I will argue that his percentage be cut. As long as the law of the jungle prevails here, I can still behave like a lion, if necessary."

I returned to my office, smiling.

FORTY-SIX

Tuesday, November 23, 1982

S chofield had elected a jury trial, probably fearing to let Judge Santangelo decide the case after the judge's annoyance with him at the chambers meeting and his denial of all of Schofield's pretrial motions. I would have preferred a trial before the judge without a jury but there was nothing I could do about it. Landauer was entitled to a jury if he wanted one.

Far more than the usual number of reporters were present in the courtroom, probably hoping for fireworks. Spellman and I were intercepted by a television reporter and cameraman on our way into the courthouse. Contrary to my standard practice, I allowed my client to speak on camera. Spellman did an effective job of setting the tone for the trial, emphasizing that the case was about his reputation—"my most treasured possession"—and that he expected the jury to conclude that the materials Landauer had spread before the public were "an ugly forgery intended to destroy my reputation."

Jury selection was a bit of an adventure since it was impossible to find a single member of the jury pool who hadn't heard about both parties and the Nazi accusation. Judge Santangelo was deeply concerned about whether a fair trial could be obtained in Nassau County. In chambers he asked me whether I wanted to move for a change of venue. Pretending to be torn between the need for the earliest possible vindication of my client's reputation and the likely prejudice against my client by a jury composed of voters in the recent election, I reluctantly declined that invitation. Neither the judge nor Schofield could know that as far as I was concerned, the only jury I cared about was the general public and I knew that they would learn about the case through the media.

I made an opening statement to the jury outlining the basic facts of the case: the delivery of the Nazi file by Weinberg to Landauer and Landauer's release of those defamatory materials to the public. Bill Schofield made a brief opening statement to the effect that his client— "Representative Landauer"—was a fine and upstanding person who wouldn't knowingly hurt anyone.

I had subpoenaed Barry Weinberg and called him as my first witness. Barry looked every bit a successful lawyer—dark gray pin-striped suit, white shirt, paisley tie, wingtip shoes, Rolex watch, perfectly combed black hair with specks of gray on the sides. He walked gracefully and confidently to the witness stand, pausing a moment to shake my hand—which surprised me—and to say good morning to Bill Schofield and the judge. After he was sworn in, his testimony began as shown in this excerpt from the trial transcript:

Direct examination by Mr. Cullen.

Q: Good morning, Barry.

A: Good morning, Mike.

Q: We used to practice law together in the same firm and then you left to join your present firm, is that correct?

A: Yes. I left your firm because I was fired by the managing partner.

Q: I realize that this was more than eight years ago and both of our memories may be a bit hazy, but didn't you tell me that you sent a letter of resignation to the managing partner?

A: Yes, but that was after he told me that I had one month to find another job.

Q: Your departure from Coburn & Perkins, my law firm, sounds like it occurred under unpleasant circumstances. Is that correct?

Mr. Schofield: Objection your honor. Mr. Cullen is leading the witness.

The Judge: Mr. Cullen, is it your position that Mr. Weinberg is a hostile witness?

Mr. Cullen: Although I regard Mr. Weinberg to be a friend and an esteemed colleague, in the circumstances of this case, I think that he is clearly adverse to my client. I can rephrase my question if necessary but I think it was really just a preliminary question.

The Judge: I am going to allow you to examine this witness as if he were under cross-examination. The objection is overruled.

—

Will, ordinarily, a lawyer is not allowed to cross-examine a witness whom the lawyer has called to testify. However, if the witness is determined by the judge to be a "hostile" witness, cross-examination is permitted. Among other things, cross-examination permits the lawyer to "lead" the witness, meaning to put words in his mouth or suggest what the answer to the question should be.

—

Q: Do you recall the question?

A: I do. The circumstances leading to my resignation from Coburn & Perkins were among the worst experiences of my life.

Q: Please explain what those circumstances were about.

A: Your client, Thomas Spellman, who was then one of the partners at Coburn & Perkins, had made pro-Nazi remarks at a luncheon at which I was present. The subject was raised by one of the other people who heard those remarks and the subject was reviewed by the firm's Executive Committee. The managing partner circulated a memorandum to the partners that I and others thought whitewashed Spellman's comments. The managing partner thought I had agitated for further action by the firm and told me I had to leave.

Q: So there was a connection between Tom Spellman and what you regarded to be your firing from the firm. Is that correct?

A: A direct connection.

Q: How did that make you feel about Tom Spellman?

A: I detested Spellman from virtually the first time I met him. As you know, I am a Jew and Spellman is an anti-Semite. He tormented me with anti-Semitic remarks and insinuations throughout the years I was in the firm. The circumstances I described a few moments ago were the last straw. I hated his guts.

Q: Please describe, in as much detail as you can, what it was that Mr. Spellman did and said that made you conclude that he was an anti-Semite.

A: I was the first Jewish lawyer ever hired by the firm of Coburn & Perkins. The day I arrived in the office Spellman stopped me in the hall and asked me to step into a vacant conference room with him. He asked me how I felt to be the only Jew in what he called, quote, "this crowd of Christians." I was surprised by that question and said something to the effect that I felt perfectly comfortable and that I hoped I would be followed into the firm by many other Jewish lawyers. He said—and I remember this well—"Sonny boy, not if I can help it, not if I can help it." That was the first of numerous exchanges we had on the subject of my being Jewish. Time and again he asked me about converting to Christianity, becoming what he called an "apostate Jew." I remember that I didn't then know the meaning of that word.

Q: Do you know the meaning now?

A: I do. It refers to someone who renounces his
religion to join another and different religion. It
has negative implications. Among its synonyms
are "traitor" and "deserter." As you might imagine,
it made me extremely uncomfortable—and,
I'll admit, angry—when he raised this subject.
Spellman kept insisting that my late father was
a kosher butcher. My father was a Holocaust
survivor and he came to this country penniless
and a broken man. He was not a butcher, kosher
or otherwise, but Spellman liked to point out to
me that kosher butchers made a lot of money
selling kosher meat to Jews. More than once
he said to me that it was typical of a Jew to be
"ripping off"—those were his words—his fellow
Jews because, quote, there was nothing a Jew
loved more than money. Shall I continue?

Q: Please do.

A: There was a time—you were there, in fact—
when he made a little speech about how the
United States chose the wrong side in the
Second World War and that we should have
allied with Nazi Germany to fight against
communist Russia. I asked him what would
have happened to the Jews of Europe if we had
done that and he said that a solution could
be found to that problem. I recall asking if he
meant a "final solution" and he said, "Exactly."
When this episode began to cause unrest in
the firm, he went to the managing partner—
we called him the Presiding Partner—and

persuaded him to tell me to find another firm,
that I never could fit into Coburn & Perkins.

I could see Schofield grinning while listening to these
questions and answers. I think he thought I had lost my
mind. I'm almost certain that Barry also didn't see where I
was leading him.

———

*Grandpa, didn't this make Spellman look bad in the eyes
of the jury?* • I'm sure it did, Will. But it did lay the
groundwork for establishing a motive for Barry's possible
forgery of the Nazi file. This is the approach that so infuriated
your grandmother. I was setting Barry Weinberg up to be the
forger of the Nazi file. I hated what I was doing in leading
Barry into that trap. • *That's why Grandma didn't want you
to handle this case.* • You got that right, Will.

———

I then asked Barry to tell the judge and the jury how
he came into possession of what I called "the Nazi file." He
repeated the story he had told me about doing research on
the American Nazi Party and its members, about making
contact with "Mr. X," and about paying Mr. X $15,000 for
the Nazi file, and, in telling this story, he used virtually the
same words he had used when he first told it to me. He even
repeated the explanation of his motive that he used when
he spoke with me. He looked directly at the jury when he
said, "The idea of having a Nazi sympathizer in the Congress

of the United States set my blood boiling. I felt that I had a special, personal, moral responsibility to do whatever I could to cause that bastard to lose the election. It was one thing for Spellman to contaminate a law firm with his obscene views. It was quite another thing for him to be in a position to infect our entire country." I could tell that the jury looked favorably on Barry at that point. There was nothing I could do, and nothing I wanted to do, to stop Barry from making those comments.

At the conclusion of Barry's lengthy response to the question of how he obtained the Nazi file, I addressed the judge:

> **Mr. Cullen:** Your Honor, at this point I am compelled to repeat my pre-trial motion to compel this witness to disclose the identity and location of the so-called Mr. X so that I can arrange to obtain his testimony in this case. That testimony, in view of Mr. Weinberg's last response, is demonstrably relevant. I am very sympathetic to Mr. Weinberg's effort to be faithful to his commitment to conceal Mr. X's identity, but the interests of justice must override that commitment.
>
> **The Judge:** Mr. Schofield, do you want to be heard on this motion?
>
> **Mr. Schofield:** I agree with Mr. Cullen.
>
> **The Judge:** Well, that's refreshing.
>
> **A voice:** If Your Honor please, I represent the witness. My name is Bradford Silverman, and I am one of Mr. Weinberg's law partners in the firm of Greenberg, Gordon & Kantor. May I be heard on the motion?

The Judge: Go ahead.

Mr. Silverman: Your Honor, Mr. Weinberg made a solemn commitment, a promise, to Mr. X, without which he could not have obtained the materials that are so central to this case.

The Judge: Can you cite any judicial authority to the effect that a witness can, by virtue of a private undertaking to a third party, deny access by a court to information relevant to subsequent litigation?

Mr. Silverman: No, Your Honor.

The Judge: I didn't think so. Mr. Cullen's motion is granted. (Addressing the witness) Mr. Weinberg, are you able to recall the name and address of this "Mr. X" without looking in your files?

Mr. Silverman: Your Honor . . .

The Judge: Be quiet. Please answer my question, Mr. Weinberg.

The Witness: Your Honor, if I am sued by this person, will I be able to claim that I am disclosing his identity by virtue of a court order?

The Judge: That's correct. I am ordering you to disclose that person's name and address.

The Witness: The person who provided the letters and photos that are in evidence in this case is named Errol Harrison and he lives in Bridgeport, Texas. I don't know the street address but I can find it in my files.

Brenda immediately asked me who in the firm we should send to take Harrison's deposition. I responded by saying that I wanted to try to bring him here to testify live. I asked the judge to call a recess so that I could set in motion an effort to obtain Mr. Harrison's testimony. The judge noted that the Thanksgiving holiday was two days away and that it might be a good idea to adjourn the proceeding until the following Monday. That would give counsel on both sides the opportunity to do whatever they thought necessary to deal with "this Harrison fellow." He also noted that an adjournment would give the members of the jury the opportunity to get an early start on their holiday traveling. Schofield and I agreed and the trial was adjourned to Monday, November 29.

Spellman had his car parked near the courthouse. We drove back to Coburn & Perkins as quickly as we could to get there in one piece. Brenda quickly obtained Harrison's address and phone number. I asked her to find out everything she possibly could about him without letting him know she was doing that. She dashed off to do that, brimming with enthusiasm.

I sat and chatted with Spellman in my office. I asked, "So, Tom, do you think I should just call the guy and ask if he'd like an all-expense-paid trip to New York City and, perhaps, some money on top of that for testifying in the case?"

Spellman mulled that suggestion for a few minutes and then said, "I think you should wait to see what Brenda comes up with. I've got a private detective who has produced some good results for me in a few cases. I'm going to hire him to go to Bridgeport, Texas, for the Thanksgiving weekend."

"I'm sure he'll love that assignment."

"He certainly will. I'll call him right now and tell him the sort of information we want about Harrison."

"You know what I'm hoping for? I would love it if that guy scammed Barry by producing fabricated documents that Barry thought were authentic."

Spellman smiled. "I don't give a hoot who forged the Nazi documents as long as that's how this thing turns out."

We then discussed Spellman's testimony, which would be the next order of business. I told him I wanted him to repeat on the witness stand everything he had told me about his treatment of Barry Weinberg and his feelings of guilt and contrition over that. He agreed that that would be a good thing to do "even if we can prove that the Nazi file was a forgery." He suggested that we go out for a drink together. That came as a surprise to me. We had been partners, working closely with each other for eight years. This would be our first drink together, assuming the wine episode at the ski lodge eight years earlier didn't count.

FORTY-SEVEN

We went to the Dingle Whiskey Bar at Fraunces Tavern on Pearl Street. It was a cozy and intimate place, stocked with a superb collection of fine scotch and other whiskeys. Knowing that we were probably going to imbibe up to and beyond my capacity for alcohol, I needed to decide whether scotch or gin would be the beverage of the day. I opted for single-malt scotch, with ice to make each drink last longer.

Was it possible that Tom and I were becoming friends? Tom could drink the way he did everything else—larger amounts of more expensive booze than ordinary people drink. That night he ordered a 1958 Highland Park from Orkney. When I saw the price, I said, "You're paying, right?"

"Of course, I'm the client," he replied.

I waited for Tom to start the conversation. He began by telling me how much he appreciated the work I'd been doing on his behalf. In what sounded somewhat like a reprise of his

confession about his treatment of Barry Weinberg, he said
he didn't deserve the effort and dedication to his interests
that I was displaying. "Frankly, I don't think I would be doing
the same thing for you if our positions were reversed. I know
that our professional relationship has largely been a one-way
street—you doing the work and me taking the credit. As far
as a personal relationship, well, we simply don't have one,
do we? You're just a better person than I am."

"It's big of you to say that, Tom. There's something to what
you say, but I've gotten benefits from our relationship too.
When Conway appointed me chairman, you gracefully stepped
aside and let me take over the running of the department."

"Yeah, I stepped aside and sulked. Hey, Mike, let's not
spend our time here exchanging niceties. You're just a better
person than I am and I'm grateful to have you on my side."

"Tom, I'm a lawyer and we find ourselves in a lawyer-client
relationship. I want you to know that I chose to represent you
because . . ." I paused to find the right words. "This is going
to sound corny. I had a Jesuit law professor at Georgetown,
Father Gerrity was his name. He taught me that, for a lawyer,
the most important words in the Old Testament were 'Justice,
justice, you shall pursue.' I chose to represent you because
as a lawyer and as a moral person, I felt obligated to pursue
justice. I think you told me the truth when you said the Nazi
file was a forgery. But I won't really know the truth until it
comes out at the trial. If it turns out that you really are the
Nazi bastard I thought you were on more than one occasion
since I met you, then justice will be served by the stigma
that will haunt you for the rest of your life. And if it turns
out that we can prove those documents are forgeries, then
justice will have been served by relieving you of that stigma.

But my real motivation came from the notion that the worst injustice, the intolerable injustice, would be if the Nazi file is a forgery but no one believed that—if you had to live with the stigma of being known as Spellman the Nazi. I couldn't be a lawyer if I just stood by and watched that happen."

I drained my glass and ordered another. Tom did likewise and told the waiter to bring some sandwiches and to "just watch for when our glasses are empty and keep the whiskey coming."

After several minutes in which neither of us said anything, Tom said, "Anne thinks you are an angel."

The mention of Tom's wife brought thoughts of Norah rushing into my head. I had to tell Tom about my personal problems. He was thunderstruck. "Oh my God. Why didn't you tell me about that? I'm going to call her, right now."

"Please don't do that," I almost shouted. "That'll make matters worse. She's not a big fan of yours, you know."

"But what are you going to do? You can't let your marriage break up because of a case. I'll get another lawyer, that's what we'll do."

"Tom, this is my problem, not yours. We need to concentrate now on the problem we share: *Spellman v. Landauer*. I'll have to deal with my family problem myself, when the trial is over."

—

This was a perfect opportunity for you to get out of the case and get back together with Grandma. • It was too late, Will. First of all, Spellman was just playing at being a nice guy. Second, I doubt that the judge would have permitted me to withdraw from the case in the middle of the trial.

But more important than any of that, I'm not sure whether your grandmother wouldn't have thought worse of me for abandoning my client at that critical point.

—

We ate a little and drank a lot until Fraunces Tavern closed and we staggered out onto the street. As we walked along Wall Street toward Coburn & Perkins, reeling from side to side on the dark and empty street, Spellman announced, "I need to pee without further delay." I stood next to him and we peed together into a sewer on Wall Street. We slept that night in the sleeping facilities that Coburn & Perkins provided for its hard-working lawyers who were working "all nighters."

FORTY-EIGHT

Wednesday, November 24, 1982

I had no idea where I was when I awoke the next morning with a roaring headache and a burning thirst. I looked up and saw Spellman standing over me with a joyful grin. "Time to get up lazybones, do you plan to sleep away the whole day? Brenda's waiting to give us a report."

"I'm not ready to go to work," I muttered. I realized I was still wearing the clothes that I had on the night before. "I need water. I need more sleep."

"Well, if this is how you're going to behave after a couple of drinks, I'll find someone else to go drinking with. Seriously, Mike, we've got stuff to do today."

I stumbled to my feet. "I feel like shit," I announced. Brenda had just walked into the lounge and said, "You don't look so great either." This day just had to get better; it couldn't get worse.

Brenda, looking bright and chipper, said, "I have some information that I think will be useful. Errol Harrison has a criminal record. Five arrests, three convictions, a total of thirty months in two different prisons, one in Texas and one in Virginia. Similar crimes in all cases."

"Come on, Brenda. Tell us what he did," said Spellman with evident excitement.

"The Virginia conviction, in 1964, was for fraud. I don't have the details yet. He was sentenced to two years in prison, released on parole after serving eight months. In Texas, in 1956, he was convicted for aiding and abetting a fraudulent pyramid scheme involving sales of cosmetic products. One year, suspended. And, in 1979, he was convicted for fraudulent sale of—get this—Confederate memorabilia. That's apparently something taken very seriously in Texas, because he spent twenty-two months of a two-year sentence in the state prison. Also charged with perjury but that was dropped when he pleaded to the other charge. That means he had been out of prison for less than a year when Barry Weinberg contacted him."

"Bingo!" Spellman exclaimed. "He's the forger or, at the very least, he hired the forger."

"That's entirely possible," I said. "Our task now is to get an admission out of him. But first, we have to get him to the courthouse in Mineola. How are we going to do that?"

"I like your idea of offering him money to come to New York," said Brenda. "There's nothing illegal about that, is there?"

"You're the lawyer in this group," I said to her. "Find out if it will cause us any problems if we pay him to testify. Get back to me with an answer as soon as possible. I'd like to call him today and extend a gracious invitation. By the way, did you find out if he has any family?"

"He's divorced, twice. Lives alone."

"What are you going to say to him when you call?" asked Tom.

"You'll hear that when I call. I need some quiet time to figure out how to approach him. In the meantime, I'm going to ask Patty to buy me a clean shirt and fresh underwear. And I'm going to shave, in case I run into Conway. Hey, Brenda, I still feel like shit."

"No comment."

I spent a couple of hours in my office writing on a yellow legal pad three alternate versions of what I would say if I reached Errol Harrison on the phone. I knew the whole time that the conversation would take off under its own power in a direction I could only imagine, but could not control. When I felt I was as prepared as possible for this critical phone call, I summoned Spellman and McGovern to my office to listen on extension phones to my call to Errol Harrison. I asked Brenda to record the conversation. I asked Patty to stand by to handle the travel details, if he agreed to come to New York.

The phone rang four times before a man's voice answered. Here is Brenda's transcript of the call:

Harrison: Hello. Who's this?

Cullen: Hi. My name's Mike Cullen. I'm a lawyer in New York City. Is this Errol Harrison I'm speaking to?

H: I don't talk to no lawyers, specially New York lawyers. Good-bye.

C: Wait please, Errol, I'm sorry to call you the day before Thanksgiving when you're probably getting together with your family, but it's really important and I think you'll really have something to be thankful for.

H: Yeah, what's that? And how the hell you know my name?

C: Your name was given to me by a lawyer named Barry Weinberg.

H: That cock-sucking Jew bastard. He swore he wouldn't mention my name.

C: Well, he really had no choice. The judge in a trial I'm working on ordered him to disclose who gave him some letters about the National Socialist White People's Party. If he didn't tell your name, he'd be in jail.

H: Be a good place for the Jew bastard.

C: Listen, he said you sold him those letters and some photos and he had them tested and found out they were phony. I want you to come to New York to tell the judge that those things are not phony. My client will make it worth your while to come up here for that purpose.

H: Worth my while? You know how much my 'while' is worth?

C: Why don't you tell me?

H: I'd say $10,000 plus expenses.

C: That's pretty expensive. Look, we'll pay your plane fare, put you up in a good hotel, and pay you $5,000 in cash for your time.

H: Smart-ass New York lawyer, my price just went up to $15,000. I don't move my ass out of Texas until I get 15K wired to my account.

C: I guess I have no choice. What's your bank?

H: Lone Star Bank, Bridgeport, Texas. Account's

in the name of Errol Harrison. What'd that Jew
bastard say about my letters?

C: He said he took them to an expert laboratory that
tested the paper and the ink and said they were
practically brand new, not years old.

H: Well that's just bullshit.

C: That's what I hope you'll say in court. Look, I
need you here on Monday. Sunday would be even
better. Give us a chance to talk.

H: Show me the money first.

C: Banks have already closed and tomorrow's a
holiday. We'll send the wire ASAP on Friday. I'll
ask my secretary, Patty Rogers, to phone you
with flight and hotel information and to arrange
for you to be picked up and brought to my office.
Watch your language when you talk to her. She's
a good Christian woman.

Harrison and I exchanged good-byes and I told Spellman
I needed a drink. Brenda said she wasn't sure whether "cock
sucking" was one word or two. Patty thanked me for calling
her a "good Christian woman."

In a more serious vein, Spellman asked me why on earth
I wanted Harrison to testify that the Nazi file was authentic. I
explained that I thought that's what Harrison would say anyway and I wanted—more than anything—to bring him here.

"I'm going to caution him about perjury. That may freak
him out sufficiently so that, if he did forge those documents,
he may choose to admit that rather than risk another felony
conviction. He may testify that Barry told him he wanted
evidence of Spellman's affiliation with the Nazi Party so he

produced that evidence to give Barry what he wanted. That's one possible scenario.

"But the main idea here is this. You heard that guy on the phone. He's going to be a terrible witness. A jury of nice folks from Nassau County are not going to believe a thing this guy says. If the judge lets us get his criminal record into evidence—Brenda, please research that issue—there is no way he is going to be believed at any point that contradicts what Barry says. He's going to be the foil who highlights Barry's credibility."

"Wait a minute," Tom jumped in, "Barry's our principal opponent in this case. He's the guy who set this whole fucking thing in motion. Why do you want to enhance his credibility?"

"Barry doesn't know whether the Nazi file is authentic or not. But I misspoke a moment ago. Harrison is not a foil for Barry; he's a foil for you. You are going to testify that that stuff is a forgery. You're going to be the most impressive, the most believable person on Long Island. Harrison says the stuff is real. You say it's false. Barry doesn't know left from right. Whose version does the jury buy?"

"You're playing a high-risk strategy, Mike," Brenda interjected. "It seems to me you're throwing a lot of balls in the air and you hope they come down in the right place. Wouldn't we be on safer ground if we could actually have a laboratory test that proves forgery?"

"Of course we would," I responded.

"She's right," said Tom. "Michael, are you afraid that an expert won't give us the result we want? If you are, then you don't believe I'm innocent."

"I have to allow for that possibility."

"Go to hell, Cullen."

"Oh, Tom, why don't you grow up?" said Brenda. "Mike is planning a remarkably sophisticated multi-dimensional strategy to clear your name."

"Is that what I'm doing?" I said, grinning. "Tom, I believe I know how stressful this is for you. But please trust me."

"I was never a Nazi."

"Is that a fact? I think I'll tell that to the jury. Better yet, maybe I'll ask you to tell that to the jury."

I was still feeling the after-effects of my irresponsible drinking bout the night before. I told Tom and Brenda that I was going to my apartment to get some much-needed sleep. I wished them a happy Thanksgiving. I wanted to leave the office because I needed to be alone to figure out how I was going to deal with Thanksgiving Day without my family. The thought of it brought me close to tears.

FORTY-NINE

called the house and Norah answered. I asked her if Kathleen and Kevin were coming home for Thanksgiving. She said, "Of course, they are."

I said, "May I come home for Thanksgiving too?"

"Michael, why must you make this so hard? Yes, okay. The kids will be arriving around noon. The others will be coming for drinks and dinner at five. You should plan to spend some time with the kids."

"Norah, this makes me very happy. Who else have you invited?"

"Jessica and Barry."

I didn't know what to say. On Monday I would be cross-examining Barry on the witness stand. I wasn't sure if it was even ethical for me to be at the same table with them. "Norah, please call Barry and ask him if it's all right with him if I'm home when they're there."

"Now that I think of it," Nora replied, "I want you to be here—*because* they are coming."

Was it possible for my life to become even more complicated? "I don't understand, Norah, I really don't. You want me there because Barry and Jessica will be there? Why?"

"Barry told Jessica that you were letting him tell the whole story of Spellman's anti-Semitism and Nazi leanings. Almost as if you were throwing Spellman under the bus. I think we should all discuss this and try to understand where things are and where we are heading."

"That sounds more like a business meeting than a Thanksgiving dinner."

"I think we can do both," Norah replied.

FIFTY

Thursday, November 25, 1982–Thanksgiving Day

Every aspect of my Thanksgiving visit required me to make a decision. What time should I arrive? How should I dress? What, if anything, should I bring? Should I volunteer to carve the turkey? What role will I be playing at this traditional family celebration? Am I a host, or a guest? Should I discuss our marital situation with Norah? With the children? With the Weinbergs—of all people? Should I embrace Norah? Perhaps kiss her? What about the case? Should it be off-limits for discussion, or, perhaps, an opportunity for discussion?

And finally, should I go, or call in sick?

Without question, I have to go; I want very much to go. That took care of the last question. As to the others, I decided to play all of them by ear. So, when I awoke—very early—on Thanksgiving morning, everything seemed to fall into place.

I planned to arrive around noon and renew my loving relationship with Jenny, who had just turned thirteen—a teenager. God, how life was fleeting by! In the afternoon, Kathleen and Kevin would arrive from Washington and I hoped to have some quality time with each of them. Their absence from my life the past eight weeks was almost more painful than the strife with Norah.

I would bring two bottles of very good wine. Fortunately, I had laid in an assortment of good wine just in case anyone should ever visit me in my apartment. Of course I would carve the turkey. It would seem weird if someone else performed that function in my home. And everything else would just play out without my orchestrating the events of the day.

I dressed in my newest suit and tried to look my best, as if I were going to an audition. In many respects, that's exactly how it felt. No, that's not right. It felt more like a trial. I was the defendant.

Jenny greeted me at the door. She jumped into my arms. Simultaneously, we each said, "I've missed you." She was still Daddy's little girl.

Norah appeared. I think we both had the same embarrassed look. Neither of us knew what to say or how to act. To break the stalemate, I hugged her gently and we touched cheeks. A quasi-kiss. "I've got a lot to do in the kitchen. Why don't you catch up with Jenny?" she said. Perfect. I was easing back into my own home.

Jenny wanted to know how I thought she looked. I told her how I had mixed feelings seeing my "little girl" looking like a grown woman. She was delighted by that remark. She told me about school, friends, how she wasn't quite ready to have a boyfriend, although she had a couple of opportunities. Those were precious moments for me, and I think for Jenny as well.

The arrival of Kathleen and Kevin should have been preceded with a trumpet fanfare. Their entry into the house was noisy, assertive, celebratory. Kevin, in what were obviously well-thought-through prepared remarks, told of how the opposing forces in the trenches in France during World War I declared an unofficial and informal truce on Christmas Day and greeted one another warmly despite the bloody battles that had raged the preceding days. "This day will always be known as the Cullen Family Thanksgiving Truce," he declared. Kathleen followed with, "I hope the war won't resume tomorrow." Norah and I stood side by side greeting— and adoring—our adult children.

Conversation flowed easily among my three children and me. The day was shaping up to be all I had prayed it would be. I was sure that Norah and the kids had discussed how to handle the sensitive renewal of diplomatic relations with their father. It was the sort of crisis management that was one of her remarkable skills. The tone of the family gathering was pitch perfect, the product of Norah's intelligence and finesse.

Kevin actually asked me to tell him about the Spellman case. I discussed the law of libel and the "public figure" issue. I stayed away from the sensitive question of how I planned to approach the proof of our contention that the Nazi file was a forgery and he seemed astute enough to understand that he shouldn't press me on that subject. I took the opportunity to refer to the conversation we had had in January when he said he wanted to be the kind of lawyer who helped "real people." I said, "You don't know him very well, but Tom Spellman is a real person. He has feelings, vulnerabilities, hopes, fears, all the emotions that all real people have. I don't want to go too far into this subject until your mother and I have worked it out, but I'm representing Spellman because, without me, his life will be destroyed if the Nazi accusation sticks to him—even if it is false. I believe justice requires me to do that. That's as far as we should talk about the case. I hope someday we can talk about it, on and on, for hours and hours."

—

Just the way you have been doing with me. • That's right, although somehow I've missed the opportunity to do it with Kevin. I'm going to force him to sit with the two of us and go through this again. • *Why with me? I will have already heard it.* • Because I want him to hear your comments as well as mine. • *If you insist. Since Uncle Kevin is now a lawyer, I want to hear what he has to say about the case of the century.*

—

Kevin responded, "I hope so too, Dad, and I hope that day doesn't turn out like that camping trip we never had."

"Oh shit, I completely forgot about that."

"I forgive you. You've got heavy stuff on your mind," Kevin said graciously.

"Thanks, I do have heavy stuff on my mind."

Throughout these wonderful conversations with my children, the imminent arrival of the Weinbergs hovered in the background of my mind. How could I not have been thinking of the impending arrival of the Weinbergs? Were

Kevin and Kathleen anxious about that too? And Norah? I wished I could have had a glimpse inside her mind.

I walked into the kitchen and asked Norah if she needed my help preparing the dinner. She nearly convulsed with laughter. I was famous in the Cullen household for my utter incompetence in the kitchen. "You can be a great help. Just stay out of the kitchen."

This was a friendly remark, not a hostile one, and we smiled broadly at each other as I said, "I can handle the drinks."

"You're definitely good at that. Just don't sample too much of the merchandise." Had my evening with Spellman at the Dingle Whiskey Bar come to Norah's attention? I was so sensitive to the subtlest nuances of Norah's every word and every gesture. I realized, upon reflection, that I was likely to behave stupidly in a vain attempt to impart meaning into the most ordinary things she said and did. I needed to try to get myself to feel and appear as natural as I would have if all the stuff in the background simply weren't there. That would be hard. Being in this house, on this day, with the Weinbergs on their way, caused me more anxiety than any situation I had ever been in—including trials, an oral argument before the U.S. Supreme Court, job interviews, final exams, hospital vigils—all because I knew that my future with Norah was at stake.

Kathleen and I discussed her job in Washington—about which she had mixed feelings that she wanted to discuss with me when we had some time alone. We also discussed what kind of drinks I should be prepared to serve and we assembled the paraphernalia that I would need to mix and serve the cocktails. I looked at my watch every five minutes as the time for the Weinbergs' arrival drew nearer. Kathleen knew I was tense and said, "Try to relax, Dad, you can handle this." I squeezed her hand in gratitude and she smiled at me.

Jenny answered the ring of the doorbell and ushered Barry and Jessica Weinberg into our living room. Unless they had been here during the weeks of my exile, this would be the first time in eight years that they were in our house—eight years since their abrupt decision to end our friendship. Norah greeted them warmly with hugs and kisses on the cheek. I shook hands with each of them. It was awkward for both Barry and me to be in this situation and I was certain that that was obvious to everyone.

"Where are your kids?" I asked.

"They're with my parents," Jessica responded coldly.

We were so stiff, so formal, so aloof from one another that Kevin and Kathleen thought our minuet was humorous.

"Loosen up guys, it's a holiday," urged Kevin and the ice was instantly broken.

Smiles appeared on everyone's face and Barry said, "How long does a guy have to wait before he's offered a drink in this house?"

Barry surprised me by asking if I had any bourbon in our drinks cabinet. "That's not your usual, Barry. I thought you were an orthodox single-malt drinker."

"A person can change," he responded, cryptically.

I poured some "single-batch" bourbon over ice for Barry, asking what single-batch meant. He said he had no idea. Jessica asked if I could mix a margarita for her. I seized the chance to display my bartending virtuosity, blending tequila and some bottled margarita mix for which she thanked me graciously. Kathleen then asked if she could have one of those as well, specifying salt around the rim of the glass.

The things your kids learn when they move out of the house. Kevin took a beer from the fridge, drinking it from the bottle. I mixed martinis for Norah and myself. Poor Jenny looked on, suffering the deprivation necessitated by her youth. She brightened when I called for a vote of everyone in the room as to whether she should have a glass of white wine. The motion passed by acclamation and Jenny accepted her glass of wine and mentioned that it wasn't quite cold enough for her taste. Laughter filled the room.

Conversation revolved around a report from Kathleen about how Washington seemed to be joyous over the fact that Ronald Reagan was president, a fact that no one in the room thought was a good thing. As I noticed the drinks glasses being drained, I asked if anyone wanted a refill. Only Barry accepted the offer and he and I walked over to the drinks cabinet together. "Do you think that you and I might find an opportunity to have a private chat sometime this evening?" he asked sotto voce.

"Sure," I said, "now or after dinner?"

"Let's talk after dinner, after we've feasted and have enjoyed that great wine I saw on the dining room table. There's something I have to tell you. But I don't want to transform this enjoyable party into a business meeting."

"That's fine," I said, wondering what this was about. Obviously it had to do with the Spellman case. It would be an understatement to say that I was burning with curiosity and anticipation. "Is it okay with Silverman if we talk about the case?"

"Michael, he doesn't matter."

That's where the main event was left during the several hours that the group spent "feasting," as Barry put it, as if the feast was the only thing that mattered.

FIFTY-ONE

Thursday, November 25, 1982–Thanksgiving Night

Norah had prepared a marvelous dinner. It would have been even better if I hadn't bungled the carving of the turkey so that most of us had something that resembled turkey hash as our main course.

"May I be excused?" Jenny asked after sitting at the dining room table for more than three hours.

Norah responded, "Everyone is excused. We have a woman in the kitchen who'll take care of cleaning up. So let's go into the living room and continue discussing the question of whether Ronald Reagan is less qualified to be president of the United States than Richard Nixon was."

As we moved away from the dining room table, I said to Norah that Barry and I were going into my study to talk. She nodded, knowingly, as if that had been her plan all along.

Barry began our discussion in my study by remarking that he was saddened to learn that Norah and I had "separated." I responded by saying, "I haven't separated; I've been kicked out."

"I know all about it. Norah is in constant contact with Jessica and I know—or at least I think I know—all the circumstances. The fact that it involves the case that I set in motion is terribly distressing to me. I wish I had never started the whole thing."

"I've often wondered whether you regretted sending those documents to Landauer."

"Michael," Barry said after a moment in which he closed his eyes and took a deep breath, "I regret it every day. I've been so consumed by hatred for Tom Spellman that I was like a slave to that hatred. Instead of it wearing away over time it became more and more intense. Sending those documents to Landauer was my way of retaliating against Spellman. I realize that it was a stupid thing to do. But, Michael, you have to believe me, I didn't forge those documents or pictures. I didn't do that. I may be a schmuck but I'm not a criminal."

"You did do a very stupid thing. I'll be perfectly frank with you. I don't think you're a criminal. And I find it almost impossible to believe that you personally forged those materials but, Barry, I can't discount the possibility that you could have hired someone to do it."

"Michael, I swear to you that I did not do anything of the kind. I beg you to believe me."

"Okay, I believe you. That brings you even with Spellman, who also swore to me that the letters and pictures are forgeries, and begged me to believe him. Where does that leave us?"

"What I wanted to tell you is that I hired a document examiner, an expert, the guy who wrote the book on forensic investigation of documents. He did all kinds of tests on the paper, the ink, and Spellman's signature. We don't have an original signature of the guy, Matt Starr, who wrote to Spellman, so there was nothing the expert could do about that. What he found was that the moisture content of the paper indicates that the letters from Spellman to the Nazi could possibly have been written in 1967 but more likely the paper is less than ten years old. This would mean they couldn't have been written fifteen years ago. That would make them forgeries, but there is a lot of uncertainty about that based just on the paper analysis. The more recent letters were all written on paper that would have existed on the dates of those letters."

Barry paused, obviously digging into his memory for more information. He then continued, "The expert is virtually certain that the Spellman letter was written using a ballpoint pen. That's based on the ink characteristics. The Spellman signature looks authentic but it has some of the characteristics of a forged signature: what he calls 'abrupt stops' in the letter *m* in both 'Thomas' and 'Spellman.' None of this is definitive, but that's what I've learned and I thought you should know it. By the way, I didn't have time to contact a photograph examiner to test whether the pictures were doctored."

"Barry, would you mind if I made some notes on what you've just told me?"

"Not at all. I assume you'll ask me to testify to what I've just said."

"I certainly will. Not only that, I'll be putting Errol Harrison on the stand."

Barry looked stunned when I said that.

I went on, saying, "I remember that you told me that your meeting with Harrison—then known to me as 'Mr. X'—took place two weeks after you told him you were interested in Spellman and the Nazi Party. That gave him time to forge those materials, or have someone do it for him, so he could have something to sell to you. Based on what that guy sounded like in the phone conversation I had with him, the contrast between the two of you will be helpful in creating serious doubt about the authenticity of the documents. You may come out looking like a bit of a simpleton, buying shit like that from a scumbag like Harrison, but that's the price you pay for dealing with real Nazis."

"Believe it or not," Barry said, "I think looking like a simpleton is a fair outcome."

"Barry, you know you and I could be friends."

We rejoined the others and the conversations gradually petered out. The Weinbergs thanked us—Norah and me—for a wonderful Thanksgiving.

After they left, I told Norah that it truly was a wonderful day, the best I'd had in a long time. She seemed pleased by that. I hugged and kissed all the kids. Norah and I looked at each other awkwardly. In order to preserve the beauty of the day and to avoid embarrassment, I said, "I guess I should be going. I love each one of you." I put on my overcoat and left to go to my empty bachelor apartment. I hugged Norah after opening the front door to leave. She hugged me back, holding on for what I hoped I was a moment or two longer than necessary, especially in view of the bitter cold that flowed in through the open door.

FIFTY-TWO

Sunday, November 28, 1982

Errol Harrison arrived at Kennedy Airport on Sunday afternoon. I picked him up in my car and drove him to the Gild Hall Hotel on Gold Street in lower Manhattan, where I checked him in as a guest of Coburn & Perkins. Patty had booked a "King Premium" room for him. I thought I heard him gasp when we entered the luxurious room. "Nice place you got here," he said as he set his bags down and plopped on the king-size bed. I told him not to get too comfortable because we had work to do. I asked him if he had brought a copy of the materials he had sold to Weinberg. He reached into his suitcase and pulled out some papers. I asked him to bring them with him when we went to my office.

We walked over to Wall Street. When he saw the street sign on the lamppost, he said, "So this here's Wall Street, where all the money is." I didn't reply. I took him up to my office.

Again, I could tell he was impressed by the appearance of the place and the view of New York Harbor. I introduced him to Brenda McGovern who, I told him, was working on the case with me. He nodded to her but said nothing. Later, he asked me if "that girl" was a lawyer.

Harrison appeared to be about sixty years old. What little hair he had on his head was gray. He appeared not to have shaved recently; his straggly beard was also gray. He was dressed casually—brown slacks, plaid shirt, cowboy boots, light-weight tan zipper jacket. The thought that popped into my head was that he looked like a character playing the role of an elderly ex-convict who also happened to be an ex-Nazi. My star witness. What a business, I thought, this being a lawyer, this pursuit of justice. It takes you to strange places.

We sat in a small conference room. Brenda was there to take notes. I asked Harrison for the papers he had brought with him. I was startled to see that they did not appear to be photocopies. They looked like originals, old paper, inked signatures, glossy photographs. I asked him about that. I was astonished by his answer. "You don't think I gave away the original letters to that Jew boy, do you?"

The following dialogue is from Brenda's notes.

"That's exactly what I thought. And please stop calling him 'Jew boy.' His name is Barry Weinberg and he is a well-regarded attorney."

"He may be a big-shot lawyer but he paid me fifteen thousand U.S. dollars for some second-hand papers."

"What do you mean by second-hand?"

"They's just copies of these papers."

"May I ask what you do for a living, Mr. Harrison?

"Oh, this and that. Odd jobs."

"You got to do better than that, Errol, when you're on the witness stand."

"Hey, that's the truth what I told you. I do odd jobs."

"Give me a few examples."

"Somebody needs his garage cleaned out, so I clean it out and sell what he don't need no more. Or somebody needs his house painted, so I do the job."

"Errol, I know about your criminal record. You can't get a regular job, can you?"

"I don't need a regular job. How'd you know about my record?"

"I have my ways. Tell me, how did you get hold of these papers?"

"What do you mean?"

"The letters, for example. They're addressed to Matt Starr and Thomas Spellman. Your name's not on any of them. So how come they're in your possession?"

"I still got contacts in the party. Matt Starr's dead. When I found out what that lawyer wanted, I made a few phone calls and a guy said he had something I might want. He showed them to me and I bought them off him. Paid him fifty bucks. Sold them to that lawyer for fifteen thou. That's one of my odd jobs."

"What's the guy's name?"

"Who?"

"Errol, stop fucking around. The guy who sold you the letters for fifty bucks."

"I think his name is Bob Smith. Don't know him very well."

"Where does he live?"

"No idea."

"Okay. That's enough for now. Errol, I know you know

what 'perjury' means. It would be in your best interests to be as truthful as you know how to be when it gets to be your turn to testify. When you walk out of this room, there will be a marshal who will hand you a subpoena requiring you to be in the courthouse of the New York Supreme Court in Mineola, Long Island, tomorrow, and to bring those letters and pictures with you. I'll have a driver pick you up at the hotel at nine o'clock tomorrow morning. I don't know if we will actually get to call you as a witness tomorrow. If not, it will be the next day or the day after. You should be in court every day until I tell you that you can go home. I think you may find the trial interesting to watch. Your hotel will provide all the food you need while you're there. Everything will be charged to my law firm. Any questions?"

"Yeah, how do I get back to that hotel?"

"I'll have someone drive you there. Don't worry. We won't lose you."

Brenda walked him out of the room and into the arms of the marshal. She came back into the conference room and said, "He's going to be the worst witness in the history of the world."

"That's what I was hoping for," I replied. "Go home, it's Sunday night. Get a life."

I was a fine one to talk.

FIFTY-THREE

Monday, November 29, 1982–Morning

I arrived at court excited at the prospect of the day's proceedings.

The main courtroom in the Mineola courthouse looked like courtrooms everywhere, even though this one seemed a bit down at the heels. The windows hadn't been washed, perhaps ever. The tables and chairs showed signs of their age and extensive use. I could envision generations of tense, agitated, nervous lawyers sitting anxiously at those tables— scratching and gouging their surfaces. Worn and cracked leather covered the seats of the chairs.

Facing the judge's bench, the plaintiff's counsel table was on the right, nearer to the jury box, and the defendant's table was on the left, nearer to the witness stand. Three wheeled chairs faced each table. Brenda and I occupied two of our chairs and one remained empty. Spellman wanted to sit with us but I vetoed that idea. Bill Schofield and Lou Galliano occupied two chairs at the defendant's table, and a third, unidentified, young person sat in the third chair taking copious notes.

The judge's bench was elevated so that one needed to be standing to see him face-to-face while he was seated in his high-backed chair. Unlike many courtrooms, this one didn't have a lectern for the lawyer who was questioning a witness. That gave me the opportunity to move around in the space in front of the judge and to stand nearer to the jury box when I thought that would be a useful tactic. My experience in court was that juries paid at least as much attention to the lawyers as they did to the witnesses.

The witness box was to the right of the judge, raised one step above the floor, and enclosed by a swinging writing surface. A clerk and a stenographer were seated at small tables directly in front of the judge's bench. There was seating for about a hundred people behind the "bar"—a three-foot-high fence that ran across the courtroom directly behind the lawyers' tables. A swinging door in the exact center of the bar gave access to and from the front of the courtroom where the action took place.

The room had an aura of seriousness about it. It contained nothing decorative. Everything in it was purely utilitarian. But despite its dour appearance, there was an electricity in the atmosphere. It was a place where adversaries came to do battle with each other. This courtroom, on this day in November of 1982, had a fearsome air. Among the many perils of the battle that was taking place was its potential effect on my life with my family. I prayed to the God I didn't believe in that my dear wife, my children, and I would not become casualties of this battle.

Judge Santangelo opened court and expressed the wish that everyone had had an enjoyable Thanksgiving. He asked if I had any further questions for the gentleman who was on the witness stand when the proceedings were recessed the previous week. I said I did have a few more points to look into with Mr. Weinberg. I announced that I would like to advise the court and Mr. Schofield that I had succeeded in contacting the person whom Mr. Weinberg, pursuant to the judge's order, identified as the source of the defamatory materials. I said that that person was available to be in the court today and I planned to call him as a witness if there were sufficient time. Schofield objected to my use of the term "defamatory." Once again, he succeeded in annoying the judge with a frivolous objection. The transcript indicates the following:

> Judge Santangelo: First of all, the jury has not yet been brought into the courtroom, so there is no possibility of prejudice to your client, Mr. Schofield, no matter what vocabulary Mr. Cullen uses. But far more important, do you mean for me to understand that your client's position is that calling a member of the bar of this state a Nazi is not defamatory? I will tell you right now that when it comes to the point in this case where I deliver a charge to the jury, I intend to instruct them that the published materials in question and the related comments of Congressman-elect Landauer, as quoted in the newspapers, are defamatory as a matter of law. I hope you do not intend to waste my time and the time of the jury contesting that conclusion.

Mr. Schofield: I withdraw my objection, Your Honor. I do, however, have another important point to raise. Mr. Cullen just indicated that he intends to call as a witness a person who was not listed as a prospective witness in the pre-trial phase of this case. I have not had the opportunity to depose that person or to formulate interrogatories relating to that person and his testimony.

The Judge: Mr. Schofield, I believe you were in this courtroom last week when Mr. Cullen attempted to learn the name and location of that person and when it became necessary for me to issue an order to the witness to disclose his identity. Under those circumstances, exactly how was the plaintiff to make pre-trial disclosure of a witness whose identity was unknown? You have had precisely the same amount of time and opportunity to contact the witness as Mr. Cullen has had. I assume you did not avail yourself of that opportunity. You will have all the opportunity you reasonably need to examine that witness after his direct examination is concluded. If your remarks constitute an objection, the objection is overruled.

It was almost as if Schofield were attempting to goad the judge into losing his temper and making an ill-considered ruling that could be challenged on appeal. I whispered to Brenda, "Learn from this. Learn how *not* to conduct yourself in court."

The jury was summoned to the courtroom and Barry was asked to return to the witness stand. I asked him about the document examination that he had caused to be performed while the trial was in recess. As he did in my home on Thanksgiving night, Barry made a lucid and even more detailed and precise description of the nature of the tests and the conclusions that were reached. All that, of course, was hearsay since Barry was simply reporting what he heard the expert say. But Schofield failed to object so the expert's analysis was now something the jury would be able to take into account. I decided to take a flyer with another probably objectionable question. From the transcript:

Cullen: Mr. Weinberg, the tests that you described were performed just this past week, is that correct?

Weinberg: That's correct.

Q: So obviously you didn't know what the forgery expert concluded when you bought the documents from Mr. Harrison in Texas. If you had had that information, would you have concluded the transaction with Mr. Harrison and paid him $15,000 for those letters?

A: I'm not sure. The test results were not definitive and it was possible that the materials were genuine. As I mentioned last week, I really wanted to ruin Spellman's election chances, but I don't think I would have used materials that might not have been authentic. I really don't know what I would have done.

Q: Thank you. Your witness, Mr. Schofield.

Schofield conducted a confused and disoriented examination of Barry. It was obvious that he didn't want to cast aspersions on Barry's credibility. After all, Landauer took the materials from Barry and ran with them, relying entirely on the fact that Barry was a highly regarded lawyer and not the kind of person who would pass on forgeries. On the other hand, a cloud now hung over the authenticity of the Nazi file. Truth is a defense to virtually any kind of defamatory statement but that defense now had a small hole in it. I intended to make that hole much larger through the testimony of my next witness, the eminent Mr. Errol Harrison of Bridgeport, Texas.

FIFTY-FOUR

An idea had occurred to me during the lunch break, which I had spent alone in the empty courtroom while Brenda took Harrison to lunch in the courthouse cafeteria. I planned to ask Harrison if he could identify Spellman in the courtroom. If he was unable to do that, it would cast substantial additional doubt on his story that the two of them were fellow Nazis.

As I had directed, Spellman was not seated with Brenda and me at the plaintiff's counsel table. He was sitting with his wife and adult son in the third row on the aisle in the center of the courtroom facing the judge's bench. During the morning testimony by Barry Weinberg, Brenda had seated Harrison in the first row of the spectator's section behind the table at which Schofield and his team were seated. That placed Harrison directly facing the witness box on the far left-hand side of the courtroom.

Harrison was sworn in and sat down in the witness chair. He had shaved and changed into a white shirt with no tie but otherwise looked exactly the way he had the previous day. I began my examination with some preliminary questions establishing that he was the source of the letters and pictures that had been introduced in evidence. He seemed not the slightest bit embarrassed when he admitted that he had been a member of the National Socialist White People's Party, formerly the American Nazi Party. I then questioned him as follows, from the trial transcript:

> Q: Was it during the time that you were a member of the Nazi party that you became acquainted with Thomas Spellman?
> A: Yeah, that was when I met him. Him and me were at plenty of meetings together.
> Q: By the way, do you see Mr. Spellman in the courtroom? Look around carefully at everyone in the spectator section.

The courtroom was packed with spectators and reporters, probably as many as 150 people, some of whom were standing along the walls. I was gambling on the possibility that Harrison had never met Spellman and wouldn't be able to recognize him. Harrison left his seat on the witness stand and strode up to the partition. He appeared to be scanning every face in the room. He then returned to the witness stand.

> A: He ain't here.
> Q: Thank you. Are you sure you'd recognize him if

he was here?

A: Unless he had plastic surgery on his face, sure I
would.

Q: Thank you. Do you have with you copies of
the letters and pictures that you sold to Mr.
Weinberg?

H: What I got ain't copies. I got the originals. I sold
copies to that lawyer.

I asked that these new items be marked as exhibits in
the case. There was a stir in the courtroom as the realization
struck that the letters Barry had had analyzed by the forensic document examiner were merely copies and could not
have been either authentic or forgeries. I asked the judge's
permission to have the new exhibits tested for authenticity
by a certified forensic document examiner to be selected
jointly by Schofield and me, with the expense borne by Mr.
Spellman, the party with the burden of proof of falsity. The
judge and Schofield agreed.

I then resumed questioning Harrison. He described how
he put one over on "that New York lawyer" by keeping the
originals and selling him photocopies. The transcript indicates the following testimony:

Q: If, as you say, the letters that you sold to that
New York lawyer were merely copies of the
originals, how do you account for the fact that all
those letters are signed in ink, blue ink?

A: No problem. I had a guy I know copy those
signatures on the letters. He was good at that
sort of thing.

Q: What's that guy's name?

A: I don't remember.

Q: Do you remember when we were talking yesterday, I asked you how you happened to be in possession of those letters when none of them are addressed to you? Do you recall your answer?

A: Sure do. I told you that I still had contacts in the party. Matt Starr's dead. He was the commander of the party that Spellman wrote to. When I found out what that lawyer wanted, I made a few phone calls and a guy said he had something I might want. He showed them to me and I bought them off him. Paid him fifty bucks. Sold them to that lawyer for fifteen thou. That's one of the ways I earn my living.

Q: You phoned this guy—what's his name, by the way?

A: I think it's Smith, Bob Smith.

Q: Where does Mr. Smith live?

A: I told you yesterday, I don't know.

Q: Is that still your answer today?

A: Are you being smart with me, Mr. Wall Street lawyer? That's my answer today and that'll be my answer tomorrow.

Q: So you called Mr. Smith and told him what you wanted—which is what Mr. Weinberg told you he wanted—and he showed up with the letters and the pictures. Is that right?

A: Yep. He wanted a hundred bucks for the stuff but I got him down to fifty.

Q: Did Mr. Smith tell you where he got the letters?

A: No.

Q: Did you ask him?

A: Nope.

Q: Did you care where he got them?

A: Not really.

Q: Did you ask him where he got the pictures?

A: Probably the same place he got the letters.

Q: But did he tell you that or are you just assuming?

A: Just guessing.

Q: Did it matter to you where he got the pictures or from whom?

A: Didn't matter to me.

Q: By the way, Mr. Harrison, you have a criminal record, don't you?

A: Yeah, what of it?

Q: How long before you met that New York lawyer did you get out of prison?

A: Few months.

Q: You needed money, didn't you?

A: What do you think? They don't pay you much in Huntsville.

Q: What's Huntsville?

A: Texas state prison.

Q: How long were you there?

A: Thirty-two months.

Q: What for?

A: Selling stuff.

Q: What kind of stuff?

A: Phony Confederate souvenirs.

Q: When you say "phony," does that mean forged?

A: You could say that.

Q: Thirty-two months just for that?

A: Also perjury.

Mr. Cullen: Your Honor, we have certified copies
of Mr. Harrison's record of arrests, convictions,
and imprisonments in Texas and Virginia. It
would expedite the trial if we could simply
mark those documents as exhibits rather than
my continuing to examine the witness on that
subject.

Schofield had no objection and Harrison's criminal record would now be available to the jury. That concluded my
questioning of Harrison.

Schofield tried to get Harrison to say that he really
believed that the letters and pictures were authentic, but
Harrison simply reiterated his indifference to that crucial
question. In answer to Schofield's questions, he kept saying,
"How would I know if they was real or phony? I don't know
any more about them than you do." Schofield concluded by
remarking to the judge that he might have more questions
after the results of the document examination were available.
The judge agreed to that.

We next turned to a witness whom Brenda had obtained,
an expert on photographic forgeries. I asked Brenda to handle his examination. Since it was now unclear whether the
pictures in Barry's Nazi file were originals or copies, she
skipped over that issue and simply had the witness explain
the techniques that could be used to create a photographic
print that was a composite of two or more original prints. He
testified that there were many ways to produce a doctored
photograph. Schofield merely had the witness confirm that
he had no opinion as to whether any of the photos that were
exhibits in the case were actually forgeries.

The judge asked me if we had any more witnesses. I said I intended to call the plaintiff, Thomas Spellman, to testify. I added that I might also call the defendant, Mr. Landauer, if Mr. Schofield did not choose to have him testify. Since it was late in the afternoon, the judge adjourned court until the next day.

I went directly to my apartment without reviewing the day's developments with Brenda and Tom. I was tired and I needed quiet time to think and rest. It was obvious to me that we had made great progress toward creating grave doubt as to the authenticity of the Nazi file. Harrison was an appallingly bad witness. It would be hard to conceive of a less reliable source of the materials in the Nazi file.

I phoned Norah and asked her if it would be possible for her to come to court to watch the Tuesday proceedings. I said that I was sure she would find them interesting. She said she would try to get there. I gave her driving directions to Mineola.

I spent the evening and well in to the night thinking about how to bring the case to a successful conclusion.

———

I don't know how anybody could believe that those letters were real. Do you agree? • You never can predict what a jury will conclude, although I do believe that there had to be substantial doubt in people's minds that anything associated with Errol Harrison could be believable. Do you want me to continue with this story? • *Are you kidding, Grandpa?*

FIFTY-FIVE

Tuesday, November 30, 1982–Morning

When court opened on Tuesday, I had a clear plan of action for the day's proceedings. But, as a great general once observed, as soon as the battle starts, you might as well throw the plan away.

Tom Spellman was sworn in as a witness. As usual, he was perfectly groomed but not so perfectly as to look like a clothing model or a movie star. Just enough to seem like a person of quality.

After a few questions to establish his identity and profession, I asked whether "you are now or ever have been a member of the American Nazi Party or any of its affiliates?"

He replied, not in his courtroom voice but rather an octave higher and decibels softer, "Not now, not ever." I directed his attention to both sets of Nazi Party letters that were in evidence and I asked him whether they were letters written or received by him. He answered, "Those documents are forgeries." I asked him about his relationship with Barry Weinberg and whether he could account for the fact that Weinberg had obtained those documents and provided them to his election opponent. Here is Spellman's answer as it appears in the trial transcript:

> **Mr. Spellman:** I've known Barry Weinberg since he joined the law firm of Coburn & Perkins in, I believe, 1965. I've had little or no contact with him since he left that firm in the summer of 1974. I was chairman of the firm's litigation department and Barry was one of our most talented litigators. We should have had a good and productive relationship but I regret to say that that was not the case. I also regret to say that it was I who poisoned that relationship. If I may, I'd like to explain what I just said.
>
> **Mr. Cullen:** Please do.
>
> **Mr. Spellman:** There was never a time—from my earliest memories through most of my career as a lawyer—when I was not an anti-Semite. Believe me, it is not easy to say what I just said. My father was an outspoken Jew hater. He blamed the Jews for the stock market crash in 1929 that nearly bankrupted him. He spoke frequently about how, quote, the Jews were responsible for everything bad that ever happened, including dragging us into the Second World War. When I was fourteen years old, my parents were divorced, a divorce caused, in part, by the fact

that my mother had sexual affairs with three Long Island politicians, two of whom were Jewish. My father was so enraged by that that he nearly burned down our house. He used that horrible experience to illustrate to me the wickedness and depravity of the Jewish people.

So I entered my adulthood as a fully trained anti-Semite. When Barry Weinberg was hired by my law firm—over my strenuous objections—I made it my mission to torment him and to drive him out of the firm. I constantly badgered him with anti-Semitic insinuations and, ultimately, I persuaded our Presiding Partner to force Barry out of our law firm.

When I learned that Barry produced those Nazi letters and pictures, it was as if I heard the other shoe drop. I expected that Barry would someday, somehow, retaliate against me for the treatment I gave him while he was in our firm. I expected it and, I must say, I felt that I deserved it. When I saw the letters, I knew immediately that they were forgeries, but I found it impossible to believe that Barry was a forger. But I had developed such a sense of guilt for my treatment of him that my instinct was to forgive him even if he was a forger since his sin against me was a direct consequence of my many sins against him. Over the past several years, whenever I thought about Barry and what I did to him, a wave of guilt, of contrition would sweep over me. If I were a better person, I would have sought him out and asked for forgiveness. But I'm not that good and now I'm facing what may be an entirely just form of retribution. I only hope that someday he can find it in his heart to forgive me. No, I am not a Nazi but, in the case of Barry Weinberg, I might as well have been. I hope I haven't imposed upon the judge and the jury with this long-winded answer.

The courtroom was utterly silent for what may have been as long as a minute. Then the room began to buzz with the sound of whispered conversations. Even the jurors were talking to one another. Finally, the judge called for order in the court-room and asked Schofield if he had any cross-examination. He did, but I remember nothing about that cross-examination and the transcript confirms that nothing of substance was elicited.

When Schofield concluded his examination of Spellman, the judge called for a one-hour lunch recess. I walked over to Schofield and told him I'd like to have a chat with him and his colleagues. I asked Brenda to get word to the judge that counsel were engaged in settlement discussions.

Seven lawyers went to a nearby diner and crowded around a table designed for four people. In addition to Schofield and his two associates and Brenda and me, we were joined, at my request, by Brad Silverman, Barry Weinberg's partner, and by Norah, whom I introduced to everyone as my wife, attorney, and wise counselor. Speaking directly to Schofield, I said, "I have a proposal for settlement."

"What's your proposal, Mike?" asked Schofield.

"My proposal is that you win the case. We stipulate for judgment in favor of the defendant."

"That's something I can accept," Schofield said with a broad smile. "What's the catch?"

"No catch," I said, "but a few sensible conditions. One, the grounds for the judgment are that the plaintiff is unable to prove actual malice or reckless disregard of the falsity of the statements by the defendant, as required in a libel suit brought by a public figure. Two, we stipulate that the plaintiff has proven the falsity of the statements by a preponderance of the evidence . . ."

"Forget about it," Schofield interrupted.

"Just wait a second, Bill, and listen to what I have to say. We stipulate that the plaintiff has proven the falsity of the statements but there is no way that the defendant, Landauer, or the person who delivered the materials to the defendant, Weinberg, could reasonably have known that those materials were forgeries."

"Let me take that up with my client," said Schofield.

"There's one more thing. I want Landauer to retract his statements about Spellman being a Nazi, repudiate the letters and pictures, and express regret for releasing the forged materials to the public."

"I will have to strongly recommend against that last point, Mike. Why should Landauer retract and regret the statements when he didn't know they were false?"

"Because that's what a decent human being would do," I said with emphasis. "Besides, it will make him look good and magnanimous. I will send you a draft of the public statement that Landauer should make. He'll sound like a hero. The only person who comes out of this soiled in any way is Barry Weinberg, who was taken for a ride by that Texas scumbag, but I think Barry can live with looking like a victim. Brad," I said, addressing Barry's partner, "I want Barry to sign on to these terms. Please discuss them with him."

"Why does Weinberg have to agree?" asked Bill Schofield.

"Because I want him to," I answered. "Let's eat lunch. Then we can talk with our clients and see the judge. I'm hungry. Bill, think about it."

Schofield looked as if this proposal was hard to understand. "I don't know, Mike, whether I can recommend this to Landauer."

I snapped at Schofield, "Landauer should agree to this in a heartbeat. If he doesn't he will have to endure a cross-examination by me exploring why it was that he took no steps whatsoever—not a single step—to authenticate the information before he publicly called my client a Nazi, before he called a prominent attorney—the congressional nominee of the Republican Party—before he said my client signed his letters, quote, Sieg Heil, just like a Nazi.

"Is there anything worse you can say about a person than to call him a Nazi? He called my client a Nazi based on a few fucking scraps of paper of unknown origin mailed to him by Barry Weinberg but he never talked to Barry about where, how, from whom he obtained those pieces of paper. I'll rip him to shreds if you force me to cross-examine him. And I think it's as likely as not that the jury will find that he acted in reckless disregard of the truth. And then we won't be talking about regret, we'll be talking about how many millions of dollars in damages Landauer has to pay Spellman. Make my day, Bill. Turn down my proposal. Let's go, Brenda. We can eat somewhere else." Norah, Brenda and I rose from our seats and left the diner.

FIFTY-SIX

Tuesday, November 30, 1982–Afternoon

I asked Brenda to leave me alone with Norah as we walked back to the courthouse.

"So, my wise counselor, what do you think? I asked.

"You know, Michael, in all these years I've never actually watched you being a lawyer. You're pretty good."

"I truly am honored that you think that. Do you think Schofield will accept my proposal?"

"I certainly do, especially after you scared the bejesus out of him with your threat to pursue your damages claim."

"What did you think of Spellman's testimony?"

"This is the hard part of this conversation. I once told you I thought he was an actor, that he can change personalities to suit his purposes. Well, this was his greatest performance. He sat there, innocence pasted on his face, and, with a plaintive voice, mixed fact and fiction to produce exactly the right combination of contrition, regret, and goodness. The jury loved it. They were almost moved to tears, as were the spectators and reporters. I can't wait to see the news reports about his performance. The media should have sent their theater reviewers, not their regular reporters."

"Norah, can't you open up to the possibility that the guy was telling the truth?"

"No, I can't and I won't. You're going to save his reputation but he deserves to be disgraced."

"I've got to go see the judge. Can we talk about this later, perhaps over dinner tonight?"

"I'll come to your office at six o'clock. Is that okay?"

"It sure is. Pick a place and book a table. See you at six."

I didn't know how to feel. On the one hand, it seemed that Norah and I would never reconcile our views about Spellman. But on the other hand, she was more communicative with me than she had been for months. It was entirely possible that the case of *Spellman v. Landauer* would come to an end by the end of the day. My reconciliation with Barry, although still somewhat fragile, could clear the way to a reconciliation with Norah. Or was I getting too far ahead of the situation? This pursuit of justice was taking me on a dangerous and twisting road.

Judge Santangelo commended us on the structure of the proposed settlement and indicated that he was prepared to enter a judgment if the text of the stipulation met with his approval. As Norah had predicted, Schofield came back with Landauer's approval of "the general outlines of the settlement." I undertook to prepare a first draft of the text of the stipulation and deliver it to counsel and the judge by noon the next day. Brenda looked at me and understood at once that drafting the stipulation would be her overnight assignment.

I had not exchanged a single word with Spellman since he had concluded his virtuoso performance on the witness stand. I really didn't feel like pandering to his need for applause but, of course, I had to obtain his approval of the settlement terms that I had already advised the judge were acceptable to my client. Tom was sitting in my chair at the counsel table when we emerged from the judge's chambers. He had a broad smile on his face and was so full of himself that he actually appeared to have expanded his dimensions. I told him what the settlement was going to be and that I didn't want to debate it with him. He said, "Why would I debate that? It's a complete victory for us. That Nazi monkey will be off my back. You are a fucking genius of a litigator. You see now why I insisted that you represent me. I will be forever grateful to you."

"You know Conway will insist that the firm bill you for all the work that Brenda and I have done."

"It will be a pleasure to pay that bill. I won't even ask for a courtesy discount."

"You know we're talking about a number well north of one hundred fifty thousand dollars."

"Worth every penny. I'm going to come back to work at the firm and I'll cut a deal with Conway to allow me to pay it off by deductions from my partnership distributions."

"That's between you and the partnership. I only do the work. I don't run the business," I said.

"You could probably do that better than Conway. I think I'll nominate you for Presiding Partner next time around. By the way, Michael, you scared the shit out of me when you asked that Texas dirtbag if he recognized me. He looked me right in the face and I almost pissed myself. I thought we were sunk. I thought the bastard would finger me."

"Am I hearing this right?" I almost hollered. "Why would he have recognized you? You told me you never met him! Did you lie to me?" At that point, as things came into focus, I was screaming at him.

"Hey, Michael, calm down. You know full well that if I told you that I had played around with the Nazis, you wouldn't have put me on the witness stand to tell that moving story I told."

"Witness stand?" I yelled. "I would never have represented you! My God, I don't believe I defended a real Nazi! I don't believe it. I just don't fucking believe it. Get out of my sight before I before I throw something at you. Go away. Go away right now. Just go!"

Spellman stomped out of the courtroom. I stood there, dripping with perspiration, my heart pounding, my head reeling. I needed to sit down but I couldn't. I paced nervously around the courtroom, muttering obscenities. I sat for an instant, then I stood, then I sat, then I walked. Finally I sat, my arms on the table, my head on my arms. After a few minutes, I looked up toward the judge's bench. On the wall behind the bench was the only decorative item in the court—raised blue lettering against a white background—bearing the message, "Equal Justice Under Law." Bile rose up into my mouth. I ran to the men's room and vomited.

—

Oh my God, Grandpa, he really was a Nazi! No wonder you vomited.

—

I returned to my office to wait for Norah at six o'clock. The haze of anger, shame and disappointment that surrounded my head gradually dissipated as I sat in those comfortable and familiar surroundings. Patty intuitively knew to shut my door and protect me from the outside world. She probably thought I had lost the case. Little did she know how much was lost.

Although I knew that the immediate and most pressing issue was how to handle the pending settlement now that I had learned that its central premise was a lie, my mind was not yet able to focus on that issue. I was completely absorbed with the question of how I had allowed myself to be captivated by Spellman's deceptively earnest denial of involvement with the Nazi Party, a denial made immensely more credible by its accompanying confession of his lifelong anti-Semitism and his remorse over his abuse of Barry Weinberg. It was one thing for the jury, the judge, even Bill Schofield, to be taken in by Spellman. It was quite another thing for me to fall for his story. I knew him. I had heard his D-Day speech. Barry had told me of Spellman's appalling treatment of him. I now remembered that I had heard Spellman refer to someone as our "Jew client." But most of all, there was Norah. She knew him—not as well as I did—but she knew him and she knew of his treatment of Barry. And she had warned me. She had implored me not to get involved with the case of the Nazi file. She was so certain he was the person he had turned out to be, the person who, in fact, he always was, that she felt that my refusal to heed her warning required us to separate—after twenty-six years of a nearly perfect marriage.

Why had I not demanded of myself that I try to fully understand the adamancy of Norah's position? She certainly was not one to trifle with her marriage, with the life that she and I had long settled into, a life full of love, respect, dignity, and joy. Was I so caught up with the real and imagined imperatives of my profession that I discounted the gravity of Norah's commitment to her principles, submerging them to what I thought was my duty as a lawyer? Was a lawyer obliged to be a martyr to his profession? What an asinine idea. What I fool I had been. How full of self-importance I was that I could think that I was taking a highly principled position in acceding to Spellman's demand that I represent him. I was pursuing justice? What bullshit! I was pursuing self-interest, ego gratification, the opportunity to be recognized as a star in a highly visible lawsuit. And for that I was willing to throw away my life with Norah, to let Kathleen and Kevin and Jenny slip away from me, to become a Homeless Rich Man playing cards in the lounge of the Graduates Club.

Soon Norah would arrive and we would go to dinner. Of course, I would tell her everything. For a moment I paused in my thinking and wondered whether telling Norah, telling anyone, telling the judge, telling Schofield, would violate the confidentiality of Spellman's disclosure of his Nazi involvement. In a flash, I concluded that I didn't give a damn about such things. If I got disbarred for violating the attorney-client privilege, I would joyously accept that.

I would tell Norah everything, including the thoughts that I had regarding the reasons for my representation of Spellman. I would beg for her forgiveness and ask her to help me find my way back to a life in which being a lawyer would not define who I am.

FIFTY-SEVEN

The first thing Norah said when she knocked on my door and walked into my office on the dot of six o'clock was, "What's wrong? You look like someone died."

"I'm fine. Just working too hard. Where are you taking me to dinner?"

"Delmonico's, where else? Meat and potatoes, the staff of life for an Irishman."

I was glad that Norah seemed to be in a good mood. I didn't think I could deal with another tense conflict with her. This conversation would be difficult enough.

We were greeted enthusiastically by the maître d' at the restaurant, a perk associated with my stature as a big-shot partner of a big-shot firm. Norah and I settled into our comfortable seats and looked across at each other with the half smiles and expectant gazes that evoked memories of what it was like to begin an evening that might lead to a romantic relationship. That quite likely could have been Norah's expectation. Mine was entirely different.

We ordered drinks. I don't remember what they were. I do remember telling Norah that I needed her help desperately. "You were right about Spellman. He admitted to me that he, quote, played around with the Nazis. I don't know what to do. I don't know what I'm obligated to do under the rules. I don't even know whether merely having this conversation doesn't break some rule that's binding on me as a lawyer. And I don't know what I'm obligated to do to restore my standing—if that's possible—as a moral person. Help me, please help me."

Norah reached across the table to take my hand, knocking over a water glass in the process. A platoon of servers raced to the table to mop up the water, to provide napkins in industrial quantities, and to assure Norah that things like that happen all the time and they hoped it wouldn't detract from the pleasure of her dinner at Delmonico's. She said, "I do that at home all the time."

With that glint in her eyes that indicated that her powerful brain was fully engaged, she looked at me and said, "As to the propriety of your telling me about Spellman, let us agree that you have engaged me as your lawyer and that your statements to me are protected by the attorney-client privilege."

I couldn't help laughing out loud at the brilliance and audacity of her comment. "What's so funny?" she asked, grinning from ear to ear. "I'm a member in good standing of the bar of the State of New York. You can afford my rates."

"You're hired. Now advise me."

"In order for me to be effective as your counsel, we need to be in close contact with each other. So my first piece of advice to you is to move home, to Brooklyn Heights." Tears came to my eyes; to hers too. I probably had not done that much weeping in one day since infancy.

Norah continued. "I was angry with you, extremely angry, but I finally figured out that the principal cause of my anger wasn't anything you did, it was my contempt for Spellman. I'm ashamed of myself for blowing that so grotesquely out of proportion. The fact that it now appears that I was right in believing that that prick was indeed a Nazi is irrelevant. This should have been about you, not him. I hope you can forgive me."

"Forgive you? Let me tell you what I figured out this afternoon while waiting for you in my office." I told her all my conclusions about my stupidity in failing to give proper consideration to her warning about Spellman, about how I was driven by ego and self-importance in taking on the Spellman case. I told her that I intended to beg for her forgiveness.

"Well," she said, "it looks like we're deadlocked. Let's flip a coin and see who should forgive who."

"Whom," I said.

"Pedant!" she retorted.

I got up from the table, walked around to Norah, who stood up, and we hugged and kissed for much longer than was appropriate for a middle-age couple in the dining room of the finest restaurant in the financial district of New York City. There was a smattering of applause as we resumed our seats. Our waiter came to our table to ask if we'd like another drink. He had a broad smile on his face and he looked much happier than he had earlier in the evening. Norah's and my happiness was reflected in his face.

As I savored the joy of our reconciliation, a joy exceeding any I could recall in my life, thoughts of Spellman, his wretched lawsuit, Coburn & Perkins, the law, everything other than Norah, faded to inconsequential annoyances in the distant background of my mind. Norah and I had found our way back to each other—each of us drawing on an understanding of the other, an understanding developed over years of paying attention to each other. We knew what mattered to each other. Norah knew that being a lawyer occupied a great deal of space in my life and sometimes took control of my judgment. I knew that Norah was a woman of deeply held principles, a woman for whom some things were simply right and others were absolutely wrong. I understood that such a view of the world could lead, on occasion, to a loss of perspective, to stubbornness. We both knew that neither of us was a flawless human being, that we were susceptible to error, and that we were entitled to understanding and forgiveness. It took some time and some effort but we were friends again, and I was jubilant. And deeply grateful.

———

I'm crying for joy, Grandpa. • I suppose you're like me, Will, and think it's okay for a man to cry.

———

"Should we call the kids?" I asked.

"Later. We have stuff to do, now that I'm your lawyer."

"Oh, yeah, I forgot about that. What do I do now, counselor?"

"While you spent the afternoon figuring out how you

screwed up our relationship, I was doing some serious legal research," Norah reported, looking quite pleased with herself.

"Why did you do that?"

"Because I was certain that Spellman had lied through his teeth in that performance he gave on the witness stand and that you would eventually, somehow, find out that your client committed perjury, I was pretty sure that you would need to know what your obligations were in that case. What I found is that New York has a rather clear rule regarding what a lawyer is required to do when he learns that his client has testified falsely. I am really going to enjoy telling you what you need to do and then watching you do it."

"I'm all ears."

"Not now. Let's have a really great dinner. And then let's go home, together."

"I don't think I left any of my pajamas at home."

"Yippee," Norah exclaimed, pumping her fist like a baseball player who has just hit a grand-slam home run.

"I hate to be a spoilsport, but I made a commitment to the judge to deliver a settlement stipulation tomorrow morning. I'm sure Brenda McGovern has already drafted a perfect document that I can't possibly submit tomorrow. We'll have to spend time tonight figuring out what I should do tomorrow morning. By the way, do I have a clean shirt and a razor at home?"

"How should I know? You did the packing. Seriously, you're not focused on the right subject. The judge won't notice your shirt or your beard, but he will be interested in the stipulation. I won't let you go to court unprepared. That's why you have a good lawyer . . . who happens to love you."

FIFTY-EIGHT

Wednesday–Thursday, November 30–December 1, 1982

About midnight, Norah and I were lying in bed, exhausted. "Well, how was it?" I asked.

"How was what?"

"My husbandly performance, that's what."

"Well, I have nothing to compare it to, but it was at least up to your usual standards."

———

Grandpa, this is embarrassing for me to hear. Why don't you just skip over this and get back to the story? • This is very much a part of the story. I think you're old enough to deal with the details of your grandparents' beautiful relationship.

———

"Frankly," I said, "I expected a burst of enthusiasm in your response."

She rolled on top of me and we did it again. "Well, how was it?" she asked.

"How was what?" I replied.

"My uxorial performance, that's what."

"Far better than average, perhaps an all-time best. But 'uxorial,' how many wives use that term?"

"At least this one," Norah replied, and we laughed and kissed, and laughed some more. "And now to work," she said. "Recess is over. Wrap a blanket around yourself. You look utterly unprofessional."

I did as she said. She then began the following presentation, reading from a sheet of paper that suddenly appeared in her hands: "The New York rule of professional responsibility that is pertinent to the Spellman case, Rule 3.3(a)(3), provides, and I quote the relevant words—'If . . . a lawyer's client . . . has offered material evidence and the lawyer comes to know of its falsity, the lawyer shall take reasonable remedial measures, including, if necessary, disclosure to the tribunal.' The term, quote, reasonable remedial measures, is open ended, leaving the nature of the remedial measures to the judgment of the lawyer. In case you're worried—as I'm sure you are—whether the duty of confidentiality that attaches to a client's communication to his lawyer gets in the way of, again I quote, 'the disclosure to the tribunal' mentioned in the rule, don't worry. Rule 1.6 takes care of that issue. A lawyer—like you, Michael—who discovers that his client has testified falsely about facts that are important to the case is not required to treat that information as a confidential communication. Now we need to discuss what remedial measures are necessary given that we know that Spellman lied when he denied that he had ever been a Nazi."

"Wait a second, Norah, you're going too fast. I have to understand this one step at a time. At the trial, I asked Spellman whether he is now or ever had been a member of the Nazi Party or any of its affiliates. I believe his answer was 'not now, not ever.' I now know that he was acquainted with that Nazi from Texas and that he, quote, played around with the Nazis. That probably means that I know that his testimony was false, at least in part. What on earth is a remedial measure? A remedial measure is something that remedies a problem. How do you remedy perjury?"

"Aha!" Norah said with enthusiasm. " I think he has to retract the testimony he gave in court, admitting that it was false—in part, as you just said—and he has to indicate what made that testimony false and correct it. But we don't know whether what I've just said is a reasonable remedy because we don't know the full extent of Spellman's Nazi involvement. I don't know what playing around with the Nazis means. Neither do you. So we have to find out. And the way we're going to find out is to have an in-depth discussion with Spellman about Nazism. Won't that be fun?"

"It will be an ordeal, for him and for me. He has been my law partner for eight years. We've worked closely together on a lot of cases. This won't be fun."

"Michael, he not only lied on the witness stand, he lied to you, over and over again. He lied to you!"

"I know. It's just hard for me to process the conclusion that he was, maybe still is, a Nazi. That is just about the worst thing a man can be, short of child molester or mass murderer."

"That's why he deserves whatever happens to him. Don't feel sorry for him."

"Okay, how do we go about this?"

Norah paused for a few moments, organizing her thoughts. "We bring him to your office in the morning. You and I, and Brenda McGovern, will be there. You will tell him about the applicable rule of professional responsibility and your need to take reasonable remedial measures. In order to do that, you will say, you need to know the whole truth about his Nazi experience. Because that is a subject so fraught with difficulty for you as his law partner, you have asked me to act as your attorney in learning the entire story and developing the appropriate remedial measures. I'll take it from there. I'll immediately point out that it is very much in his interest to try to fix this problem because right now he is facing a felony charge for perjury."

"We've got to do what we've got to do," I said. "Let's do it."

"First, let's try to get some sleep. It's past two o'clock in the morning."

Neither of us really fell asleep before we showered, dressed, and rode the subway to Wall Street.

FIFTY-NINE

As soon as we arrived at my office, I phoned Bill Schofield and told him there had been a development and that I would not be able to meet with him and Judge Santangelo as planned. I fended off his insistent questions about the nature of the development and assured him that I wouldn't be postponing our session with the judge if it wasn't absolutely necessary. I then called the judge's clerk and delivered the same message.

I asked Brenda to come to my office. As soon as she arrived, she handed me the draft of the settlement stipulation that she had prepared overnight. Without looking at the document, I told Brenda about Spellman, our Nazi client. She seemed dazed; her pale face became ghostly white as I told the story. However, she quickly recovered and, again displaying the acute insights that were typical of her, said, "Don't you think it's necessary to advise Mr. Conway of this situation? It seems to me it directly affects the firm's interests."

"Oh boy, you're so right," I said. I immediately called the Presiding Partner's office and was told by his gatekeeper, the fearsome Mrs. Hadden, that he was flying to London as we spoke. I asked her to call our London office and leave a message asking him to call me as soon as possible to discuss an urgent matter. I hung up before she could cross-examine me about "the nature of the matter."

The next step was to summon Spellman to my office. As I expected, he was nowhere to be found at the offices of Coburn & Perkins. I phoned his home. Anne answered and immediately asked me what was wrong. She said that Tom was very upset and wouldn't tell her anything. I said that the best thing she could do would be to see to it that Tom hustled down to my office as quickly as possible. I said that a problem had arisen in our effort to settle the case and we needed to work to try to resolve it. For that purpose, I needed Tom as soon as possible. It wasn't my place to tell Anne, a lovely and decent woman, that her husband was a Nazi. Tom got on the phone and when I made it clear that I would not discuss anything with him on the phone, he said he'd be at my office within the hour.

A few minutes later, I received a phone call from the judge. He said, "I assume there's some problem with the terms of the settlement we discussed yesterday."

"Yes, there is, Your Honor."

"Is it Schofield?"

"No, Your Honor, the problem is on my side."

"I can't believe your client is balking at the terms you worked out for him. He can't get a better outcome."

"I wish I could give you more specifics at this point, Judge, but I'm not in a position to do so."

"What would you have me do?" the judge asked.

"Well, I think you should send the jury home. I doubt that this trial is going to be resumed. I must tell you that I am in a terrible pickle."

"I think I'm getting the picture, Mr. Cullen. I know I can count on you to do the right thing."

"That's my intention, Judge."

It had only been an hour since Norah and I had arrived at the office. I still needed to hear from Conway and to turn Norah loose on Spellman. It promised to be an interesting day.

As we waited for Spellman's arrival, I thought it would be prudent to inform the other members of the firm's Executive Committee about the fact that Spellman, a partner on leave of absence from the firm, had committed perjury and that I was about to begin to take the "remedial measures" required by the Rules of Professional Conduct. With the dramatic growth of the firm in the past several years, the Executive Committee had been expanded from three to seven members. One was in our London office, one in Washington, and the other five worked in our Wall Street office. Conway was en route to London, leaving four members of the committee in New York. One of them was my old friend Henry Stevens, the tax lawyer who had wanted me to do something about Spellman eight years ago when the "Perkins matter" had evolved into the "Spellman might be a Nazi matter." I walked down the hall to Henry's office. He still had the boyish appearance he had had as a young partner but he was now a fully matured and highly regarded partner. He invited me to take a seat and asked what he might do for me. He was fully aware of the fact that I had undertaken to represent Tom Spellman in a libel suit against his election opponent. He knew about the Nazi letters and Spellman's claim that they were forgeries. He even knew about my proposed settlement terms, having been told about them by Brenda when she asked him to look at her draft of the settlement stipulation.

The only significant thing about the case that Henry Stevens didn't know was that Spellman had lied on the witness stand and actually did have Nazi Party affiliations.

"Holy shit!" Henry exclaimed. "What do we do in a case like that?"

I explained about the remedial measures clause in the Rules of Professional Conduct and that it might be necessary to inform the judge that Spellman had given false testimony. Henry was thunderstruck. "This is a firm matter," he said. "I've got to get the Executive Committee together." He picked up his phone and instructed his secretary to ask the other members of the committee to come to his office as soon as possible. "Tell them it's urgent." He turned to me and said, "Michael, it may be necessary to convene a full partners' meeting. We have to kick Spellman out of the firm. It's bad enough that we had grounds to do it eight years ago and sat back and did nothing."

Henry's secretary stepped into the office to inform him that only Mr. Schultz was available and that the others were either in court or otherwise out of the office.

"Schultz is worthless," Henry said. "He'll add nothing to the solution to this problem." I remembered Schultz as either Tweedledum or Tweedledee, Conway's silent colleagues on the old Executive Committee.

"Henry, I plan to demand that Spellman resign from this firm as one of the remedial measures that I require in view of his false testimony."

"That will help a lot. It's important that his resignation be portrayed as having been forced by you and not just something he does because his conscience is bothering him. If you can possibly make it appear that he kept his Nazi affiliations a deep secret from the firm all the years he was a partner, that too will be helpful to the firm. Goddammit, how did we wind up being a law firm with a Nazi partner? I hate that son of a bitch. Do me a favor, Mike, tear him to pieces."

"I have to try to handle this the right way. I have my wife helping me. She has exceptionally good judgment and she has no love for Spellman, never liked him, never trusted him."

"Norah is smarter than anyone in Perkins & Coburn, including you, Mike. Better looking too." Henry seemed to be unwinding a bit from the strain that was apparent the moment I told him about the situation.

"Do you want to join us in confronting Spellman? He'll be here in twenty or thirty minutes."

"Michael, I'm a tax lawyer. I'm famous for not knowing how to talk to people. Thanks for the invitation, but we don't want to overpower him with too many people in the room. You and Norah are sufficient."

"And Brenda McGovern," I added.

"She's good, isn't she?"

"None better. I'll keep you posted on how this goes. I'd appreciate it if you would tell the Executive Committee that I tried to report this matter to them but wound up with you being the only one available. Not counting Schultz." I returned to my office. Spellman had not yet arrived.

SIXTY

Thursday, December 1, 1982–Early afternoon

B renda, Norah, and I sat in my office waiting for Spellman. Patty arranged to have sandwiches sent up from the cafeteria. As we chatted casually and ate our lunch, Brenda said, "I think it's so nice that the two of you can be working together on this extraordinary matter. If I had a husband, I'd like to have the opportunity to do something like that."

"It's not so easy to be married to a lawyer," said Norah.

"You know, Brenda, if you weren't so much older than our son, Kevin, I'd insist that you marry him. I'd leave you no choice in the matter," I interjected.

"Is he good-looking?" Brenda asked, in a way that made me wonder if she were serious.

"You're much better looking, and also smarter, than Kevin. Let's talk about Spellman," said Norah. "It's not as pleasant as talking about the forthcoming wedding of Brenda and Kevin, but he could show up here any minute and we're not focused on what we have to do."

"She's all business, isn't she?" Brenda said with a grin.

"Norah, it may surprise you to be reminded that we've already fully discussed what we're going to do with Tom. I believe we concluded that you are going to carve him up and pass slices of Spellman around the firm as hors d'oeuvres."

A court stenographer was led into my office by Patty at that moment, ending a few moments of enjoyable repartee. I had earlier decided that it would be a good idea to have a record of the impending showdown. I then had the bright idea that Norah should sit in my desk chair as if this were her office. She liked that idea. I asked Patty to tell anyone who asked for me that I was in a deposition and could not be disturbed. She asked if that applied to Mr. Conway or the judge. I told her, "No interruptions, period."

As if on cue, Patty stepped back into the office a moment later to announce that Mr. Spellman had arrived. "Here we go," I announced. "Show him in. No smiles anyone."

Spellman looked shocked when he saw Norah. "I didn't expect to see you here. How have you been?"

In an icy voice, Norah responded, "I've been well. Tom, we have no time for small talk, so let's get right down to what we are all here to try to accomplish. Michael, why don't you begin?"

I handed Spellman a copy of the New York Bar Rules of Professional Conduct, opened to the page on which Rule 3.3(a) appeared. "Look at Rule 3.3(a). That will provide you with the context for the discussion we're about to have."

"Mike, let's talk like old friends for a minute."

"We've never been friends."

"Okay, we've been colleagues, partners, we've worked closely together. We even got drunk and pissed in the gutter together."

"Where are you going with this, Tom?"

"I'm asking you to give me a break. You yourself said I was running for my life. Well, now you've got my life in your hands. Can't you just erase what I said to you when we were alone in the courtroom yesterday?"

"You really are ethically obtuse, aren't you? How can you have the audacity to stand there in front of my wife and my associate and ask me to lie to a state Supreme Court judge, to file a stipulation that recites a bunch of lies as if they were facts? I guess that's what happens when you spend years and years cavorting with Nazis. Spellman, you make me sick. I learned yesterday—from you—that the testimony you gave earlier in the day was false. I learned that you lied about having no affiliation with the American Nazi Party. You correctly observed that if you had told me about that affiliation, I would not have permitted you to testify as you did. You threw me for a fucking loop. Now you want me to conspire with you to commit a fraud on the court. Except for the expensive suit and the New York accent, there's no difference between you and your fellow storm trooper, that guy who sold you down the river, Harrison. There is one difference—he didn't lie under oath. Enough of this bullshit. We have work to do."

—

Didn't Harrison lie when he said that Mr. Spellman was not in the courtroom? • My goodness, Will, I never thought

of that. That SOB committed perjury and I let him get away
with it. It's far too late to do anything about that now. Wait
until I tell your grandmother about this. I want you to be
there so you can watch her slap her forehead. But now I
have to get on with the story.

—

I paced the floor to blow off some steam. I pointed to
a chair. "Sit there. I'm sure you've noticed that we have a
stenographer in the room. We intend to record this entire
interview. I asked Norah to help me determine what my
responsibilities were in light of what I learned about your
false testimony. She directed me to the rule that you have
before you. Note the reference to remedial measures. It's
my obligation to take reasonable remedial measures. I can't
fairly determine what measures are reasonable because I
only have a small glimpse at this point of the nature and
extent of your involvement with the American Nazi Party, and
I think I need to know everything about that involvement
in order to comply with the rule. You're going to tell us the
whole truth about that subject today. Tom, as you said a few
minutes ago, you and I have worked together for eight years.
We know each other well—although not as well as I thought
we did yesterday at this time. I find myself in an impossibly
difficult position right now. As must be apparent to you, I am
absolutely infuriated with you. You deceived me. You swore
to me on the heads of your children that you had nothing
to do with Nazis. You made me pursue a false position in
court, to make arguments based on a lie. And then you come
in here today and ask me to get down in the ethical pigpen

with you. I am so angry, I don't feel capable of dealing with this subject. I've asked my wife to act as my personal counsel in attempting to comply with Rule 3.3(a). I am telling you to respond to her questions fully and honestly. Norah, please take it from here."

Spellman raised his arm like a traffic cop. "I'd like to say something before you begin whatever you intend to do."

He cleared his throat and was about to begin talking when Norah said, "Tom, you can make whatever statement you care to make after I've concluded my questions. You're not in charge here." I thought his eyes would pop out.

Norah continued. "I heard your testimony in court yesterday and Michael has told me what you said to him afterwards. You committed perjury, almost certainly first-degree perjury, a felony punishable by imprisonment. The proper course for Michael to take might well include reporting that fact to the Nassau County district attorney. He would prefer not to have to do so. Or at least that was how he felt last night. I think whether he will continue to feel that way depends on your cooperation with us today."

"Can't we just discuss this? Why do we have to treat this like some sort of star chamber proceeding?" Spellman burst out.

I jumped in. "Tom, I have the right to phone Judge Santangelo right now and tell him that you deliberately lied in testimony in his court yesterday and ask him what he'd like me to do about it. One more outburst like that and that is precisely what I'll do. You've used up all your credits with me."

"Okay. I'll be a good little boy while little Mrs. Cullen gets to play trial lawyer."

"That kind of remark is not going to get you any place. Norah doesn't know this, but I've been hoping to develop as a, quote, remedial measure, a carefully constructed retraction and correction of your testimony that might convince the judge not to seek criminal proceedings and possibly even avoid disbarment. Why I do things like that for a shit like you is a mystery to me. You'd do well to think about whether insulting my wife is in your best interests."

Here is the transcript of Norah's questioning of Spellman:

Q: In your testimony yesterday before Judge Santangelo and the jury you denied ever having had any affiliation with the American Nazi Party. Was that part of your testimony true or false?

A: I regret to say it was false.

Q: Do you now have any affiliation or involvement with the American Nazi Party or the National Socialist White People's Party? For convenience let's refer to those parties as the Nazi Parties.

A: I do not presently have any such affiliation or involvement with the Nazi Parties.

Q: When did such affiliation or involvement terminate?

A: I'm not sure of the date.

Q: Well, was it more than a year ago or, perhaps, was it this morning?

A: Look, you don't terminate your relationship with the Nazi Parties by sending in a formal resignation. You just stop having contact or participation with their activities. There was a period of time—I'd estimate it was more than

five years ago—when my involvement began to
diminish and eventually it just came to an end.

Q: Let's leave the ending for later and turn to the
beginning. When did your involvement with the
Nazi Parties begin?

A: I think it was when I was in college, the
University of Virginia, in the late 1940s, 1948
or '49. I had learned about how Roosevelt and
Truman had agreed to give Soviet Russia control
over half of Europe and the Cold War was taking
shape. I was strongly anti-Communist.

Q: Well, you didn't have to become a Nazi to be anti-
Communist did you?

A: Hey, look. This is a complicated subject. I don't
want to drag this out with a long narrative about
my thoughts when I was in my twenties.

Q: I'm sorry, but we need to know all about your
thoughts that led you into the Nazi Parties.

A: First of all, you don't fill out an application to join
the Nazi Parties. You just do it.

Q: What was on your mind when you first just did it?

A: Russia, Communism.

Q: Couldn't you have just joined the Republican Party?

A: I did, but I didn't think they were sufficiently
militant. Don't forget, Eisenhower was a liberal
and he led the war against Germany that let
Russia gobble up Europe.

Q: What did you actually do as a member of the
Nazi Party?

A: I'm glad you asked that question. The answer is
I didn't do much of anything. I contributed some

money. I don't think it came to more than one
or two thousand dollars a year. I helped write
a few propaganda pieces, and on a handful of
occasions—not more than five or six—in all those
years, I went to meetings and rallies.

Q: At those meetings or rallies, did you wear a
swastika armband?

A: Yes. We made believe we were storm troopers
fighting for the rights of white Christians. It was
silly role-playing and I'm embarrassed to admit
that I took part in it.

Q: In your testimony yesterday, you mentioned that
you were trained by your anti-Semitic father
to be an anti-Semite. Was that part of your
testimony truthful?

A: Yes.

Q: Was anti-Semitism among your thoughts when
you began your involvement with the Nazi Parties?

A: I suppose so.

Q: Suppose?

A: Hey, Norah, we're talking about something that
happened more than thirty years ago. It's difficult
to remember precisely what was in my mind
back then. It's true I was an anti-Semite and that
anti-Semitism was part of the platform of the
Nazi Parties, so it would be logical to assume that
anti-Semitism had something to do with it.

Q: Let's talk about anti-Semitism. Have you ever
committed an act of violence against a Jew?

A: Oh, please.

Q: What is you answer?

A: That question is insulting. The answer is no. Put an exclamation mark after that.

Q: For someone who has committed perjury, affiliated himself with a group that thought the mass murder of Jews was a good thing, who ran around wearing a swastika armband, who has admitted to spending years tormenting a Jewish colleague in order to drive him out of your law firm, you are a remarkably thin-skinned person. I would think it is impossible to insult a Nazi. Is it correct that your feelings about Jews were a factor in your decision to become involved with the Nazi Parties?

A: One factor out of several.

Q: I'd like to explore your feelings about Jews. Do you believe they killed Christ?

A: Yes, I believe the Jews of the time were instrumental in bringing about the crucifixion. I don't think it's possible to read the Gospels any other way.

Q: Do you believe that Jews are, on the average, more dishonest than non-Jews?

A: I think that would be hard to prove but, anecdotally, there's evidence to support that conclusion.

Q: How about money? Do you believe Jews have a love of money that is greater, on the average, than non-Jews?

A: I'd answer that the same way I answered the previous question.

Q: Do you have any Jewish friends?

A: No. My primary care physician is a Jew. Where is

this line of questioning going? What is its purpose?

Q: In your testimony yesterday, you stated that you have for some time felt guilty about your treatment of Barry Weinberg. Was that part of your testimony truthful?

A: Yes.

Q: When did you begin to feel guilty about Weinberg?

A: Sometime, a year or more, after he left Coburn & Perkins.

Q: Did you participate in the Nazi march in Skokie, Illinois, in 1977?

A: There was no march in Skokie.

Q: How about a Nazi rally in Marquette Park in Chicago on July 9, 1977. Did you participate in that?

A: Yes, I did.

Q: That was an anti-Semitic rally with guys wearing swastikas, was it not?

A: Yes.

Q: That took place about three years after Barry Weinberg left your law firm, didn't it?

A: Yes.

Q: Would it be fair to conclude that while you were busy at a Jew-hating rally in Chicago, you were not yet experiencing feelings of guilt about your anti-Jewish treatment of Weinberg?

A: One thing had nothing to do with the other.

Q: Oh, then your guilt about the anti-Semitism that led you to torment Barry Weinberg was personal to him and didn't reflect a change in your general attitude toward Jews?

A: I'm not going to answer that or any more

questions about my private feelings and beliefs.

Q: Earlier this afternoon, you estimated that your involvement with the Nazi Parties began to diminish about five years ago. That was about the same time as the Nazi rally in Chicago. Are those things connected, or did your interest in the Nazis begin to diminish more recently than five years ago?

A: When I went to the rally in 1977, I was still active in the Nazi Party. So my involvement would have started to decline more recently.

Q: Were you still involved in any way with the Nazi Parties when you decided early this year to seek the Republican nomination to run for Congress?

A: Definitely not.

Q: Therefore you would have to have severed your connection with the Nazi Parties before 1982 but after 1977, is that correct?

A: It would seem to be correct.

Q: Can you recall any reason or event that caused you to move away from the Nazi Parties?

A: Nothing specific, but now that you ask, it was probably something to do with the rally in Marquette Park. That was probably the single occasion in which I was in the company of more Nazi Party people than any other time. I recall feeling revolted by many of those people.

Q: Because of their anti-Semitism?

A: No, because of their appearance. Many, if not most, of them were like that character, Harrison, who testified at the trial.

Q: That reminds me. Those letters. They are not forgeries, are they?

A: I don't have a distinct memory of writing or receiving each one of them, but they are not forgeries.

Q: So your testimony on that point was also false, correct?

A: Regrettably.

Q: So, Tom, why the hell did you lie?

A: It's obvious, isn't it? I'm not proud of my former association with Nazis. I'm embarrassed, humiliated, now that it has been made public. And I fear that my career and reputation have been ruined. This afternoon's experience has only deepened my humiliation and I'd like to stop.

Q: Fine. I am finished.

I gave Norah a gentle hug and a brief peck on the cheek and said, "Thank you, Norah, for handling that. I know it was difficult for you, and for Tom. It would have been impossible for me to ask those questions."

I turned to Spellman and said, "Tom, I know this was an ordeal for you too. I think it must be apparent to you that you now have to resign from Coburn & Perkins, before all this becomes public and you are expelled from the firm. I strongly recommend that you resign from the bar and surrender your license to practice law. If you do those things—and do them today—I will try to persuade Judge Santangelo that reasonable remedial measures have been implemented. I will ask him to permit you to retract the perjured testimony and correct the record by way of new testimony admitting the truth of the allegations of Nazi affiliations. I will indicate that judgment should enter for Landauer in the lawsuit. I will argue to the judge that these measures obviate the need to refer the matter to the district attorney for criminal prosecution. That's the best I can do for you. Frankly, it's far better than you deserve. You can dictate your resignation letters to Patty. She'll type them for you. Plan to be in court tomorrow morning. Give my regards, and my sympathy, to Anne."

Spellman slowly lifted himself out of his chair, looking as if he had a physical disability, and without a word or a glance toward any of us, he left my office. He was broken. Brenda, Norah and I just stood silently together looking out over New York Harbor as the darkness of late autumn began to gather over the water.

Patty typed the letters that Spellman dictated to her. She said he was outside waiting to sign them but he wanted me to read them first. I could tell that she was astonished by the content of the letters, each of which was typed on Spellman's personal stationary retrieved from his unused office. I approved the letters and stepped outside my office to watch Spellman sign them. Neither of us said anything, but I briefly put my hand on his shoulder as he turned to leave and bring home with him the news of the end of his career.

Patty told me that Paul Conway had called from London. I decided that I wasn't ready to speak with him. I remember thinking that I hoped Henry Stevens had briefed him on what was going on with Spellman.

I called Schofield and Judge Santangelo and asked for a meeting in chambers the next morning. I thanked Brenda for her help and suggested that she go home early, although it wasn't really early. There was no rejoicing in my office.

SIXTY-ONE

When we returned home, we found that Jenny had prepared her meatloaf and mashed potatoes specialty in the hope that we all might have dinner together. This was a small thing that loomed extraordinarily large. For Norah and me, it helped us to emerge from the distress of the ordeal that Tom Spellman had caused us to endure. It was an act of kindness, thoughtfulness, communion, and love. It was the polar opposite of the things we had heard from Spellman, the opposite of hate and arrogance, ugliness and deceit. How could Jenny know that we needed this small act from her? She knew because she was Norah's daughter, because she was a witness to the stress and pain that Norah and I had experienced in the past weeks. We had had mixed feelings about having a third child who would be eleven years younger than her brother, who would still be a child as we approached middle age. But I remember thinking that she would be a comfort to us, that she would extend the years of our youth and vitality. We were right. She was a blessing.

—

Thanks for saying those beautiful things about my mother. • Will, there aren't words enough in the English language to fully describe what a beautiful person your mother is.

—

Jenny asked perceptive questions at the dinner table. Why did Mr. Spellman hate Mr. Weinberg? What, exactly, is a Nazi? What's going to happen to Mr. Spellman now? Why do some people hate Jews? Are Jews different from us? How are they different? Are we going to be friends with Mr. and Mrs. Weinberg and their children? When you go to court, is the judge fair? When lawyers argue with other lawyers, do they dislike each other?

We spent the evening discussing Jenny's questions. In the course of the discussion, Jenny learned a lot. But not nearly as much as Norah and I learned. This was a time to take an inventory of our lives, to separate the important from the trivial, the good from the evil, the mandatory from the optional, the permitted from the prohibited, the holy from the profane. No, I didn't suddenly get religion, but Norah and I did give sustained and focused attention to things of preeminent value to us. Maybe that's what religion is about.

It became apparent to Norah and me—and to Jenny, who participated in the evening's discussions—that we had to emerge from the Spellman case changed in some fundamental ways. I didn't think I could go back to Coburn & Perkins and pick up the next litigation case involving a hostile corporate takeover or the defense of a stock manipulator. Norah didn't think she should resume working on residential real estate closings. Those conclusions were rather obvious to all of us. It was easier to identify things that were no longer appropriate for us to be doing with the remainder of our productive lives than to conceive of suitable substitutes.

At one point, Jenny asked, "Do you have to be lawyers?"

"What could we be instead?" Norah responded.

"How about teachers? You'd both be good at that."

"Do you really think so?" I asked.

In typical Jenny fashion she said, "Look, I don't have nearly as much experience at anything as both of you have. The only job I've really seen anyone do is being a teacher. That's because all I've ever been is a student." I was about to say that that was a perceptive comment when Jenny popped up with, "Do we have enough money for you both to do whatever you want?"

"I don't know. Do we?" asked Norah.

"Last year I earned more money than my father did in his entire life driving a bus for the Fifth Avenue Coach Company. The Cullen family didn't starve, we didn't freeze in the winter, we had clothes to wear, we went to Coney Island in the summer. We seemed to have enough money to do whatever we wanted. The problem, Jenny, is that the more money people have the more things they think they need and the more things they want."

"Well I think that's stupid," Jenny opined.

That comment was, to say the least, thought provoking. After a few minutes in which the three of us were thinking, not talking, I said, "During Christmas vacation, I told Kevin that I wanted to go on a camping trip with him. We both loved that idea. We haven't done it, mostly because I was spending too much time making money. I assume, Jenny, that you would think that was stupid too."

And on into the night this conversation continued, and this examination by my wife and me, illuminated by the insights of our thirteen-year-old daughter, led us further and deeper into a realization that we were in the wrong place. We went to bed, however, without having discovered the right place.

The next morning I had to convince Judge Santangelo to go easy on Spellman, a person whom I held in utter contempt.

SIXTY-TWO

S pellman's letters of resignation had been delivered by a Coburn & Perkins messenger to Henry Stevens as a representative of the Executive Committee of the law firm, and to the appropriate representative of the bar of the State of New York, all as arranged and overseen by Brenda McGovern.

Judge Santangelo had ordered that the transcript of Norah's examination of Spellman be transformed into an affidavit and that Spellman should sign that document, swearing before the clerk of the court that his responses set forth in it were the truth, the whole truth, and nothing but the truth. The document was then entered into the record of the case of *Spellman v. Landauer.* Judgment was entered in favor of Landauer and Judge Santangelo concluded that nothing further remained to be done in connection with that case or with Spellman's testimony of the previous day. Spellman was ordered to pay court costs and the legal fees incurred by Landauer in the defense of the libel case, by far the least of his problems.

I returned to the offices of Coburn & Perkins before noon that day. Patty told me that Henry Stevens had called for a special partners' meeting, with participation by speakerphone of all partners in London and Washington who were available to participate. I met briefly with Henry, who said he wanted me to give a full report to the partners on the Spellman case and the circumstances of Spellman's resignation. I told him that a "full" report was impossible, that I did not understand how Spellman's mind worked or what the real character of the man was. I said those were the most pertinent questions and that I was not competent to answer them. He understood and asked me simply to outline the factual narrative. Paul Conway called from London and I gave him a preview of my intended presentation to the partners. He said I had done a great service to the firm. I thanked him but derived no real gratification from his commendation.

It was late afternoon before all the New York partners had assembled in the firm auditorium. Hardly anyone was missing. Phone connections were established with the Washington and London offices. Paul Conway reported that all of the London partners had returned to the office and gathered in a conference room for a late-night meeting. Someone gave a similar report from Washington. I don't remember which member of the Executive Committee presided at the meeting while Conway was in London. It doesn't matter. Whoever he was, all he did was call the meeting to order and announce that it was a special meeting to hear a report from Michael Cullen concerning the case of Thomas Spellman. He called upon me to speak. I stood at the lectern and decided to use the microphone.

I dispensed with any light-hearted opening remarks, intending to impart an air of the highest level of seriousness. I began my report by saying that during his entire tenure with the firm, Thomas Spellman was either a member of the American Nazi Party and its successor organization, the National Socialist White People's Party, or he was sympathetic to their anti-Semitic and racist positions. I said I didn't know how many partners, if any, were aware of those facts but it seemed likely to me that more than just a few partners had to be aware of Spellman's radical ideas. No doubt, I pointed out, some of those partners were sitting in this room. I said it was my fervent hope that no partner in this distinguished firm actually shared Spellman's views but that it was impossible to deny that most of us chose to look the other way when he spouted his Nazi-inspired perspectives.

"We did that," I said, "because Tom Spellman was a charming man, because he was larger than life, because he was a hard-working and excellent lawyer, and mostly because he brought in a great deal of business and helped every one of us to take home a great deal of money. Because we looked the other way, Coburn & Perkins will be known in our profession as the law firm that was the professional home to a Nazi, a card-carrying Nazi if I can use that term, from 1955 to 1982, for twenty-seven years. He's gone now, his resignation from the partnership has been delivered to the Executive Committee, and he has resigned from the New York Bar. How much of his character, how much of his presence, how much of his bigotry remain as shadows on the name of this firm is a subject that demands the attention of the partnership."

I then narrated the chronology of the Spellman case, beginning with the D-Day luncheon, continuing through the *de facto* expulsion of our only Jewish partner, the congressional election and the disclosure of the contents of the Nazi file. I described my representation of Spellman in the libel suit against his election opponent and my reasons for undertaking that representation. I told of how Spellman had lied to me about his Nazi affiliations and how I had believed him. I told of his perjured testimony and how he inadvertently disclosed to me that he lied in his testimony. I told of how, with the assistance of my wife and Brenda McGovern, we took the actions that led to Spellman's resignations and how, based upon the admissions and resignations that we extracted from him, I was able to convince the judge that criminal proceedings against him were unnecessary. I think I told the partners everything about the Spellman case that I could think of, with the important omission of the strife that it caused in my home and marriage. That was no one's business but mine.

I came to the end of this presentation and looked around the room, amazed that the firm had so many partners, noting in passing that none of them were women. "I hope the past fifteen or twenty minutes have not been boring to you . . ."

"It was forty-five minutes, but not at all boring," someone shouted.

I laughed. But then, without intending to do so, and actually to my surprise, I continued to speak: "Gentlemen, my involvement with Spellman the past couple of months has been an epiphany for me. I saw things I had never seen before, I understood things I had not previously understood, I gained insights into myself, into our profession. I gave a great deal of thought to the idea of justice and what I, as a lawyer, was obliged to do to serve the interests of justice.

"I concluded that what I have been doing throughout my career as a lawyer has not been faithful to that obligation. I was horrified by the fact that I came within a millimeter of assisting Tom Spellman to escape from the consequences of his deliberate affiliation with people whose ideas are an abomination. Gentlemen, I've concluded that I must change directions, walk on a different path. I don't know what I'm going to do, but I must tell you that I have decided to resign from Coburn & Perkins as soon as we can manage an orderly transition of my cases to other lawyers."

This was followed by a minor uproar. Paul Conway shouted across the Atlantic, "Michael, don't do that! Don't be hasty. I'll be back on Wednesday. No, I'll change my schedule; I'll be back tomorrow. Let's meet tomorrow."

"Paul," I replied, "I'm sorry but I can't meet with you. I have plans to be with my family this weekend."

EPILOGUE

So, my dear grandson, that's the story of my Nazi law partner. But—as I am sure you realized—it's a story of much more than that. Thirty-two years have flown by since that story ended but hardly a day goes by without my thinking about it.

I think I've told the story accurately. At least, that's what I've tried very hard to do. I don't think I've made myself appear either too good or too bad, because I'm neither of those. I made a terrible, unforgiveable mistake in placing my marriage to your grandmother in jeopardy. But she forgave me, and together our lives after the Spellman case flourished.

Your grandmother and I started what came to be known as a public interest law firm. We called it Cullen and Cullen. The first "Cullen" is your grandmother. We've done a lot of things that I think have been useful to our country and our city. We've done work to help preserve the environment, to help poor people assert their rights; we have pursued justice wherever it led us.

Your Aunt Kathleen became a powerful figure in national Democratic politics. She was consulted frequently about strategy and policy positions. She appeared regularly on television talk programs and her views were important to many people. Somehow she managed to have a good marriage to your Uncle George and be a good mother to your cousins Robert and Richard. It makes me happy that they are your friends as well as your cousins.

Your Uncle Kevin joined our practice and is now running it. The firm of Cullen and Cullen now has over twenty lawyers, all of whom work hard and none of whom are getting rich.

Kevin lives nearby in Brooklyn Heights and is married to your Aunt Marge, who also works at Cullen and Cullen. I think their son Pat will be heading to law school next year. Somehow I've failed to impress upon my children and grandchildren that there are better things one can do with one's life than be a lawyer. But I'm not as sure of that as I was thirty years ago.

Your mom, our daughter Jenny, the baby of the family, is, as you know, a social worker. She converted to Judaism and married your father, David Rosenberg, still another lawyer in the family—but I love him. You are in a family of observant Jews and, looking in from the outside, I envy all of you for the certainty of your beliefs, the closeness of your community, and the values that guide the way you live.

You might want to know that Barry and Jessica Weinberg were at your mother's wedding. So were several of my former partners at Coburn & Perkins, including Paul Conway, who was about ninety years old and was in a wheelchair.

Tom Spellman became a hedge fund manager and made a fortune. I've not had any contact with him since December 2, 1982, thirty-two years ago. I don't expect ever to hear from him again.

Arthur Landauer, by the way, served two terms in Congress but was eventually driven from office and convicted of accepting bribes. He went to jail.

Coburn & Perkins was eventually swallowed up by a much bigger law firm which, ironically, also acquired Greenberg, Gordon & Kantor, so Barry Weinberg again became a partner of several lawyers whose attitudes about Jews were—shall I say?—ambiguous.

Brenda McGovern married a lawyer and they work together in a small law firm. Your grandmother and I see her and her husband from time to time, and I keep trying to persuade them to join Cullen and Cullen.

The Weinbergs became our good friends again, this time for good.

I think I have pursued justice, but I'm not sure I ever really caught up to it. But pursuit seems to be all that the Bible wants us to do.

CPSIA information can be obtained
at www.ICGtesting.com
Printed in the USA
LVOW12s1825040916

503171LV00009B/612/P